Burning Vengeance

A Fireman Romantic Suspense

Tricia T. LaRochelle

Manufactured in the United States of America

ISBN 979-8-9909107-7-5 (paperback)

ISBN 979-8-9909107-6-8 (ebook)

Published by Flaming Heart Press, United States of America

Distributed by Ingram Book Group

Cover design by Damonza

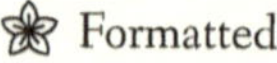 Formatted with Vellum

I dedicate this book to my pup, Daisy, and her sister, Sadie (my grand pup), two sisters who bring light and joy into our lives. To Cheri, Julie, and Noreen, my sisters in all ways but one, and to all the brave firefighters who run toward danger when the rest of us flee.

Daisy

Sadie

Sisters

Burning Vengeance

Chapter 1

The Beginning of Their End

As I approached the warehouse on the eastern side of Charlottesville, VA, the cold night air biting at my cheeks, I was reborn. My limbs grew antsy, eager to get busy. Anticipation filled my chest as I stalked the 17,000 square foot building, peering in windows and making sure the night shift had vacated. No noise or voices reached my ears. *Good.* This would be my biggest score yet. The small house I had torched last week was barely worth the effort, as was the pathetic excuse for a gift shop that the owners had just put up for sale. Both were necessary steps in my revenge that had begun on March 17th. My own D-Day. I'd been waiting five years for this, planning, patient, waiting for my time to come. I wiggled my fingers, every cell in my body ready to party.

"Yeah, you'll go up nicely, burning a big hole in Logan's pocket. Just wait, asshole, things are gonna get so much worse for you." I lifted the containers of accelerant from the ground, the liquid sloshing like a violent sea, waiting to unleash its fury. The pungent odor coiled my senses.

I had always believed fire to be a threat and a danger—something to avoid and protect the world from.

I was wrong. Fire was brave and strong. Humanity was weak and selfish, especially rich pricks who believed they could control the world. I would show *him* that he couldn't.

Fire didn't apologize for its arrogance, and neither would I. It took what it wanted, never asking for permission, relentless and unforgiving.

Fire was the ultimate weapon, and for too long, I had refused to appreciate its power. But now that I was alone, pain and anger would fuel my efforts. No longer would I turn my back on fire's command.

Together, we would repay the debts of my life.

Chapter 2

Natalie

A wailing siren and horns pierced the walls of the medical building as a notification popped up.

Breaking News: Industrial Fire in East Charlottesville, VA

"Huh." I pocketed my phone.

"What's, huh?" My mother asked.

"Nothing. Just another fire. Seems like there's been a lot lately. How are Bea and Nigel doing?"

"They're pretty shaken up. The fire destroyed their gift shop."

"I remember you telling me about it. I'm just glad they weren't injured." I sat next to my mom in a brightly lit doctor's office, awaiting news. An adjustable examination table remained off to the side, lined with disposable paper, while various framed posters of exposed muscles, organs, and circulatory systems stared down at us from the walls. A small basket attached to the wall held a blood-pressure cuff, neighboring a collection of scopes for peering into ears or down throats. The walls and counters were different shades of nondescript tan. A distinctive antiseptic smell hung heavy in the air, the sound of people's voices drifting down the hallway outside our door.

Behind Doctor Clark's desk, several framed diplomas assured us we were in the right hands.

We'd known Dr. Marion Clark for years. She set my brother's broken leg when he was a boy, prescribed antibiotics for me when a bad cold had turned into a sinus infection, and monitored our health for decades. Dr. Clark was the woman who counseled me about birth control when I was seventeen. And she wasn't one to rush you in or out. She cared, which I came to appreciate when I encountered doctors in other facilities. We trusted her, so when Mom's health took a turn, Dr. Clark was the first person we called.

A sigh escaped from my mother's lips as she sat beside me, her hands restless in her lap.

I reached out and took one of those anxious hands, her clammy palms an understandable byproduct of our visit. Dr. Clark had run multiple tests, which took several appointments, before delivering my mother's diagnosis two years ago. At sixty-six years old, my mother had lupus, which explained her constant fatigue and joint pain, not to mention the rash inflaming her cheeks.

"It's okay, Ma. Don't worry. She's going to have good news. I know it. You've been feeling so much better, right?" I did my best to sound persuasive, even though I was worried right along with her. Back when her diagnosis threw us into a tailspin, I'd done my research. If untreated, lupus could be debilitating. "You've been taking your meds. You eat well. And since you've started working for me, your body looks incredible." I wasn't lying. A bountiful crop of silver hair had replaced her younger shades of light brown, and crow's feet radiated from the corners of her blue-and-gold eyes—a few more lines defining the edges of her mouth—but Rose Dugan was still a catch, despite what my asshole father had done to her self-esteem.

She nodded, her eyes uncertain. "Yes, but I can't help but worry." She touched her face repeatedly before lifting her purse from the floor and placing it in her lap. She pulled out a tissue to wipe her nose, something she often did, especially during the winter months. "You know how I get."

I *did* know. All too well. Anxiety had taken its toll, especially after my father had deserted her twenty years ago. She didn't handle it well. And while some people resorted to alcohol or drugs, my mother chose other coping mechanisms. She withdrew. She isolated. And she cleaned. My mother had always been a neat person before my father had left us, but something shifted during the divorce. She took cleanliness to an almost OCD level. Looking back, keeping her house spotless seemed to be the one aspect of her life she could control. It was beyond anything I had ever encountered. Balled-up Christmas wrapping paper could send her over the edge.

But when she became sick, her energy flatlined. The frantic woman I came to know in my teenage years was still frantic, but she didn't have the vigor to carry out her obsessions. The final straw was when a bottle of honey had spilled, and she'd forgotten about it—or maybe she was too tired to deal with it at the time—inviting an army of ants to invade. It was bad. At one point, a trail of them ran up our kitchen walls. I had to call an exterminator. And that was when she broke down. Wouldn't get out of bed. "What do I have to live for?" she'd said.

I knew I had to do something. I put a plan together. Many plans, including exercise, diet, and even a way to pay the medical bills.

My mother's voice cut through my ruminations. "You're right, though. I *did* notice my clothes are getting a little less loose." The corners of her mouth tilted a notch upward.

Most women celebrated weight loss. Not *my* mother, who had dwindled over the years. At one point, I feared she was wasting away. The extra weight, as of late, had firmed her body up in a healthy way.

"See. I knew it." I nudged her with my elbow. "Dr. Clark is going to have good news."

"Thank you, Natalie. You're a good daughter. You'd have to be to hire your own mother."

I scoffed. "Ma, I can't think of anyone who can clean better than you can."

It was still hard for me to fathom that my BFF, Yazmine Mounivong, and I had been in business together for twenty-two months. Even more bizarre? We were starting to show a sizable profit from our cleaning business, which we cleverly coined Dust Bunnies. Coming from a background in mathematics, this was a huge shift for me, but it was necessary. Desperate times and all.

"I know you started Dust Bunnies for me, Natalie. I just hope you won't regret it." My mother glanced over, her gaze surveying.

"What? Are you kidding? I hated working at Old Dominion CPA. Don't you remember? I used to complain about Stewart all the time." I thought about my old boss. *Stewart Howard.* Behind his back, I called him *Stewie.* No reason, other than it sounded demeaning when I said it. He was one of those people who wasn't the tallest guy in the room (at five foot, five inches, he was three inches shorter than I was) or the best looking. He was losing his hair at the ripe old age of thirty-eight. His gray eyes were too big for his head, and he had a chin that was determined to sink into his neck.

Stewie and I had seemed to really hit it off in my job interview. At one point, I hoped we could be friends. Until he had asked me out on a date, and I had turned him down. Everything changed after that. I found out later that he'd asked out most of the female hires. What a douchebag. Of course, he never said or did anything I could accuse him of, such as harassment. His uncle, *the tightwad*, owned the firm, so no point in going over his head.

"I can't tell you how nice it is not having to report to bosses like him. Or anyone. I never saw myself staying there forever, anyway. I just wasn't sure what I wanted to do."

My mom's tone wavered. "Yeah, but you love math and running numbers."

"I didn't stop running numbers, Ma. I still handle our books. This is much more rewarding. Believe me. No one tells me what to do anymore."

When my mom became sick, Stewie wasn't going to support any effort I made to take time off. A day here and there was fine. I had my two weeks of vacation, but none of that would help her in the long term. *And* Stewie made sure I knew that there was always a file overflowing with applicants who would be more than happy to do the job for me should I complain. The hours were nuts. I worked most weekends.

"I'm not stupid, Natalie. You had benefits there. Insurance. And a steady paycheck." My mother wadded up her tissue and stuffed it into her purse, which she hugged close to her abdomen.

"Yeah, we had some tight months. But don't forget the reason we hired you is that we are making a profit now. And we have more customers coming in. It's all good, Ma. Yaz is checking on finding us better insurance. We can afford it now."

"I just hope—"

"Ma. Stop. We're fine. I hated working in that cubicle with those fluorescent lights humming over my head. The sad part is, even as a business owner, I work fewer hours now than I did when I was there. I'm glad I left. You did me a favor."

My mother's head flinched back. "I doubt that. You're just being nice." Her tone was unconvinced.

"I was stuck. I had no idea what I wanted to do. You helped me figure that out. Remember those people we hired to clean your house?"

Since I didn't have time to do it myself, I'd hired people to clean my mother's house when she was ill—the same ranch-style home where I had grown up.

She made a face. "I remember they were awful."

"What was that one woman's name? Was it Helen?" I searched my memory banks.

"Yeah, I think her name *was* Helen."

"Remember how she used carpet cleaner on your hard-wood floors?"

My mother threw her hands up. "What a mess she made. I thought she had ruined my floors. She barely dusted. And didn't do laundry."

"None of them would do laundry. We hired three different companies. And none of them did a very good job. Plus, they were way too expensive. You gave me a reason to quit that crappy job. I should be thanking you." I pointed with emphasis. "And don't forget, I even clean for Old Dominion now."

What a surprise *that* was. The day I gave my notice was one of the most surprising in my years working there. I had explained to Stewart that I wanted to be my own boss, admitting that the circumstances surrounding my mother had inspired me to start my own business.

"I can't see myself doing this job for the rest of my life. The hours are long, and there isn't enough time off. I feel like I work all the time. No offense." I *did* mean to offend until Stewart spoke.

"My uncle is a difficult man to please. He gives me shit about productivity all the time. For years, he's been threatening to replace me." Stewart rubbed his jaw contemplatively. "I guess the stress of it turned me into the same tyrant he is. I'm sorry, Natalie. You've done a good job for the firm. We'll miss you. And if you ever need a good reference, don't hesitate to ask."

Wow, a feather could have knocked me over. Trying to close my slackened jaw, I thanked him and turned to leave his office.

"Hey, the cleaning crew for this place leaves something to be desired. If you can match their rate, we'll hire you to clean *our* offices."

"Uh, sure, Stewart."

I explained all of this to my mother whose tone turned hopeful. "I remember you telling me that. So, if this cleaning business doesn't work out, maybe you can return there?"

Hmph. She wasn't getting it.

Knock, knock, knock.

Saved by the door. Sporting short, silvery hair, high cheekbones, and friendly brown eyes, Dr. Clark stuck her head in the door. "Are you two ready for me?" She always wore a smile on her face and had a spring in her step. Aside from her demanding schedule, the woman did triathlons in her early sixties.

I could feel my mother clench as she sucked in a lungful of nervous air.

Clasping her hand in mine, I whispered, "We've got this." I turned my head toward the door. "Yup. Come on in, Dr. Clark."

She hustled in the door. "Sorry to make you wait. I had an emergency to deal with this morning at the ER. It was my brother-in-law, actually." Wearing a white lab coat over her pink button-down shirt and a pair of black slacks, Dr. Clark rounded her desk and took a seat in front of us.

"I hope everything is okay." My mother's voice hinted at concern.

"We could have rescheduled, Dr. Clark." I suddenly felt guilty for being there, taking her away from her family in need.

She made a dismissive gesture with her hand. "He's going to be okay. He works at a warehouse that burned down last night. His lungs suffered smoke inhalation, but he'll be fine."

I hadn't noticed the dark rings bottoming out her eyes until now. "Wow, it seems like there have been a lot of fires lately. Ma has some friends whose gift shop burned."

Dr. Clark met my mother's gaze. "Really? I hope they weren't injured."

My mother raised a palm. "Thankfully, they weren't."

"I'm glad to hear it. And I agree about the number of fires. It's troublesome." She drew in a deep breath and released it. "Okay, let's get you taken care of." She opened her laptop and punched a few keys. "You're looking well, Rose. How is the cleaning business going, Natalie?" Her gaze traveled over my work attire. I didn't have time to change, not that Dr. Clark would care.

I sat straighter in my chair. "Excellent. Going very well."

"And how's your business partner, Yazmine?"

Yaz was born in the US, but her family was from Thailand. We'd met our freshman year of high school and had been in each other's lives ever since. I honestly wouldn't know what I would have done without her. During the divorce all those years ago, she was my rock. Her mother, now a widow, could pass for her older sister. They both had beautifully shaped dark eyes and flawless skin. I was always so jealous. Yaz's current boyfriend, Ross Parker, whom she met through an online dating service, adored her. And I could see why. Yaz had a heart of gold. Always had.

"Yaz is doing great. We hired her mother to clean for us."

With people like my mother and Mrs. M. on the payroll, it didn't take long for our reputation to spread. We also offered introductory discounts to attract business, and if the client had financial difficulties, we offered lower rates. That was our mission statement: *clean houses at an honest price*. Only we actually meant what we said. Word got out. I even networked with a friend of mine named Miles, who was an RN at Charlottesville Physicians. He put flyers up in their break room, encouraging his friends to do the same around town.

A smile tugged at my cheeks. We were busting our asses with a few bucks in our pockets and the promise of much more to come. Soon, we'd have office space and maybe a receptionist. Given all the ups and downs in my thirty-six years on this planet, I felt like my life was turning around.

Dr. Clark planted her elbows on her desk, clasped her hands together, and leaned her chin over them. I suspected she was tired from the rigorous morning she had told us about.

"That's good news. And don't you also work for Natalie, Rose?"

"So far. She hasn't fired me yet." My mother lifted her chin at me.

I pretended to whack her, swatting the air instead. "Don't listen to her. She does a great job."

So did Yaz. She never went to college because, as with most people, she didn't have the money, but she was smart and motivated.

We were a good team. I was proficient with numbers, so I took care of the books as well as my share of cleaning services, permits, taxes, and other necessary details. Yaz was great at promotion. She also became our cover model. Her beautiful face adorned our website.

It wasn't long before I had sold my townhouse and moved back in with my mom. The sale went a long way toward financing this dream of ours. We were able to purchase a minivan and rent a storage unit for our equipment.

"Well, I am happy to report some good news. Rose, your bloodwork came in, and you are still in remission. I'm so impressed by your progress. And your weight is up. Whatever you are doing, keep up the good work."

My mother's shoulders eased. In fact, her entire body seemed to take one long exhale.

"I knew it! And you can also thank her new boyfriend."

This time, my mother whacked *me*. "You stop that, young lady."

"Oooh. New boyfriend, huh? Good for you, Rose." Dr. Clark beamed.

Not only did having a job breathe new life into my mom—she even renewed her driver's license that had lapsed and bought a small car—but so did meeting Harry. She bumped into his cart at the grocery store. Harry was recently retired, handsome, and very interested in my mother. Mom said he looked like Denzel Washington, and I had to agree. So far, they were enjoying the early stages of a golden-age romance, which my mother more than deserved.

She sputtered a few times. "Well, I don't know. . . . We've only been seeing each other for a short time. . . . Who knows where it will go?"

Dr. Clark leaned back in her chair. "Go for it. Have fun, Rose. Enjoy life. You deserve it."

On that, we could both agree.

* * *

Out in the parking lot, I stood by my mother's car, ready to get back to work. Not knowing how this appointment was going to go, I had given her the afternoon off. But *I* still had one more job for the day.

A red-and-white fire engine flew past, its lights flashing, and its siren loud and daunting. Several cars on the road above moved over to get out of its way. *Another fire?* Was it the same one I heard earlier? I thought of Dr. Clark's brother-in-law and my mother's friends.

Once the noise subsided, the fire engine long gone, I gathered my mother in my arms. "I'm so happy for you, Ma. I knew you could do it. Now you can tell Harry all about it." I pulled back and winked at her. "He's got a sixty-eight-year-old hottie who is healthier than a horse."

She shook her head at me, her eyes bashful. "I wouldn't go *that* far." She stared at her reflection in her car window. "I may get my hair cut. Why not? I have the afternoon off, right?" She was glowing. And she had every right to be. She'd suffered long enough. It was time for her to live.

"That's a great idea, Ma." I fished my keys from my purse, ready to climb into my minivan and finish my workday.

"Speaking of boyfriends, how are things going with Justin?"

My mother wasn't the only one enjoying the dating scene. After a long relationship drought, I managed to land *myself* a boyfriend. His name was Justin, and he was the landscaper for one of my clients. He was very knowledgeable about vegetation, which was how I had struck up our initial conversation, explaining that my mother could use some advice about weeds in her front yard. Total bullshit, but it got us communicating.

As with my mom and Harry, we were in the early stages of our relationship. Was he the one? I wasn't sure. I'd never felt that *spark* with a man, and I was starting to wonder if it was a myth. But, for all intents and purposes, Justin was fine by me. And a good kisser.

"Justin is good. I haven't been seeing him long enough to

know much about him yet. Not like you and Harry. How long has it been for you two?"

Her cheeks fired up. "I don't know. A month or two. I'm not sure I'm up for dating another man." A shadow flickered in her eyes that spoke of years of solitude and self-deprecation.

I bent over and kissed her cheek. "There is no rush, Ma. Take your time. You've got your whole life ahead of you. Try not to second-guess so much. Like Dr. Clark said, 'Have fun. Enjoy life.'" I snagged my keys and unlocked my van. "Okay, I gotta go. See you back at the house later." I took a step away. "And congratulations. We need to celebrate." A *woo-hoo* flew from my lips as I climbed into my minivan and fired up the engine.

* * *

I called my best friend, who was home suffering from the flu.

"How'd it go?"

"Excellent. Her bloodwork looked good, Yaz. She's still in remission."

"Yay! I'm so happ—" My poor friend couldn't finish her sentence. A coughing fit forbade it.

"Save your voice. So, tell me where I'm going next."

Using as few words as possible, Yaz did just that.

"Okay, thanks. And you think he's . . . safe, right?"

"His creds checked out. He used to be a fireman. Why? Are you worried? Want me to get more references?" She coughed and then cleared her throat. "We can always reschedule until I can go with you." Another cough stole her voice, and then a sneeze.

I thought about Yaz's offer before realizing it wasn't necessary. To date, we'd both been pretty good about vetting new clients. If she hadn't seen any potential problems with this new one, I could trust her judgment.

"Nah, text me his address, and I'll get over there as soon as I can. I gotta stop by the storage unit to grab our new vacuum cleaner. The one I used yesterday afternoon kept crapping out on me."

Cough, cough, cough. "Okay, hey, tell your mom I'm so happy for her. That is wonderful news."

"I will. Get some rest. And feel better. I'll be in touch."

Soon, I was back on the road, heading toward my next job. I hoped our new client would like my work and want to schedule regularly. According to the text Yaz had sent me, this guy was over thirty minutes west of where I was located, which was on the eastern side of Charlottesville. I turned up the radio and let my mind wander, basking in the news about Mom. The time flew.

"In one mile, take Exit 22 for Crozet, Route 250."

A bundle of nerves forced my feelings of gratitude aside, my stomach transforming into a hive of bees. I used my CarPlay to listen to Yaz's earlier text again, which included the name of the homeowner, Aaron Marino.

I took the exit, then turned right onto Route 250.

This was one aspect of the business that still made me leery. New jobs. Especially ones at the home of a man. Not a husband and a wife, which felt different.

Whenever either of us visited a new customer for the first time, we took the other one along to make sure everything was safe. The moms cleaned for repeat customers only. The last thing we wanted was some crazy dude abducting one of us and torturing us in his basement.

Unfortunately, that pesky flu bug had bitten my best friend *and hard.* I didn't want to catch it. As the end of March approached, I was eager to leave the cold-and-flu season behind. My hands were raw from constant washing.

The navigator's voice cut through my thoughts, instructing me to take my next right at the upcoming stop sign. Another pang of dread pulled at my abdomen. *Knock it off. You're fine.* What was my deal, anyway? Aaron's home was a tad farther from Charlottesville than most of my jobs, in a place called Crozet. Was that it? Crozet was a nice little town, really, just not as close as I had hoped. I tried to keep my jobs within half an hour, and this one was turning into forty minutes.

I took the right, traveling down a secondary road as my GPS instructed me to do. The trees in my periphery sprouted early buds, a welcome sign that spring was on its way. And the Blue Ridge Mountains moved closer, allowing me to appreciate their brilliance. I loved living in Charlottesville, with its historical landmarks and energetic culture, but I missed being able to see those mountains. At least you didn't have to travel far to take in some spectacular views.

As far as my nervous stomach, I had to remind myself that Yaz had assured me earlier that she'd spoken to Aaron over the phone. Said his credentials were good. A fireman, no less. Or maybe he used to be one. I couldn't quite remember. It reminded me of those recent fires. Did Aaron help put any of them out?

I'd grown accustomed to a certain level of jitters when it came to any new job, but something felt different about this one. Was my sixth sense trying to warn me? Or was I just being paranoid, which happened often. "Firefighters are heroes. They don't kill people; they save them." I sucked in a calming breath. "Okay, time for protocol."

I texted Yaz to remain on standby, *just in case*. If she didn't hear from me within the first ten minutes of my arrival, she'd be calling 911. I'd already pinned my location. Not only did I have a full selection of cleaning supplies, but I came equipped with pepper spray and a rape whistle, nestled in the pocket of my jacket. Plus, there was knowledge from various self-defense training videos that Yaz and I had practiced together in our living rooms.

More turns and three miles later, the words "Your destination is on your right" alerted me to my location.

I peered out my side window, trying to see the place, but several stubborn maple and oak trees fenced me out. Then the roof appeared, its height telling me the house had at least two stories, before the rest of the dwelling revealed itself.

That was when my mouth dropped open. "Wow."

I had seen this place before.

Chapter 3

Natalie

How did I know this house?

The answer came to me. About five years ago, I had gone winery hopping in this area with Luis, a man I had dated for a brief period. Luis was loud and all-knowing when it came to pretty much any topic. But he was cute—expressive brown eyes and a yummy body—so I went along. He was also a cop, so there was that man-in-uniform sort of thing. Not bad in bed, either.

Everyone knew Nelson and Albemarle counties in Virginia for their variety of local wineries, cideries, breweries, and distilleries—rivaling anything one could find in California, only much closer. And therefore, much less expensive to visit.

We found ourselves in Crozet, as I recalled. Luis wasn't great with directions—atypical for a cop—and kept telling me to take this turn and that to find a winery that he *swore* he had been to once. *Best wine in the region,* according to him, *won multiple awards.* He claimed it was remote, which was why it hadn't shown up on my navigator. *Yeah, right,* I had thought to myself. We got lost so often that at times I wasn't completely sure we were still in Virginia. (Given Luis's profession, I trusted he wasn't abducting me.)

After a series of wrong turns and unsuccessful attempts to find this winery, we ended up in front of the house I was staring at now. A white Craftsman cottage—although it was larger than a cottage—with a porch that spanned the front and a triple roof with dormers. Back then, a For Sale sign stood firm in the front lawn, or what remained of one.

What I remembered most about the place was how run-down it appeared. The white paint suffered chips and fading, the windows old, and the roof streaked with black mold. One section of the porch roof was definitely sagging. A realtor had probably mowed the yard. There was no landscaping, and patches of dirt revealed too much brown and too little grass. It didn't matter. The location was pristine, with several mansions surrounding it, remote but not isolated. With the right owner, the house definitely promised potential.

"I would love to buy a house like that one and fix it up," I had told Luis, admiring the picturesque horse pasture across the road. "Could you imagine? This is such a great area." I had no means to do this, but it was fun to imagine.

It seemed two minutes had passed before Luis was proposing. *What?* Did he think my interest in a random house had translated into me wanting to marry the man? As quickly as he had come up with his harebrained idea, I had turned him down. I mean, I actually laughed at first, assuming he was joking. He didn't appreciate the humor.

Needless to say, it was a strange day. I drove Luis home after that, and he never called me again. Probably for the best. He was cute, but not my type. To be honest, I wasn't sure what my type was. Men came and went from my life (with long spans in between). No one I had regretted losing . . . yet.

How odd that I was here once again. Only the house I

admired all those years ago for its potential must have found an owner who shared my vision. The chipped paint was gone. The white exterior was unblemished. Under a white aluminum porch roof, a red door provided entry, bound by two beveled stained-glass sidelights. The lawn was thick and ready for springtime green. A stretch of mulch for planting shrubs extended all the way up the long driveway to the house. A few small inhabitants had already taken root.

"So, this is where you live, Aaron?" I was impressed as I pulled into the lengthy paved driveway and parked next to a large silver GMC truck. Two red gas cans, along with saw blades and other hand tools, rope, a tarp, and what looked like a dark coat, littered the bed.

Pulling up now. I'll text when I'm about to go in.

Good luck.

Aaron had to be wealthy. Or a talented handyman. For some reason, that only made me more skittish. Why? I wasn't quite sure. Yes, I was in the country, but it was also an affluent area.

Suspense thrillers were my go-to for books and movies. The problem was, they let my imagination run a tad wild every now and then. This wasn't my first case of the jitters. When we had first started cleaning houses, I got pretty freaked out at a few, none of which resulted in anything sinister. A hoarder. A less-than-friendly old man.

Regardless of the situation, benign or otherwise, I checked my hair in the rearview. I took a moment to admire the caramel highlights that my hairdresser had woven into my wavy brown hair the week prior. Sharon had been talking about doing this for months, claiming it would bring out my eyes, which were the same blue and gold as my mother's. As I stared at myself in the mirror, I had to agree with her.

"Okay, time to go to work."

Heading in now. Keep your phone close.

Of course.

A headline flashed on the screen of my phone as I was exiting my vehicle.

> Authorities investigating a series of fires in the local area, one linked to a commercial public warehouse in eastern Charlottesville. Two men in the hospital due to smoke inhalation. No fatalities. Authorities suspect arson.

"A series. Arson?" I mumbled to myself. I thought about Dr. Clark's brother-in-law. "What kind of idiot would start a fire on purpose? You have to be absolutely nuts to do something like that."

My jaw clenched thinking about all the casualties, not to mention the men and women who had risked their lives to stop the insanity. It never ceased to amaze me how destructive *certain* people could be.

I thought about that fire that broke out at my mother's old neighbor's gift shop last week. Bea and Nigel were nearing retirement and had just put the place up for sale. They lost all their inventory in that blaze. At least the fire hadn't injured anyone. Bea had told my mom that she swore she had seen a dark, hooded figure in the woods nearby on the night of the fire. Was the person watching the place? Bea and Nigel were careful people. They didn't smoke or take unnecessary risks. A late-night call had informed them that their place was now a pile of rubble . . . *charred* rubble.

Baffled didn't begin to describe it. I hoped they had insurance.

I strolled up the walkway covered in light-and-dark gray pavers toward a porch supported by square pillars and anchored by natural stone accents. The shining sun gleamed against the beveled sidelights as I rang the doorbell and waited. It wasn't long before footfalls approached, the door swinging open to reveal a tall man with strawberry-blond hair and a slight curl to it. A trimmed beard of the same shade revealed a few wisps of white, suggesting Aaron was probably older than I was, but not by much, his face relatively free of wrinkles.

My pulse ramped. Every cell in my body went berserk.

The thin red-and-black flannel shirt Aaron wore did little to hide the robust shoulders of this guy or his pecs. And I had thought Justin was in shape. His faded jeans hung casually from his hips and toned waistline. White socks covered his feet. His amber eyes emphasized warm honey with a slight slant in a Ryan Gosling sort of way, his lips full, and his overall facial structure rather scrumptious. If this guy wanted to abduct me, I'd have a difficult time putting up a fight. *Not really, but man.* How many men and women had he rescued in a fire who were swooning over him still?

Zing. I felt it. As though an electrical shock had zapped me.

Suddenly, I wished I had put on makeup. *Damn.* My hair was back up in a neat ponytail, but my outfit was about as unflattering as it got: bright-orange sneakers and scrubs in pale yellow with a doggy print splattered all over them.

Yaz and I were the new owners of cockapoos. Daisy was my baby, and Sadie was Yaz's. We adopted the two sisters six months ago, when we had both decided to try our hand at pet parenting. And we were smitten. Our little spitfires kept us busy.

Embracing the doggy craze, I'd bought pj's with images of

dogs adorning them, tote bags, and throws of the same type of pattern, and of course, the scrubs. Hell, I even had stemless wine glasses with doggy prints etched into the glass—a gift from Mom last Christmas. She doted on Daisy more than I did.

"You the cleaning lady?"

Aaron's voice brought me back to the moment.

I do have a name.

Other than his gaze lingering on my outfit for a millisecond longer than normal, Aaron never really looked at me as he spoke. He stayed focused on the area behind me, mostly. He also kept lightly scratching at his beard, like someone would do when they were either anxious or prone to such habits.

Handsome or not, I kept my mind on high alert as I watched for signs of crazy from this guy. One hand remained in my pocket, gripping my pepper spray.

"Yes, I'm Natalie. Natalie Dugan." I reached my free hand out, and he shook it, quickly releasing his grip.

As with Justin, Aaron had the hands of a man who performed manual labor: strong and slightly rough. I preferred that to the clammy hands of my ex-boss.

"I believe you spoke with my partner, Yazmine?" I paused for him to acknowledge my words, my gaze drifting over to a small hall table in the center of the foyer, stacked high with mail. Had he just gotten back from vacation? That was a lot of mail. Behind the table, a wide staircase with wrought iron spindles ascended to the second floor, a herringbone-patterned runner providing traction for the hardwood steps.

"Yup." He stepped out of the way while rubbing the back of his neck. "I, uh, have some friends coming this weekend, and my place needs . . . an overhaul." He turned, his feet shuffling along a section of golden marble, covered by a tan woven rug that spanned throughout his beautiful foyer. Natural light from the beveled glass created a stunning prismatic effect.

I waited for a *Come on in. Let me show you around.* But none arrived.

Red flag number one.

Aaron disappeared around the corner for a moment, leaving me standing there until his head poked out. "Uh, are you coming in? Or do you need to get your equipment?" Confusion narrowed his eyes, which made no sense to me since he hadn't invited me in yet.

"Uh, yeah." I stepped over the threshold. "I wasn't sure what you wanted me to do." That probably sounded foolish, but I was feeling a tad awkward around this guy. Handsome, definitely. In fact, he was probably one of the most attractive men I'd ever seen. But a bit strange for sure. Well, maybe strange wasn't the appropriate word. *Unapproachable? Rude?* It was unclear.

"Once I show you around, I'll be working in the basement, so I won't interrupt you. I don't need you to clean the basement. . . . I'm remodeling it. . . . I prefer to keep that part of the house private. . . . If you need me, you can knock on the door at the top of the stairs. . . . I'll show you where it is." He scratched at his beard again. "Is something wrong?"

Good question. I pulled my cell phone from my other coat pocket and stared down at it with my protocol in mind. Did I need to call for backup? Aaron hadn't behaved aggressively. Quite the opposite. He'd made it clear he *wasn't* planning on dragging me into his basement. Then again, he could have just been saying that to lure me in. I doubted it. Why bring the basement up at all? I'd cleaned for all sorts of people, some a little quirkier than others.

Enough ruminating. Now you're the one acting weird. "Give me just a sec. I need to answer a quick text from my partner." I held my phone up. "Uh, I have it on silent."

Releasing my hand from the pepper spray, I texted with fast fingers.

I'm not sure about this guy.

Are you able to get out of there? Or do you need me to call 911?

Yes, I'm able to leave, and no, not yet.

Aaron cleared his throat. "All set?" I could feel his eyes studying me.

Since nothing terrible had transpired, I decided to wait another minute or two to make sure all was well. Trepidation filled my chest as I closed the door and followed Aaron into his house. Had I just become the idiot girl in the horror movie who walked into a dangerous situation when all the warning signs had told her otherwise? Or was I being overdramatic? I'd find out soon enough.

Aaron opened a door in the foyer. "Hall closet. You'll find the vacuum in there." He opened a second door on the other side of a wide opening into an adjacent room. "Half bath, which probably needs cleaning. I don't use it much. I use the one in my bedroom."

Okay, getting down to business. That seemed to satisfy my butterflies, or whatever my stomach was dealing with. "I brought my own vacuum, unless you prefer I use yours." I knew how well, or sometimes, how *not so well*, my equipment worked. At least it was predictable. And no learning curve.

"Yours is fine."

My sneakers squeaked along the marble floor until they met wide planks of natural wood that matched the stairs and opened up into a sizable living room on our left. Within the eggshell-colored walls, a leather sofa faced a large screen TV that hung proudly over a white mantel. No curtains outfitted the windows with curved tops, inviting the beautiful front yard to be part of the experience. A large pasture across the street and a small mountain enriched the scenic background.

A cream-colored throw made of soft-looking material curled on the sofa like a big, fluffy cat. Another one in brown bunched up on the floor next to a pair of work boots with a few crumbles of dirt beneath their tread.

Against another wall stood a waist-high oak cabinet with glass doors. A turntable and several other stereo components told me this guy leaned toward old school when it came to his music. A few boxes filled with what appeared to be vinyl records neighbored the cabinet, and I found myself curious about what type of music Aaron liked.

No knickknacks, mementos, or decorative *somethings* like you'd see in homes such as these.

I counted six water bottles on the end tables and the oak coffee table, some empty and lying on their sides, plus two coffee mugs, which I assumed were also empty. A takeout container took refuge on the coffee table, along with a stack of newspapers.

Not many people still read actual newspapers these days, but my mom did. She claimed she liked the *smell of the news*, her clever way of trying to be funny.

Flanking the fireplace, two bookcases recessed into the wall, each one housing a small collection of books and not much else.

In addition to the light mess, an inch of dust had gathered on all the surfaces not covered by newspapers and trash. The brown shag rug that centered the room came with a half-empty laundry basket and two pairs of sneakers, several balled-up socks as their loyal companions. The air smelled of wood and must.

Aaron cleared his throat. As he spoke, he waved one hand in one direction or another, depending on his focus. "I'd like you to straighten up, wash the throws, and whatever you find left out, mop, and dust. Shoes can go in the hall closet, newspapers and leftover containers in the trash can in the kitchen." He used the same hand to point to our right, where a wide doorway presented access to more of his house. "The kitchen is this way."

Yaz texted me.

Everything okay?

Yeah. So far.

We continued into the kitchen, which wasn't all that messy, either. Maple cabinets peered down at us, most without doors, exposing the contents within. A few plates stacked in one, a small selection of glasses in another. Most remained bare. The marble flooring matched the foyer.

A small selection of mismatched dishes, glasses, mugs, and utensils sat stacked and dirty on the side of an oversized sink, a dishwasher waiting nearby to clean them. A window overlooked the backyard above the sink, but I couldn't see out of it. On the other side of the kitchen, a medium-sized table of light-colored wood and four chairs provided a place to dine, since the breakfast bar didn't offer any barstools.

"I'd like you to unload the dishwasher, put the dishes away, and load it back up with whatever you find. Mop the floor and polish the countertops. You'll find polish under the sink. I have a different cleaner for the marble flooring than I do for the hardwoods. You'll find it under the sink as well." He quirked a brow. "I meant to ask, you do mop, right?"

"Yes. I have a special cleaner for hardwoods and for the marble, unless you prefer I use something else." On this issue, I was flexible, especially if the customer was particular about that sort of thing.

"What you have should be fine."

My job was easy enough, considering the room was vacant, other than a small mug tree and its partner, a large coffee pot near the fridge. The sapphire-blue granite countertops held a dull film, preventing them from properly reflecting the recessed lighting from above.

Where were the small appliances, or toaster, most kitchens included? *Pantry?* There were a few doors around the room, one of which had to lead to one.

Something told me that if I checked the fridge, I wouldn't find much there as well. Probably because the trash can near the back door stretched way past its capacity with takeout containers.

"I'll empty the trash. I meant to do that earlier."

I nodded. "Okay. But I don't mind."

Aaron raised a palm. "Nah, I got it."

To the right of the kitchen, we came upon what I assumed was a dining room that sat empty. A few dust bunnies were the only residents keeping the hardwood flooring from utter solitude. "This just needs a vacuum and a mop."

The last room he showed me brought us nearly full circle. In the corner of this lonely room sat a wooden desk with a computer and a chair. That was it. Was it intended as a formal living room instead of a makeshift office as it appeared now? This house was way too large for one person.

"Same instructions here. Vacuum and mop. I'll show you the upstairs." We returned to the kitchen, where a back staircase provided entry to the second floor. Aaron led me through three sizable bedrooms and two hall bathrooms (one Jack and Jill style), none of which were overly messy, just dusty and lackluster from nonuse, something you would find in an old house, not a fairly new remodel such as this one.

Only one bedroom included furniture, which consisted of a queen-sized bed, a nightstand, a clock, and a dresser large enough to store a minimal amount of clothing. I could tell the cotton seersucker bedspread used to be white, but dust and age had turned it more of a light gray. The beige area rugs suffered the same fate.

Mustiness continued to permeate the air, the sound of creaking floors or a ticking clock suggesting a life of solitude. In fact, the only room that showed any signs of *significant* life in the house was the living room, and *maybe* the kitchen. It was as if Aaron stayed here but didn't quite *live* here.

All I could think was that a house of this size deserved a family, with plenty of space for kids to run around, dogs to play with, and families to gather. There was none of that here, not a remnant or a photo to suggest Aaron knew *people*.

Although he did say he had visitors coming. Whoever they were, maybe they could breathe new life within these walls.

Not only did the house seem unusually quiet, so did Aaron.

Any attempt I made at small talk *Are you from Virginia? . . . Do you have family in the area? . . . Yaz had mentioned you are or used to be a fireman. Is that true?* didn't amount to much. He responded with a shake of his head or a nod, depending on the question. From that alone, I learned Aaron wasn't from the area, didn't have family in the area, and *was* or *used to be* a fireman.

"I saw this house about five years ago when I got lost trying to find a winery in the area. It was for sale. Were you the one who bought it back then, or did you buy the place more recently?"

"Yup, been here four years."

At least he offered a solid answer this time. "Well, you've

done a great job fixing it up." I teetered my head back and forth. "Well, I never saw the inside. Just the front. But even that looks so much nicer now."

Nothing but silence came back at me. Was Aaron being rude? Hard to tell. Shut down would be my guess. Something in his amber eyes spoke of sadness. Had he lost someone close to him? Was it a wife? I imagined him fixing up this house for her, trying to make her happy. Or was I confusing his life with movies like *The Notebook*.

He does have those Ryan Gosling eyes.

Aaron opened the double doors to a generous-sized closet positioned at the top of the stairs. "Sheets are in here. They could use a wash. And my guests will need some for their air mattresses, so wash them all. Towels are in the bathroom closets, same instructions with those. Laundry room is downstairs off the kitchen. I forgot to show that to you. It's easy to find. You do laundry, right?"

"Yes, I can do laundry. And I can do windows if you'd like."

He waved me off. "Not necessary. Windows are fine. Carpets need vacuuming . . . furniture dusted. All the stuff we've discussed." He waved one arm out. "I haven't been on this floor in . . . months."

Months?

"When you're done washing everything, I'd like you to put sheets on the bed. No one has used the bathrooms in a while, but I'm sure they need . . . something. Bleach and cleaners are under the bathroom sinks. Once you've washed the towels, put them in each of the bathrooms, along with any washcloths and hand towels you find. Maybe stack them on the side of the sink or something." He scratched at his jaw again. "That's about it." He made a feeble attempt at a cough. "I would have done it myself, but I've been working on some projects in the basement. Sort of lost track of time."

"Oh, that's cool. Are you turning the basement into a game room or something?"

True to form, Aaron simply shook his head and led me back down the stairs.

Hmm.

When we reached the living room, I pointed upward. "Those are your guest bedrooms, correct? Do you have an owner's suite that you want me to clean?" I was curious what his bedroom looked like. Why? I had no idea.

He shook his head again. "No. I'll take care of my room. No one goes in there but me."

Not a great thing to admit, dude. You're not getting laid. That seemed to fit his persona. Aaron was a recluse. And yet, he was also a fireman. An interesting juxtaposition of personality traits. Then again, who was I to talk?

We returned to the foyer where a moment of silence brought the discomfort level up a notch. At least he wasn't a serial killer. I didn't get that particular vibe from him.

I took a breath and exhaled as I spoke. "Okay, I better get started. The laundry will take some time." I ticked tasks off with my fingers. "Other than dusting, vacuuming, laundry, mopping, washing dishes, and scouring bathrooms, is there anything else you need done?"

"Nope, that about covers it. Your partner mentioned an introductory discount, but I'll pay the regular fee." He placed his hands on his hips and stared off.

My phone vibrated again in my pocket. It was Yaz checking on me.

All good?

All good.

Aaron grasped the knob of a door that he hadn't opened yet. I suspected it led to the basement. "You like dogs?" His gaze washed over my outfit once again.

I stared down at myself and chuckled. "Yeah, I just got a cockapoo named Daisy. She's still a pup."

He nodded. "Cool." And then he was gone.

* * *

Three hours later, I had washed most of the laundry, and the house was starting to sparkle. It wasn't that difficult, really, and the washing machine was one of those large capacity models, so I could throw in hefty loads of blankets and towels, which Aaron didn't have a lot of to begin with. I was able to return the bedspread to its original white. Mostly.

I went through the laundry basket in the living room, not entirely sure what was clean or dirty, so I washed it all. Interestingly enough, no undergarments. Aaron had said he wanted to take care of his own bedroom, so I assumed he felt the same way about his underwear. Or maybe he didn't wear any. *Girl, you have a dirty mind.*

To his word, the owner of the house kept to himself, staying out of my way. He checked on me once after the first couple of hours and offered me a cup of water from the tap. *What a guy.* What bothered me most about Aaron was his inability to look directly at me. One thing I remembered vividly about my father was how he never made eye contact with me or my brother, especially when he was guilty of something. After the divorce, he stopped making eye contact out of apathy. Neither sat well with me.

Aaron's reclusiveness made it hard to imagine him as a firefighter. Then again, wearing a thick coat and helmet, eyes shielded, victims didn't care much how personable their firefighters were. They were more interested in surviving or saving their home. How many firefighters did I actually know? None. Perhaps the fictionalized, outgoing, hot fireman was a myth.

In the living room, while dusting, I did a quick perusal of his albums to discover that Aaron was a classic rock fan. Bands such as The Who, Bruce Springsteen, and Tom Petty were some of his favorites, if quantity had anything to say about it.

I found something else in the box of albums that caught my eye. Sandwiched within those retro sheets of vinyl hid an 11 x 17 framed canvas of what was called "The Fireman's Prayer." Beautifully written and poetic, The Prayer asked God to watch over the firefighter, providing the courage to do what was right. Considering these bare walls, why was it here? The frame was solid, and the canvas nicely decorated with images of a hydrant and a helmet that supported the hero's profession.

When I thought I heard footfalls coming up from the basement, I slid the Prayer back into its hiding place and moved on to other projects.

A recluse and a firefighter. What else was there to know about this man? Other than his obvious good looks. Somehow, I knew I would have to find out.

Chapter 4

Casualties of War

I hadn't planned on hurting people, except for the guilty ones, yet I knew that could happen. Most people were expendable, especially rich clowns with no conscience or care for others. Civilian casualties were unavoidable. It was all part of the war I had waged. I had lost everyone who had mattered to me, and the life that went with them. I understood loss.

After the *so-called* accident, there was nothing left to aspire to. So, I gave up trying. I turned away from everything good. It was in the dark recesses of my soul that I realized I was punishing the wrong person. A plan grew like a weed inside my mind, all the steps taking root. A good plan, one that would restore my life to its former self.

Once I held those accountable responsible, I'd move past the hate. It was what got me out of bed in the morning. No more would I turn the other cheek. I could pretend all was well. I had done such a good job of it. On several occasions, I had almost convinced myself. When I finished my plan, I would revisit who I used to be. Not here, but somewhere. My second rebirth.

I had too much to do first. So far, I had outsmarted the authorities. They suspected arson, but they had no idea who was causing the fires. I'd done my homework. I had to. This wasn't a time for sloppiness.

When *and if* they ever figured out who was behind the chaos, I'd be long gone, my enemies strewn about like carcasses on the side of the highway. My hourglass would refill, my life restored. Only then would I be able to say, *Bye-bye, Virginia* and to the shattered life I had suffered.

Chapter 5

Natalie

Aaron paid for my services, and I was on my way. I checked the amount. *No tip. Hmph.* Although I had to consider that he *had* paid the full-service fee, not our introductory rate, so I guessed I shouldn't complain. The house wasn't really all that messy.

When I left him my business card, I asked if he wanted me to return to clean again after his guests had left, and he said he'd let me know. Door closed. It was like a mic drop, only slightly ruder.

Oh well. I drove home, my yawns bordering on jaw cracking. Fatigue reached into my bones, and I was ready for some rest.

My CarPlay indicated a call coming in. It was Justin.

"Hey, Cleaning Lady. How was your day?"

This was one of two nicknames that Justin coined me with, Cupcake being another. I didn't mind being called Cupcake—although it wasn't my favorite—but Cleaning Lady felt derogatory, even if he didn't mean it that way. Aaron had used the same moniker.

Men.

"Ha. You don't need to keep calling me that, you know." *Maybe I'll start calling you Lawn Boy. How'd you like that one?* "My day was . . . tiring." Another yawn stole my voice.

"That sucks. Are you up for dinner tonight, or are you too tired?" The sound of something heavy collided with a metal surface in the background.

"Are you still at work?"

"Yeah. Just putting my shit away in the back of my truck. I did the house of a banker dude, and this pool lady parked her goddamn van right behind my trailer. I wasn't able to get out for an hour, which was how long it took me to find the b . . . *woman*."

My eyebrows shot up. "Were you just going to call her a bitch?" I half chuckled, not sure if I thought it was funny or sexist.

Justin exhaled a heavy breath. "Sorry. I wanted to be done an hour ago, but I couldn't find her *or her* scrawny assistant. Dude looks about thirteen. I guess they were down at the pool house . . . or whatever you call it. While I was waiting, I didn't want to just sit around. This owner has cameras everywhere. Rich asshole type, and he signed a contract with me last fall for a year. That means I can finally get some new equipment that I've been needing. My mower is about to shit the bed, if you know what I mean." He grunted a little as though lifting something else, making louder *bangs* in the background.

I had to get used to some of Justin's idiosyncrasies. At times, he came off a bit rough around the edges, and I wasn't entirely sure he held a positive view of women. He called his sister a gold digger because she was dating a man with means, even though she worked full time as a nurse. Whenever he analyzed a celebrity, if say we were watching a movie, his criticisms focused more on the way the actress wore her hair, or how aggressive he felt she was behaving, often referring to her as a bitch, much like the pool person. Nothing earth-shattering, but the men never earned the same judgment from him. Aggressive men were always *bad ass*.

The door to his truck opened and closed with a *clunk*. "Anyway, I can take you to dinner if you'd like, or we can make it another night. I've got some work I need to catch up on later." The truck's engine grumbled to life.

Most of the time, Justin was a sweetheart. He'd brought me flowers on two occasions and always opened the door for me, even though that was old school in my mind. When he was tired or stressed, an impatient man emerged, one who was quiet, preoccupied, and sometimes short in his responses. I suspected by the tone of his voice, impatient man was taking the reins for the evening.

I spoke through more yawns. "I'm beat. If you don't mind, I'm gonna take a shower, eat a bowl of cereal, and plop into bed." I thought for a moment. "I only have one job tomorrow. How does your schedule look?"

"I've got a full day, but I can make it work. Why? What did you have in mind?"

Since tomorrow was Thursday, an idea came to me. "How about we try that new Mexican place off Main Street? Do you know which one I mean? The one that just opened last month. I read some reviews, and it sounds like their food is pretty good."

"You mean the one with the big cactus on the roof? A bit gaudy, if you ask me."

"Yup. That's the one. They have five-dollar margaritas during happy hour. I'll treat. And then, we can go to a movie or hang out at my place and watch a movie." I hadn't had Justin over before, mostly because I lived with my mom. And he hadn't invited me over to his place yet, either. We were still newbies at this.

I did have a nice big TV in my room, where I envisioned a round of cuddling along with some extracurriculars if he was up for it. The man was certainly fit. Justin was tall and thin, from what I could tell, I'd yet to discover his *other* attributes. He was not my usual type, but as I'd reasoned many times; I wasn't sure what my type was.

Aaron came to mind. *That* was my type. Not the recluse aspect of his personality, but the solid body and full muscles, amber eyes that a girl could lose her mind over. Larger than life. In my experience, men who looked like Aaron were often full of themselves—or unapproachable—although in Aaron's case, I suspected vanity wasn't the cause of his reclusiveness.

"I could try to cut out early. What time were you thinking?"

The ticking of his truck's blinker told me he was turning one way or another.

"Well, happy hour is four to six-thirty. What time do you think you'd be free?"

* * *

Wearing a brown quarter-zip sweater with a white T-shirt underneath and jeans, Justin sat across from me in our booth, enjoying his five-dollar margarita. Justin was cute and kept his brown hair very short, almost a military cut, probably to beat the heat. His blue eyes smiled when he spoke.

"Yup, this was a good idea, Cupcake."

There was that nickname again. Did I like being referred to as a food item? The first time we met, I was wearing hot pink scrubs with those doggy prints splattered all over them (I had sets in many colors), along with my go-to bright-orange sneakers. He said I was dressed like a cupcake, and the name stuck. Since I liked cupcakes, it didn't bother me at the time. For me, it seemed like an endearment a father would bestow upon his daughter, and besides, I wore different clothing on our dates. Tonight, I donned a button-down olive cardigan with a matching camisole and a pair of thick black leggings that coordinated well with my brown-and-black riding boots. I had on makeup and pulled my hair back into a barrette, a few curly wisps falling around my face. Not bad, if I said so myself.

Justin took a generous sip and smacked his lips. "I'll be ready for a second one of these soon."

I crunched a chip dipped in pico de gallo and nodded, ranchero and mariachi music emanating from hidden speakers around the restaurant. Colorful murals, intricate paper lanterns, and what were called sugar skulls decorated the room, providing an authentic ambiance. The chairs shone in vibrant red, the tables boasting large patterns of Mexican flowers, thick plexiglass used as an overlay to protect the artwork.

"Told ya. Hey, did you hear about those fires in the area? Sounds like some lunatic is causing them."

Justin glanced out the window at a cluster of young women walking by. If he heard my question, he wasn't acknowledging it. Or maybe the size of one woman's boobs preoccupied him.

I cleared my throat. "So, how was your day?" I chased the chip with a sip of margarita, the tangy lime exciting my taste buds.

"Same old, same old. Yours?" He grabbed a few chips and stuffed them into his mouth. *Crunch, crunch, crunch.*

"Hmm. Let's see. I cleaned the office where I used to work today. It's an accounting firm downtown. Old Dominion. Anyway, I never used to care for my boss, Stewart, but since I left there, he's been a lot nicer to me. He even stuck around and chatted it up while I worked." I took another sip of my drink, the glass cold against my palm. "I got to hear the office gossip. I guess Stewart's uncle, who owns the firm, suffered a heart attack, so he's eased up on him for the time being. From what I've heard, he's a real piece of work. Oh, and our office manager, Gretchen, just found out she's pregnant—"

"He was probably hitting on you." Justin's eyes narrowed. He sat straighter in his seat, the corners of his mouth crimping downward.

"Huh?" I waved him off and scoffed. "*Please.* Stewart is not . . . " How to say this without sounding conceited or judgmental? "Handsome. *At all.* He's kind of a nerd. Not even close to anyone I'd be interested in. He asked me out once, and I turned him down immediately." I lifted my palm to emphasize the apprehension in my voice.

"Ooh. So, he *was* hitting on you." Justin raised his chin slightly as though I had divulged something that confirmed his suspicions.

I wrinkled my face at him, setting my glass down on the table. "I worked with him for several years, Justin. He wasn't hitting on me, and even if he were, it wouldn't matter." I met his gaze, trying to determine what he was implying. "I'm not interested. And he's well aware of that."

Are you the jealous type, Justin? If he told me not to clean for Stewart anymore, this would most definitely be our last date. I wasn't into possessive men.

Our waitress, who had already introduced herself as Sophia when we had arrived, cut through our little chat when she delivered our soft tacos, the smell of Mexican key lime and spices teasing my hungry stomach. "Here you go." After she placed our entrees on the table, her attention went to our nearly empty basket of chips. "Can I get you any more chips?"

Justin was already nodding, his gaze pivoting to her ample

breasts. "Sure. Thanks." I hated it when men did that, and Justin had done it twice already.

The Latina woman with long black hair, pulled tight into a ponytail, took the basket from the table. "I'll be right back with more chips. Is there anything else I can get you?" She glanced over at me.

"Maybe a couple of extra napkins, and that should do it."

"And another margarita." Justin lifted his glass, now filled with ice and not much else. He handed the glass over to Sophia.

"Was that with salt on the rim or no salt?"

"Salt." Justin stared down at his phone as it vibrated on the table. He picked it up and examined the screen. "Sorry, work thing."

"No worries." I stared over at Sophia, who had just asked if I also wanted another drink. My head was starting to swim. "No, I'm good, but thanks."

"Okay. I'll be right back with your chips and one more margarita." Sophia left us as the words "Hey there" reached my ears from a different location.

I leaned out of my booth as my mother, rocking a mid-thigh-length plum cardigan, a black camisole underneath, approached. Jean leggings covered her toned legs, brown leather flats on her feet. I had to say that the woman was slaying it with her new outfit and pixie-styled, natural gray hair. Since she'd gone into remission, started working for Yaz and me, and had met Harry (the icing on the cake), she was full of life as though twenty years had melted away. I was so proud of her.

I had always wished my mother had more going for her when she was younger. Pictures of her, donning shiny brown hair and unique blue-and-gold eyes, a movie-star-quality smile, Rose Natalie Sullivan was a catch. She met my father in high school. He was a popular running back on the high school football team. And of course, she was a cheerleader. Neither one of my parents came from money, which was why they had decided to send Dad to college after they married. Apparently, my mother took accounting classes at night, offered by the local community college, until her time would come. I knew this from my grandmother (who had since passed). Nanna told me how hard my mother had worked to support my father. Coming from a different generation, Nanna felt it was proper to allow the man to achieve his professional goals first, so she didn't criticize, only reported the goings-on. The one detail Nanna didn't reveal was why my mother never went to college full-time. Even later on. She had me at thirty-two, so there was definitely time. I always wondered about that.

And so, Jack Dugan Sr. went to college, studying business management and eventually working for the power company with a good, stable salary. He had a pension, which was unheard of nowadays. He had set himself up well.

Aside from her night classes, my mother continued her job as a bookkeeper until I arrived, and then she stayed home with me to save on daycare. My brother, Jack, arrived three years later. I remember her planning our playdates, which was probably the only time she had to herself. Sometimes she'd come with us if the parents were friends. From my young age, she seemed happy and doting. But as the years passed, that winning smile faded. My father was so wrapped up in his job and his friends, he'd barely come home for dinner. He worked out at the local gym. He drank at the local bar. Or so he said. Was he seeing other women by then?

My mother was still a beautiful woman in her own right. As far as I was concerned, she had many good years ahead of her, a small nest egg, and a house with no mortgage. (Awarded to her as part of the settlement.) Now, she also had a handsome piece of eye candy.

On her arm, Harry offered a nice pairing in his black wool

pea coat and tan cashmere scarf. He kept his gray hair cut short, against his nearly flawless dark skin. Together, these two were as hip as it got.

"Well, hello there. I didn't expect to see *you* here." I stood from the booth and gave my mom a quick hug, followed by one for Harry, whose cologne smelled of sweet vanilla.

"You mentioned this place to me last week, and we thought we'd give it a try." My mom's cheeks reddened, but only a little, which happened when she was excited or upset.

My mom turned toward Justin, who was accepting a new margarita from Sophia, causing the small area around us to feel cramped. "Hello, Justin, so nice to see you again."

"Yeah, you too." Justin took a quick sip of his drink and placed the glass on the table. What he didn't do was get out of the booth and address my mother properly. Not cool in my mind. Being so new in our relationship, I found myself rating Justin on my invisible scale from time to time. This particular moment sagged his approval rating below a five, if ten were Keanu Reeves, who I had read had a considerate heart.

It had never been easy meeting men when I was younger, but the older I got, the more challenging it had become to find anyone who liked to go camping, or take long walks, or even cuddle on the couch while watching a good movie. Those were my preferences. I also enjoyed following local musicians and a night of dancing whenever the opportunity presented itself. I settled for ESPN, lectures at the local university—about topics I had little interest in or knowledge of—or a night out at a sports bar, pretending I was interested, just to go out with a guy.

I did try golf once with a professor I had dated, but I was bad at it and unwilling to invest hundreds of dollars in equipment to improve, something he suggested I do.

Over the past few years, I'd dated a cop, a financial advisor, a professor from the local university, and one bartender. Justin was my first landscaper. On our third date, Justin had asked that we be exclusive. "I don't want to share you," he'd said.

For me, it felt sudden. But I hadn't dated anyone for so long that I decided to give it a try. The more frogs I kissed, the less I expected a prince to *poof* out in front of my eyes. Was Justin a frog or a prince? Time would tell.

"Would you like to join us? We just ordered, and I'm sure we can get you some menus quickly." I gazed at my boyfriend of almost three weeks, who nodded.

"Sure. We've got room." Justin slid over on his wooden bench, which left more than enough seating space for me. "You can sit next to me, Cupcake." He patted the wooden bench for emphasis.

My mom hesitated, her attention drawn to Harry. "Well, we don't want to impose." Her voice wavered as though she had other plans but didn't want to be rude.

Harry slid his hand along her lower back. "If you don't mind, we'd love to join you. It looks like the place is filling up right quick."

He was right. Customers were piling in, ready for those happy-hour prices.

Keeping his hand on her lower back, Harry guided my mother into the bench seat across from Justin, taking his spot on the outer edge. "So, what's good here?" He peeled off his coat to reveal a button-down shirt with a pastel windowpane pattern, the material a nice complement to his tan chinos.

I slid in next to Justin, who said, "Margaritas!"

* * *

With our bellies full and my head starting to float from my second margarita—I ordered an encore when Mom ordered hers—the four of us were able to talk more freely.

"I hear you're a landscaper, Justin." Harry balled up his napkin and tossed it onto his plate, which contained a few left-over crumbs from his taco salad. "Is the work steady enough in the winter months around here? Enough to keep you busy?"

Justin had just returned from the restroom. He'd had four margaritas to my two, but I was driving, so it didn't matter much.

"Not always. I've got one, year-round contract with a client who keeps me somewhat busy, pruning, trimming, and doing mulch beds. I'm hoping to get more contracts soon that will carry me through the winter months. If I'm lucky, the rich dude will recommend me. Most of my clients want six-month contracts to save money. Spring is here, so work will pick up." He exhaled and draped his arm around my shoulders, the scent of his last margarita ripe on his breath. "If it gets too slow, I clean gutters and sometimes do some pressure washing for a buddy of mine who has his own business. I haven't had to do that this year, though. That one contract is with a banker dude who lives in a mansion out in Afton. He signed last fall, and he's kept me pretty busy with all sorts of shit." He pursed his lips, his gaze going sheepish in front of my mother. "Sorry. Pardon my language."

My mom waved a dismissive hand. "I curse all the time, young man. You can ask Natalie about that one." She smirked and gazed over at me.

"She sure does. *Shit* is one of her favorite words."

My mother scoffed. "Now, let's not exaggerate. Don't be a brat." She gave me *the look*, the one that warned me to watch my manners.

I giggled inwardly, mostly because I was only kidding. My mother wasn't much for curse words. She was being polite.

"A banker, huh? Where in Afton?" Harry sat straighter in

his seat, his attention piqued. "I did some work for a man out there years ago, electrical stuff."

Justin removed his arm from my shoulders and fiddled with the edges of his used napkin. "Oh, really? So, you're an electrician?"

The muscles in Harry's jaw flexed. "I used to be. Until I worked for a man named James Logan. Ever heard of him? He also has a place out in Afton." Something in Harry's friendly brown eyes darkened.

When Justin didn't answer right away, I gazed over at him, which seemed to prompt his response. "Yeah, same dude. Should I be worried? The only thing worse than a rich asshole is a rich *banker* asshole. They're all just a bunch of criminals. And this guy wasn't easygoing at all. He barely spoke to me when he signed the contract. And he keeps me busy doing crazy shit, like hanging Christmas lights over the holidays and cleaning up dog shit from his yard. But he pays well." He quirked a brow. "So far, anyway."

Harry's chin seemed to rise as he stared down at Justin. He crossed his arms over his broad chest. "James cost me my license. He *claimed* I did shoddy work that caused a fire in his garage, the oversized one that's separate from his house, which also contained two of his sports cars. Fire destroyed them both." He stared off. "If you ask me, it wasn't the work that he didn't like. It was the color of my skin." His exhale carried a hint of a growl to it. Or maybe it was more of a low groan.

My mother's brow lowered, and her eyes filled with concern. "My heavens."

"Really? That's awful, Harry." I reached across the table and placed my hand over his, which remained resting on the table, until he pulled it back, not out of rudeness, but more in an *I'm fine* sort of way. "Can you get your license back?" Harry seemed like such a nice man. He didn't deserve that sort of treatment. The guy was a racist? *What year is this, anyway?*

He shook his head. "No, and I'm retired now. But he soiled my reputation in the community. I used to live out in Nellysford, which wasn't far from his . . . complex, but I sold my small home and moved into town." His gaze fell to the empty plate in front of him. "I just want to put it behind me."

He sounded so defeated as though the experience still haunted him.

"When did this happen?" I asked.

My mother nodded as though she meant to ask herself. I could tell this news had shocked her.

"About five years ago."

My mother patted his leg from under the table, her head leaning over onto his shoulder for a brief moment. "You had said you used to be an electrician, Harry, but you never told me about any of this. I'm terribly sorry, hon. That's just awful. Didn't anyone stand up for you? You must've had customers who liked your work, right?"

Harry's brow rose and then fell. He exhaled a tense breath. "Well, yeah, I did. A few spoke on my behalf, but it didn't do any good. One of the firefighters who came to put out the flames even claimed the incident in question wasn't due to any recent electrical problems, but more of an area in the garage where either mice or some other rodent had chewed on the wires. According to him, that was what had caused the hazard."

"How were you able to speak to the firefighter? Were you there when the fire broke out?" My mind was growing more curious by the second.

"No, I wasn't there, but I talked with the fire department about it afterward to find out what *they* thought had happened. They directed me to the captain in charge on that day."

"Can I get you anything else?" Puncturing our airspace, Sophia gathered up the decorative plates and silverware.

"No, we're good. Thank you. Just the check." I helped stack plates together to make her job easier.

"Will this be on one check or two?"

Feeling sorry for poor Harry, I piped in immediately. "One check. My treat." I offered a comforting smile, but Harry was already searching his pea coat for a wallet.

"No, no. Let me get this. We crashed your dinner."

My mom nodded alongside him.

Justin just sat there staring at his empty drink as though he wished for another.

I raised a palm. "Listen, Harry. This is happy hour. The check isn't that much. You can get it next time." I gazed up at Sophia. "One check. Whenever you're ready." While Sophie rushed off, I fished through my purse to retrieve my wallet, pulling out a credit card before Harry could stop me. Justin sat there, offering nothing.

Hmm. More demerits on the approval scale. Although, I *had* already offered to pay.

"It seems to me that if an actual firefighter can vouch for you, I would think that should carry some weight." Concern, mixed with an equal measure of ire, forged a wrinkle across my mother's forehead.

"It's fine, Rose. I just want to put it behind me." Harry's shoulders slumped.

From my perspective, my mother's boyfriend was still dealing with the emotional wreckage from what had happened. Who wouldn't feel that way? I remember worrying at one point in my career as an accountant that I'd audit a client and they'd retaliate somehow. Those types of things were possible anywhere, even now, in the houses or businesses we cleaned. It was a good reason why it was wise to always bring a partner along. People could accuse you of anything. Stealing was one of those accusations that would be hard to recover from. We'd been lucky so far.

Sophia returned and collected my card. As we were gathering up our things, a thought came to mind. "You know, Harry, it may be worth talking to that firefighter again. I mean, you lost your profession because of this. He ruined your reputation. That's defamation, right?" I'd seen a few shows featuring lawyers along the way.

Harry stood and shouldered his arms into his pea coat, then helped my mother out of the booth. He nodded once. "Yes, it is, young lady, and there's also something called business disparagement. I looked into them both, but unless I had the firefighter's statement in writing, there wasn't much I could do about it. Friends could be character witnesses, and so could previous clients, but that wasn't enough. Not with a man like Logan, who has his hands in every pocket around town, including politicians."

I suddenly wished Justin didn't know Logan. "But still. Wasn't it worth asking him for an official statement? It sounded like he was on your side."

Justin gave my knee a slight squeeze, telling me he either agreed or thought I should shut up. I wasn't sure which.

After I signed the credit card bill, I slid out of the booth as more people came bustling through the door.

"The firefighter had his own problems going on. In fact, he quit when an apartment building in Charlottesville went up in flames, resulting in two casualties: an older couple. Apparently, he tried to rescue them both and almost died in the process. Sustained a considerable number of injuries."

The four of us stepped outside, the streetlights not yet aglow as a stiff March breeze offered a splash of refreshment to my margarita-flushed cheeks. Regardless of the chill, the days were growing longer. A few early birds chirped from branches bursting with springtime buds to prove it. Cars drove past on the highway in the distance, a shopping center next door, a flurry of activity. Carts clanked and rattled in and out of the main grocery store.

"That sucks about the firefighter." Justin took my hand. "I could never do a job like that one. Too much risk."

Harry and my mother stood by the curb, ready to take their leave.

"I'm sure Aaron Marino agrees with you, Justin."

I'd let go of Justin's hand to fish my keys from my purse. My head sprang up. "Wait! What did you say his name was?"

"Aaron Marino. He was a fire captain at the time. From what I heard, he also taught CPR classes and was an EMT. After the incident, he quit all of it, according to one of his friends at the station. Of course, he could be doing much better now."

What were the odds? "You're not going to believe this, but Aaron just hired me to clean his house this week. And from what I could see, he isn't doing much better . . . at all. The man barely spoke to me."

Chapter 6

Natalie

Because Justin wanted to see a movie, I wasn't able to grill my mother's boyfriend any further about the circumstances regarding Aaron, but I hoped to do just that when the situation presented itself again. When I returned home, Harry was gone and Mom was already in bed, Daisy sleeping by the door waiting for me. And after those two margaritas—plus sitting in a darkened theater for two hours—I was beyond tired. I barely had enough energy to let Daisy out to pee and brush my teeth before collapsing into bed.

That night, while Daisy slept soundly against my side, I had some bizarre dreams, mostly about fires, but nothing that made any sense. At one point, I was battling a blaze with a large snake in my hands. I'd always been prone to dreams that were as vivid as they were strange. I chalked it up to hearing about Aaron from Harry and moved on.

It was now Friday morning, which meant I had three houses to clean and a church on the west side of town. Since Yaz was still sick (I had already texted her), Mom came along with me. Cleaning was always a lot less strenuous when you had someone to talk to—plus that whole worrying about people accusing you of stealing their stuff thing. Not only that, my mother could clean circles around me, which also made my day much easier.

I fed Daisy and ate a quick breakfast, consisting of yogurt with fresh fruit, topped off with a bowl of oatmeal, something my mom said agreed with her digestion.

With breakfast behind us, and Daisy fenced off in the front living room, we hopped in my minivan and took off. I always made sure to check on my little pup several times throughout the day; another reason I didn't take jobs that were too far from home.

Riding shotgun, my mom strapped herself in. "So, how was the movie last night?"

I clicked my seatbelt and started the engine. "Good." I giggled. "I think I fell asleep during part of it. Those margaritas were good, but they also made me tired."

I backed the van into a small, paved turnaround in the driveway and drove out onto the street, my eyes scanning our relatively new neighbor's overgrown lawn. "How was *your* night? Did Harry stay long?" I wiggled my eyebrows for effect, which only made my mother scorn me with her gaze.

"Now, you stop that, young lady. Don't forget I *am* your mother. And no, Harry didn't stay long. We watched *Wheel of Fortune*, *Jeopardy*, and the news." She stared out her side window.

"Harry was quiet after dinner." She glanced over at me with worry in her eyes. "I didn't know anything about what had happened to his career. We've been together for two months, and I would have thought he'd told me something that important." Her tone leaned toward edgy, yet sympathetic.

I pulled up to a stoplight. "Well, you can't exactly blame him, Ma. It sounds like what he went through was humiliating.

I just can't believe that man was so awful to him." When the light flashed green, I proceeded forward. "Harry is a nicer person than I am. I would have sued . . . what was his name?"

"James Logan." My mother's voice came out deadpan as though she had no sympathy for the rich banker with an oversized garage and sports cars, all of which had burned.

"What an ass." I turned onto Water Street, which would bring us to our first job of the day. "I just can't believe that I cleaned Aaron's house this week."

My mother scrunched her face at me. "Who?" She grabbed her purse from the floor and searched through it, pulling out a tissue to wipe her nose. Postnasal drip was a daily occurrence for her.

"Aaron. You know, the fireman who vouched for Harry. The one who fell on hard times."

"Yes, I remember." She wadded up her tissue and tossed it into a small trash bag hooked to the console in front of her. "Poor man."

"Speaking of firefighters, have you heard from Bea? How are she and Nigel doing?"

"I haven't. But I owe her a phone call. I'm sure she's got her hands full with the insurance company."

"Oh, good. I wondered if they had insurance. Do they know how the fire started? Or if it was intentional?" Those headlines continued to intrigue me.

"I don't know."

We pulled up to the two-story house for a family of six, an unusually large number for the times. "Okay, I'll grab the vacuum and the mop. You grab the bucket of cleaners."

* * *

After returning home for a Daisy potty break, we were on our way to the second job of the day, a small house of an elderly woman who managed to get around with a walker. Mrs. Armstrong was my favorite customer, and not just because she loved small dogs, allowing me to bring Daisy along with me. At eighty-six, the woman hadn't lost an ounce of spunk. While she played with and cooed at Daisy, who ate up all her loving attention like peanut butter, Mom and I cleaned her house. We also offered her a large discount to allow the sweet woman with short curly gray hair the means to afford our services. Hell, I'd clean her house for free if she hadn't professed more than once, "I won't have your charity, Natalie. I am a proud woman, and I will pay a fair wage for your services."

I got the message. It was a pride thing, which only made me love the woman more. I found out about her from Miles.

It was a partly sunny day, the temperatures climbing into the upper 60s, a nice change from the winter chill. The awakening of nature had a unique smell to it, earthy and fresh. And the sun felt warmer as it positioned itself for longer days ahead. I enjoyed knowing all of this was happening around me. And the birds. They were coming back in droves—the ones that had left—their music sweet to my ears.

We were ten minutes from Mrs. Armstrong's, with Daisy cuddled in the passenger seat on Mom's lap. I turned the radio down. "Okay, revisiting our earlier conversation. Do you remember me telling you I had cleaned for Aaron *the firefighter* this week? The man Harry had said revealed the real reason for the fire at James Logan's estate?"

Mom stroked Daisy's patchwork of black-and-white fur, which the pup seemed to appreciate, considering her Almond Joy shaped eyes were fluttering.

"I told you, I remembered. I had just forgotten for a moment. What a coincidence, though, huh? That's awful how he tried to save those people, and he was injured in the process. I wonder how badly he was hurt. Is Aaron married, or does he have any kids that you are aware of? How old would you say he is?"

I shook my head. "No family that I saw or am aware of. I'd guess he was in his late thirties. I'd been to his house one other time, you know. About five years ago, when this all must've happened." I went on to explain about my date with Luis, the police officer who had me searching high and low for a winery that never appeared.

My mom wagged her finger. "*That* I remember. Didn't Luis propose to you? I seem to recall something about that." As she scratched the back of her neck, she grinned over at me. "It's not every day that my only daughter receives a proposal from a police officer." Her gaze found the road in front of us. "That's so strange that you went to Aaron's house and didn't even know it. Where does he live, anyway? Is his house nice? What's it like? Is he a neat man or a slob?"

My mother and her inquisitive mind. When I was in high school, she was like the Spanish Inquisition whenever I started dating someone new or went to a party. *What is he like? Does he have good parents? Where does he live? Who was at the party? Was there any drinking going on?* It was endless, but I never minded so much. It only showed me how much she cared. I had friends whose parents barely spoke to them. And then, there was my dad, the opposite end of the spectrum.

When good ole *Daddio* divorced my mother, he divorced Jack and me in the process. I was sixteen when Dad took off, and Jack was thirteen. In what seemed like no time, he had a *new* wife named Krista (who I suspected he'd been seeing long before the split) to focus his limited attention on, and then, his *new* kids, Danny and Tabitha, who came years later. *Asshole.*

Who starts a new family at fifty? We weren't exactly close. I considered myself lucky. I had my mom.

"He lives in Crozet, and yes, the house is very nice. But empty. I mean, he has some furniture, but not much. The place was dusty. He has three guest bedrooms upstairs and one main suite on the first floor. The bedrooms looked like they've been sitting empty for years. I didn't see his room, though."

"Hmm. What was Aaron like?"

I removed one hand from the steering wheel to stroke Daisy's head. "Very handsome. And yet, quiet. Just like his house."

Mom sighed. "That's what men do when they suffer a loss or fall on hard times. They shut down. My father was like that. Your grandfather. I remember when the mill closed. Gosh, I couldn't have been more than six at the time. My father didn't speak to anyone for weeks. Except for my mother, who had a way of reaching him that none of us kids could. Eventually, he got a new job doing carpentry work, so everything worked out, and he was a saver. Hoarded every spare penny. Other men shut you out because they are selfish, like your father." Her face fell into a frown. "He was a hard man to love." Her eyes unfocused, her mind lost to a difficult time in her life.

"Dad shut us all out, Ma."

"Yeah, well, after we were married, he wanted a family right away. Did I ever tell you that?"

"No, you didn't." I remained quiet, hoping she'd reveal more about that time in her life. I had always wondered.

"After he got his master's, we tried to get pregnant. It took me a year, but then it happened." She sighed. "I was so happy. Until three months later, I miscarried. I was devastated."

The pain in her voice was evident. I never liked hearing it.

"We waited six months, and then we tried again." Her pause extended as though the memory was too painful to finish.

I was her firstborn. That much I knew. And she had me at thirty-two. She must've been in her mid-twenties when this all happened.

"I'm sorry, Ma. That must've been so hard." I touched her shoulder, my heart reaching out to her.

"The second pregnancy ended the same way." A painful tremor invaded her voice. "I felt like such a failure. I knew your father wanted kids. And I was so afraid I couldn't give him any." Her troubled gaze found me. "That was when he first turned away from me. Shut me out. I could feel it. And I wasn't up for trying again. Not for years. I didn't think I could handle another loss. I didn't want to go to school anymore. I was too old. I took a class every now and then. And I worked as a bookkeeper for Mr. Wright. He was our dentist back then." Tears glimmered in her eyes. "I felt dead inside." Her spirit lightened, as did her tone. "Until *you* came along. You were my blessing. Those first few years with you and Jack were some of the best memories of my life. I foolishly believed that everything was going to be okay."

I had no idea. What a bastard my father was. Why couldn't he have supported my mother? Been there when she needed him most. I truly hated the man. "Gosh, Ma. I feel so bad that you had to go through that alone. Not to repeat myself, but I'm so sorry."

She wiped a few tears away and snapped out of her cloud of sorrow. "It's okay. That was years and years ago. I don't know why I even brought it up. Anyway, Harry is very sweet, but he can also be private at times."

"Do you mean about what he told us last night?"

"Yes, about last night, but there are also times when he's unavailable, and I can't reach him. I know he lives in a small house in town, but he's never invited me over." She wobbled her head. "We're still getting to know each other. And we're not teenagers. He's the sweetest man I've ever met. Very doting. I know I'm being silly. It's just . . ." She pursed her lips.

"No, you're not being silly, Ma. Especially after what you went through. Harry is very different from Dad. I can see that. And if it's any consolation, Justin hasn't had me over yet, either." I smirked. "We also haven't been together all that long. Monday, we'll have been dating for three weeks. Do you believe Wednesday will be April already? Anyway, from the state of his truck, I get the feeling he's not all that neat, and considering my profession, maybe he's self-conscious. He calls me 'Cleaning Lady,' and I hate it. And he better not expect me to clean *his* place." I kept my tone jocular, since I wasn't all that serious. Most people had messy vehicles, and I would consider cleaning his place if he helped me. That was, if we made it that long.

I expected my mother to laugh or at least smile at my observation, but she didn't.

Her silence spoke volumes. She was worried.

"What's on your mind, Ma? You can tell me anything."

"Nothing. It's just that there is so much I don't know about Harry. I'm not even sure if he's ever been married or had any children. When I ask him about these things, he tells me we'll have plenty of time for *those* types of conversations."

"Hmm. Maybe he had a bad divorce, or he's estranged from his kids. It happens." Hard to imagine when Harry had been nothing but kind toward me. "Remember how he said his friends and customers had vouched for him, but he never mentioned any family."

"Yes, I do remember that." My mother's voice drifted off as Daisy shifted in her lap. The little pup buried her nose in the crook of her arm as though trying to hide herself away from the world outside of our minivan. *She is so adorable.*

"I wonder if he didn't tell me about what happened with

his job because he was afraid I'd judge him for it." Her eyes watched the trees and houses pass by on the side of the road.

I kept my focus forward, knowing I had several turns coming up, and traffic around me was heavy, typical for a Friday. It didn't help that Mrs. Armstrong lived near UVA. Sort of. She wasn't right on campus, but close enough, requiring me to navigate students and faculty as I drove through town. I loved this section of Charlottesville, where the younger generation walked about chatting it up, probably about a hookup or a class that was driving them crazy. *Man, when did I get so old?*

"He may have worried about that, Ma. I'm glad he did finally tell you, though. And now that he's told you, he knows you would never do that. Don't forget, Mr. Logan sounded like a major racist. Those are touchy subjects. And you're white, which may add a little uneasiness to the subject." I blinked, my smile meant to offer comfort. "Maybe now that he's breached that barrier with you, he'll be willing to share more."

My mother's warmth reached me as her hand touched my shoulder before she returned it to Daisy's back. "You are sweet to say that. I do hope Harry shares more about his life with me. I really like him. He's so considerate. He gives me back rubs all the time and dotes more than anyone I've ever known. A real gentleman. As far as that Aaron person goes, I can't imagine being brave enough to run into a burning building and risk my life for total strangers. And to have something even worse happen as a result, like losing people, would have to be devastating."

I agreed with her. It made me wish I had offered to clean his place for free. And here I was, silently grumbling to myself that he hadn't left me a tip. When I had first met Aaron, his good looks threw me off. And his size. There was something extraordinary about him. Knowing what I did only added to his exceptionalism. Of course, he was reclusive. Who wouldn't be?

Mrs. Armstrong's house came into view, steering my thoughts toward work. I pulled up to the curb and shifted the van into park.

"Okay. How about you bring Daisy inside, and I'll grab the vacuum, mop, and the bucket of cleaners. Sound good?"

* * *

We were on our way to our next job when a call appeared on the vehicle's center display. It was Yaz.

"Hey there. I just got a call from the Fletchers. They're also sick right now and asked me to reschedule." She coughed before clearing her throat. "Not sure if it's the flu or a stomach bug."

"Yuck. That sucks. Okay, go ahead and reschedule, but make sure you wait until they're better." I exchanged a look with my mom. "We don't want to catch any of what they've got."

Even though my mom wore a mask at all her jobs due to her compromised immune system, she still nodded her approval.

"Hi, Yaz. I hope you are feeling better, dear."

"Oh, hey, Mrs. D."

"How *are* you feeling, by the way? Your voice sounds a little better." It did. A few days ago, Yaz could barely finish a sentence without hacking up a lung. She'd only coughed once so far.

"Better." She cleared her throat with gusto. "It's all stuck in my throat now, so I need to clear it. But I do feel much better. No fever, and I have my appetite back. Ross has been gone for a week at a wedding expo, trying to attract potential customers, so he's been spared. The minute I felt symptoms coming on, I told him to stay away until I was better."

Ross was one of those men who kept himself busy all the

time. Not only was he a foreman at a natural gas plant, but he also did part-time survey work and appraisals for the county, and dabbled in wedding photography, which, according to Yaz, was something he had always loved to do. The guy had endless energy and probably a healthy bank account from his efforts. His positive attitude meshed well with my best friend's. If I could have picked the perfect man for her out of a catalog, it would have been Ross.

The late March sun glared down at me, its brilliance unrestrained by clouds that had drifted off aimlessly. It felt like a spotlight to my retinas—probably due to the double margaritas from the night before—causing me to pull the visor down and throw on a pair of sunglasses.

"Hey, before you go, Yaz. Can you see if Holy Souls would allow us to come clean their church early? I'm driving right now, and Ma has Daisy on her lap. We are supposed to be there at five, but if we could come now, that could finish our day early." The clock on the dash flashed 1:14 p.m. Ending my workday early on a Friday sounded good to me. I could even see if Justin could get out early as well. We hadn't made plans.

"Sure. I'll call you right back." *Click.* The call disconnected.

As it turned out, the church couldn't reschedule, which was a bummer. Working until eight on a Friday night didn't thrill me. Such was the life of an entrepreneur.

Since I was already headed toward the western edge of town, in hopes the church could accommodate, I thought of an idea. "Since we're on this end of town, why don't I drive us to that really good sandwich shop off Route 250 in Ivy near the country club? Remember? It's called Cork and Board. You can stay in the car with Daisy, and I'll get us something to eat. They have those heaters out front as well, so we may be able to sit at one of the outdoor tables." The car's temperature gauge told me that the glaring sun was pushing the temperatures into the mid-sixties. A spring heatwave.

My mother's stomach rumbled. "Sounds good, Natalie. I'd love one of those turkey and cheddar sandwiches with the pickled red onions, and I'm hungry. Did you bring food for little miss, here?" She rubbed Daisy's belly from the side.

As though she could understand Mom's question, Daisy gazed over at me. The bright sunlight made her dark eyes, normally camouflaged against the dark fur of her face, now clearly visible. They glistened like two black diamonds.

I scratched under her chin. "You hungry, Daisy Dew?" I cooed, causing her eyes to widen and her ears to flutter.

"Yes, I brought her some food. And we definitely have time to kill."

"Let's do it!" My mother thought for a moment. "Isn't Ivy near Crozet?" She gave me a look, excitement sparking in her eyes.

"Yeaaah. Why?"

"Let's have lunch and wander over to that man, Aaron's, house. You've got me intrigued. I'd love to see what his place looks like."

"Really?" I quirked a brow at her. "Why would you want to see *his* house?"

I had to admit, I was curious about Aaron, too, and *I'd* seen his place.

She shrugged. "I don't know. What else do we have to do? And maybe ... oh, never mind."

I rolled my eyes. "Maybe, what, Ma?"

"Well, maybe we could ask him about Harry."

Aha. Her ulterior motive. If my mother ever decided on a new profession, private eye would suit her well.

I shook my head. "No way. I don't even know the man. That feels creepy. And it sounds like Aaron has been through a lot himself. It's not professional of me to be asking customers questions about their personal lives."

She nodded, but it was subtle. "Fine. I get it. You have a reputation to uphold. Maybe we could just drive by. Or does he live on a private road or something?"

"No, it's not a private road."

"So, could we just drive by and see what it looks like?"

I tried not to laugh. "I already know what it looks like, *remember*? I was there. I cleaned the place?" I flailed one hand.

"Yeah, but *I* don't." She turned in her seat and readjusted Daisy in the process, who was now watching the world outside the minivan's windows with wide eyes.

Before it got cold last fall, and when Daisy was just a baby, she loved to go for car rides with the window down. I looked forward to introducing her to summer soon.

"Call me curious. It would be fun."

I shook my head at my mother and her inquisitive mind. "Why do you care what his house looks like, Ma?"

"I don't know, honey. What else have we got to do? It's a beautiful day for a drive."

She had me there. What else *did* we have to do? I also loved spending time with her, whatever the reason.

I exhaled. "Okay. We'll have lunch, and then, we'll head over." I wagged a finger in her direction. "But no jumping out of the van and banging on his door, asking a million questions."

She shot me an intense, unwavering glare. "Now, Natalie, you know better than that."

Did I? I chuckled to myself.

* * *

Lunch was as delicious as I had hoped. Cork and Board had those outdoor heaters, so Daisy could walk around within leash range, and Mom and I could enjoy our sandwiches. An unfettered March sun provided heat to our backs. I'd forgotten how tasty the food was: mayo infused with cranberry, and turkey and cheese loaded with flavor. It was a party on my tongue. Since we arrived at 1:30 p.m., the lunch crowd had dispersed, leaving us with the place to ourselves.

Even though I gave my mother a hard time about it, I had to admit, I rather liked the idea of driving by Aaron's house, but I wasn't sure why. Maybe I had that same curious mind as my mother had. Or maybe it was nice to see this adventurous side of her. She'd been so down after the divorce. For years, she had turned inward, not an ounce of vitality within her. When lupus struck her out of nowhere, I feared it would be the fatal last straw.

Not so. Lady Luck had dealt her a second chance, and not just for her, but for me too. I had my mother back, only a happier version of the woman I grew up with. If she wanted to take a brief detour and play Inspector Clouseau, who was I to tamp out her fun?

Who are you kidding? You just want to see Aaron again.

I had to argue with my inner voice that the odds of me seeing him were remote. Not from the road.

Regardless, off we went in search of Aaron's dwelling.

"If he ever asks me to clean for him again, I may be able to find out a few things, but I wouldn't get your hopes up. The man barely speaks. And I'd have to wait until I've cleaned his house a few times, so he sort of knows me." If only I could get to know a man like him. A hero. Someone who would do without question what most of us would run away from.

When she didn't reply, I gazed over at the duo fast asleep. With the sun beating through the windshield and both of their bellies full—soft rock playing from the radio—it was the perfect prelude for a nap.

We reached Crozet in no time. I woke my mother, who wiped her mouth clean of sleepy saliva and took several stabilizing breaths.

"I didn't mean to fall asleep. How long was I out?"

"Not long. Fifteen minutes or so."

Daisy yawned in her lap, her tongue so long it would make Gene Simmons envious. Hard to believe with such a small mouth.

"This is Aaron's road."

My mother stared out of all the windows in the van, her eyes curious. "Which side of the road does he live on?"

"Right side."

"Wow, this is a nice area. Well-to-do."

"Yeah, it is."

She pointed to a gorgeous brick house, pediments above large windows with black shutters, and even a widow's walk atop an impressively high roof. A second-floor balcony with a curved frame gave the house a unique quality. The mowed lawn was impeccable, and the shrubbery tailored to commercial standards. A wrought iron gate remained closed to keep passersby away. People like us who wanted nothing more than a tour of the place and dreamed of what it would be like for ourselves.

"I wonder what the owners around here do for a living?"

"I have no idea. Maybe they own one of the wineries in the area. Or they're doctors or lawyers." I glanced at Daisy, who watched with interest, yet knew nothing about what we were discussing. "There is a lot of old money in this area."

A horse pasture appeared on our right—one I remembered from my last visit—just before Aaron's driveway.

I took comfort in knowing that the mystery man had a long driveway as well as several old oak and maple trees that framed the road, providing cover.

"Is Aaron's house as nice as these other houses?"

I shook my head. "Not really. It's nice, though, but nowhere near as large. We're coming up on it now. Keep your eyes peeled."

And that was when my heart started beating out of my chest. I expected this to be a drive-by, Aaron none the wiser about our little excursion. But that wasn't going to happen, considering the man in question was standing at his mailbox glaring at us.

Chapter 7

Natalie

What in the hell was I supposed to do now? As my tires slowed, crunching stones on the pavement, Aaron's gaze fixed on me, his brow furrowed in a curious sort of way. Of course, we'd baffled him. In his eyes, what were we doing here? I was twenty feet away and not sure what to do.

"Is that the fireman?"

"Yes," I said with as little movement from my lips as possible.

My mom stared over at me as Daisy barked, jumping up on all fours. She had spotted him too.

Last month, Daisy and her sister, Sadie, had found their voices. So, when Daisy spotted Aaron through the windshield, ear-piercing barks echoed off the interior walls of the van, enough to make my brain hurt.

"Calm down, Daisy. It's okay. It's just Aaron." Why I felt the need to explain things to a dog who probably heard the same *wah-wah* sounds coming from my mouth that Charlie Brown had heard from his teacher was beyond me. She heard tone, though, so when she wouldn't stop barking, I tried a firmer one.

"Stop! Daisy. It's okay. You're okay."

The spectacle only drew more attention to us as we approached. *Christ on a cracker!*

I had two choices: I could drive away and wave, hoping I didn't seem too obvious—who knew if he'd ever hire me again anyway—or I could stop and try to come up with a plausible excuse as to why I was driving by his house.

Down came my window. Decision made. A fresh burst of March air offered my racing heart and clammy chest some relief, a slight musk wafting off Aaron as he approached. When I had first met the ex-firefighter, I had felt something. I wasn't sure what. Nerves, maybe, but as I met his gaze once again, that same spark excited my heart. On the outside, I remained calm as a cucumber. On the inside, dopamine flooded my brain with feelings of euphoria and giddiness. The reaction was not only visceral, it overwhelmed, nearly stealing every breath. My palms grew sweaty.

Keep it together.

"Oh, hi, Aaron. I was telling my mother how nice your house was, and since we had a job in this area, she asked me to show it to her. I hope you don't mind." *Did that sound legit?* I sure hoped so.

Aaron removed a few pieces of mail from his black mailbox, the post painted white to match his house. Given the pile in his foyer when I had first arrived, I assumed he was checking his mail randomly, but I could have been wrong. He could've been checking the mail, just not opening it. Hopefully, his guests—the owners of the Jeep and the truck sitting vacant in his driveway—encouraged him to resume normal activity. He crossed the road to greet us, no cars in sight.

"Yeah, I guess so. I wondered if maybe I hadn't paid you enough."

Bark, bark, bark. Daisy was beside herself. She jumped from my mother's lap onto mine, making me grunt. I shifted the vehicle into park.

Embarrassment had me shrinking in my seat. "Sorry. She's a puppy. Hasn't gotten used to strangers yet." I cupped the pup's head and stared directly into her soft eyes. Those Almond Joys stared back at me, full of innocence and wonder. I kissed the end of her wet nose. "Now you stop that barking, Daisy Dew." I held my tone even, trying not to add to her fears. "You're okay. Mommy and Grandma are right here with you." *Again, why the need to try and reason with a dog who didn't understand English, much less words?*

Aaron watched me, his gaze landing on my scrub top. "Nice outfit." The humor in his voice was nearly imperceptible, but I heard it. He scratched his upper lip with his index finger.

And then he did something unexpected. He reached through the open window and scratched the black fur growing rampant on Daisy's crown, his manly hands showing a gentler side. The gesture seemed to settle my pup as she licked his fingers relentlessly, the ones she could reach as she moved her head this way and that. And the barking had ceased. Thank god! A popular quote came to mind: "Never trust a person who doesn't like dogs. But always trust a dog that doesn't like a person." It seemed Daisy trusted Aaron.

The corners of Aaron's mouth lifted just a tad, his face brightening. His amber eyes almost glowed with possibilities of what this man was all about. It was like watching the sun come out from behind a dark cloud, warming the air around us.

My heart melted. "You like dogs?" Something inside me grew ecstatic by this new development, almost giddy.

Aaron hadn't done anything extraordinary, other than show

he had a pulse, yet I appreciated this moment more than I wanted to admit.

"I used to have one. A golden . . . CB. Her coat was almost white."

This was more than Aaron had spoken to me in the hours I'd spent at his house. I was determined to keep the conversation going. "What does CB stand for?"

Aaron's eyes glazed over as he continued to pamper my dog. "Cotton Ball." His cheeks flushed as another smirk flirted with his lips. "*I* didn't name her."

Who did, then? Sister, mother, or past lover? I was dying to know.

"Aren't you a little cutie?" As Aaron scratched behind Daisy's ear, a light wind kicked up a few of his auburn locks, his scent encircling me in a state of wooziness. He'd trimmed his hair leaving it short around the base, thick and full at the top.

I wanted him to remain in this moment with me for as long as I could, even if I didn't understand why. I liked Justin, but what I was feeling now didn't compare. If I had to put this feeling, whatever it was, into words, I'd say I was crushing on Aaron. *If only I could switch places with Daisy right now and enjoy those pampering hands.*

My mother straightened herself in her seat. "Natalie tells me you were a fireman. Is that true?" Like an ice pick, my mother's question stabbed through our tranquil moment.

And that was when the warmth in Aaron's eyes vanished, the dark cloud returning to block out the amber suns. In fact, Aaron's expression became impassive to the point of deadpan. He removed his hand from Daisy's fur and let it drop by his side.

"I need to go." And off he went toward his beautiful house. Did my eyes linger on his backside and the jeans that fit him like a glove? It wasn't as if I had a choice.

"Well, that was strange." My mother raised her brows at me. "Was he like that when you cleaned his house?" She leaned toward my window, watching him walk away. "Handsome man."

I closed the window, wishing my mother hadn't been with me. What would have happened had she not asked him that question? Something flickered in Aaron's austere demeanor, something that offered a warmer side of him.

I handed Daisy back to my mother and shifted the car into drive. "Yeah, that was pretty much how it went. To be honest, he wasn't *that* nice when I saw him last." My tires rolled forward. "What did you think of the house?"

"It was nice, from what I could see of it." My mom resumed grooming Daisy with her grandmotherly fingers. "Poor man." She never spoke of him again.

Poor man.

Those words resonated with me all afternoon.

That night, after Mom went to bed and I had chatted with Justin over the phone, we'd made plans to drive over the Blue Ridge Parkway on Saturday and have lunch, I sat in my bed with my back against the headboard and opened my laptop. Seeing Aaron today only heightened my curiosity about his life. Harry had said that the apartment fire had happened about five years ago, so I typed in the year along with "Fire in Charlottesville apartment building."

Several stories appeared from all over the area, so I had to narrow my search to certain sections of Charlottesville, not knowing any of the specifics. Most of the fires had caused injuries, leaving people displaced.

It wasn't long before I found what I was looking for.

> Two dead and thirty displaced following a fire at a Charlottesville apartment complex Monday evening. At 10:30 p.m. on Monday, March 17, Charlottesville Fire and EMS received a call regarding a fire at Shetland Apartments, located at 1602 Monument Avenue. When officials arrived, they rescued over thirty residents, some from apartment windows.
>
> Firefighters extinguished the blaze, leaving a partially collapsed roof, the building severely damaged and uninhabitable, according to officials. One firefighter suffered severe burns in the incident. The cause is still under investigation.

It had to be Aaron's story. I kept searching for more articles to be sure. None of the other reports I read included anything about a firefighter being injured, aside from this one. I wish they had included his name, but I realized that wasn't how these articles read. It was only when something controversial happened that names came forward.

I switched gears and read about the recent fires. I realized that the first one, at a small home on the eastern side of town, had also happened on March 17th. The incident was one of three in recent history that had officials suspecting arson. Was the date a coincidence, or did it relate somehow to the apartment fire? But it had been five years. For all I knew, it could have been random. *Or maybe the arsonist has a problem with Saint Patrick's Day*, I thought in jest.

Now you're being silly. But? What if?

At the foot of my queen-sized bed, Daisy cuddled into a fluffy ball, her patchwork of white-and-black fur resembling a little pillow.

I yawned, the clock on my nightstand warning me it was getting late. It was Friday night, and I was going to bed at ten-thirty, two-and-a-half hours after finishing work. I thought about calling Justin again, but from our earlier conversation, I learned he had a friend in town who was meeting him for a drink and to watch a hockey game at a local bar. We had plans for the next day, and that was enough. The days of me barhopping on a Friday night were long gone. Watching a movie and cuddling on the couch sounded like a plan. Maybe a nice bottle of wine to relax me. Since Harry had also been busy, Mom had been my couch-time date for the evening, until she grew tired and went to bed halfway through *Downton Abbey*.

As I snuggled into my sheets, Aaron's past continued to gnaw at my thoughts. There was something about him I couldn't shake. This was unusual for me. I had never been overly interested in people, excluding my friends and family, of course. I suspected my father had put a sour taste in my mouth regarding how awful humans could behave. During the divorce, my mother lost all her "couple" friends, the ones who they had met for cookouts, happy hours, or whatever event was happening at the time. Losing them didn't help her feelings of loneliness, which set the stage for her introversion over the next two decades. It was only now that she was coming out of her shell. Meeting Harry and rekindling her friendship with Yaz's mom, not to mention, the people whom she encountered on the jobs she worked—people like Mrs. Armstrong, the wise, old sweetheart who loved on Daisy—filled her up.

Somehow, Aaron had the same effect on me. He wasn't particularly friendly. Yet something drew me to him. And when he smiled, sort of, I was ecstatic. *I am also crazy.*

A yawn reminded me it was time to put my thoughts to rest. I'd have to save this problem for another day.

* * *

"I need to take care of some things before I can pick you up." Justin's tone carried an edge.

"Is everything okay?"

He huffed. "I don't have time to explain. I'll call you when I'm ready to head over to your place." He rushed his words, tone curt.

"No problem. I'll go check on Yaz. I think she's better now. And if you get too tied up, we can reschedule."

"Okay, bye."

Hmm. I really hated dating, especially in the early phases of getting to know people. It made it difficult to understand what was really going on with Justin. Was he angry about something? Did it have anything to do with me? We'd kissed many times, but that was about it. Considering I hadn't gone out with anyone in a while; I wasn't sure what the rules were anymore. The way Justin gawked at every breast within eyesight, I had wondered if he wasn't that attracted to me. Or could it be that I wasn't all that attracted to him? It seemed like I'd be feeling more *oomph* by now. Teenagers experienced these types of emotions, not thirty-six-year-old women.

When was the last time I felt that sort of zing, anyway? I wasn't sure why I asked myself these questions when the answer was obvious: *Aaron.* The hermit with the gorgeous amber eyes and the mysterious aura. I saw something when he lowered his guard with Daisy. I just wasn't sure what. My mother admitted later that she thought he was weird. *Galant but strange.* And she could be right about that. My taste in men was far from perfect.

I took a shower and dressed, choosing an oversized flannel shirt with an off-white camisole underneath and a brown pair of cotton leggings for a day in the car, sneakers on my feet. Feeling the need for protein, I made myself a plate of scrambled eggs with toast and a large cup of coffee to chase it.

I sent a quick text to Yaz to make sure she was up for visitors and brought Daisy out to do her business before I left. Mom had slept in but agreed to watch the pup for the day. Harry was out of town.

Later, Mom planned to have dinner with Mrs. Mounivong, whose first name was Neenah, but I could never call her that. Since freshman year of high school, I'd referred to Yaz's mom as Mrs. Mounivong, and that was the way it would remain.

Since I hadn't grabbed yesterday's mail, I brought Daisy out front instead of out back, killing two birds with one stone. And that was where I caught sight of Mom's new neighbor, Alan *something or other*. Mom's old neighbors, Bea and Nigel—the owners of the gift shop that burned—had rented their old place out to a small family. When that family had moved out of state, they were free to sell. Alan moved into the raised ranch last summer as the new owner.

Alan was a big man with long brown hair and a thick beard. He wore dark T-shirts and baggy pants regularly, lending a sort of sloppy appearance. I tried not to be judgmental, but when it came to cleanliness, my mother had rubbed off on me. The man couldn't have been much over forty, so not old, just unkempt.

Anytime I tried to strike up a conversation, Alan simply walked away. And his idea of lawn care was—how to put this—nonexistent. He let his yard grow thigh-high and then thought a clunker of a mower was going to fix it, which clogged and stalled every few feet. His solution was to tamp the grass down, only to have it spring back up when it was ready. After a couple of months of this, Alan stuck to cutting his front yard only, leaving the sides and backyard long enough to produce hay. And ticks! Leaf season was a whole new nightmare. Last fall's offerings still piled high.

Mom called the county at one point, which helped, but didn't make the man any friendlier toward us. When I saw him these days, he just scowled at me. Like Aaron, Alan appeared to be alone. I hadn't seen another car in his driveway since he'd moved in last year. Only his trashcans and a pile of wooden pallets remained permanent residents out front, along with his old maroon sedan.

"Hi, Alan." I waved, trying to be neighborly, knowing it was a wasted effort. My hand gripped Daisy's leash.

True to form, he behaved as though he hadn't heard me. He opened his large garage door and entered. Did he know Mom had called the county on him? According to her, they hadn't asked her name. It was entirely possible Alan was just a curmudgeon. He disappeared into his garage and came out carrying two large jugs. I caught the word *GAS* with the image of a flame on the side. When he reached the trunk of his large sedan, covered in rust and several dings, he popped it open and put them inside.

Preparing for some spring mowing? I suspected not.

He returned to his garage and grabbed two more, repeating the process.

Four?

When he came out carrying the last two, totaling six gas cans, I stood there baffled. What in the hell would he need six cans of gasoline for? By the ease with which he carried them, I assumed they were now empty. So, he was going to the gas station? I sifted through my mind, wondering what he was up to. Did he have a generator? Or maybe a boat somewhere? I'd never seen either in the months he'd been living here. Something else loitered at the recesses of my mind: the fires. The news app indicated the authorities suspected arson. Was I witnessing someone plan their next crime?

I'd watched a crime drama on Netflix once about a man whose life unraveled, until he took matters into his own hands, kidnapping various women, each one imprisoned in his basement. The darkened house, the creaking of the floorboards, and the soiled bed sheets covering his windows, gave me the willies. I couldn't remember the name of the show (there were so many) or the character, but I remembered those bedsheets. And Alan had bedsheets for curtains.

Alan slammed his trunk closed and stared over at me. "You need somethin'?"

I snapped out of my haze, flustered. "Oh, no. I was just . . ." Nothing came to mind, so I simply turned and headed for the door.

As he drove off, I made a mental note to pay more attention to the people around me. If Alan were up to nefarious activities, it would come out eventually.

I couldn't wait to tell my mother about it.

Chapter 8

Natalie

I stopped by Panera to grab some soup and a sandwich on my way to Yaz's place. It was the least I could do for my ailing BFF.

"How are you feeling?" I lifted my bag of goodies as I stood outside her door. "I got you lunch, plus one of those big chocolate chip cookies you always like."

Her pup, Sadie, jumped up and down with excitement, Yaz doing her best to keep her inside.

Wearing a velour top with a scoop neck in plum and matching pants that accentuated Yaz's toned legs, she smiled at me, her long hair gathered up into a ponytail. Yaz was one of those people who never appeared haggard, even when I knew she was. Her black hair remained shiny, her clothes coordinated and flattering to her shape. She even smelled fresh. How she managed to pull that off while suffering from the flu was beyond me. Then again, I had no idea what she looked like last week.

"Thanks, Nat. You're the best! I'm actually pretty hungry, and my fridge is so empty it echoes." She grinned and gestured with her hand. "Come on in." She picked up Sadie as I closed the door behind me.

Like Daisy, Sadie did little to control her young self, wiggling inside Yaz's hold. Though sisters, Sadie and Daisy looked nothing alike. Daisy had a tiny face with a patchwork of black-and-white fur. Sadie, three pounds heavier and much taller already, donned reddish-brown fur with white patches over her adorable body. Behavior-wise, they were two peas in a pod, wild and silly. "Hey, Sadie, girl." I petted her as best I could, which was difficult considering she moved around like a jackrabbit.

"Calm down, Sadie." Yaz put her pup down, who ran around as though her feet were on fire.

"I left Daisy with my mother. I didn't want to inundate you with the two of them while you were sick." Each pup on their own was a handful, but if you put them together, it was nothing short of pure craziness. They chased each other, tumbled over each other, and played without restraint. It was cute and rather scary at times, the fear that one could hurt the other without meaning to. No floppy ear or ankle was safe. It was survival of the fittest with them.

I followed Yaz deeper inside, where a medicinal odor hung heavy in the air. "I sprayed disinfectant everywhere and wiped down all the surfaces." A passing truck's rumble brought my eyes to an open window in the living room.

"Yeah, I've got a few windows open to get some fresh air in here. I do feel a lot better, though. I'm not even coughing anymore. I think you're safe, but if you want to wear a mask, I've got a ton of them." She waited for my answer.

I waved her off. "Nah. It sounds like you've got it covered." I carried the food toward her galley kitchen and placed it on a small glass table in her quaint dining area. The four cushioned chairs adorned with tan fabric, the kind with a bow tied around the back, always reminded me of something one would see at a wedding venue.

Yaz's apartment wasn't large, but it was always clean, her walls a splash of earth tones. She chose modern furniture and artwork, along with a few area rugs to coordinate various color schemes, giving the space a welcoming ambiance. Unique-looking lamps with frosted glass shades that she'd found at an estate sale, waited patiently for nighttime to emit their glow while a generous selection of decorative pillows supported her efforts to comfort any occupants who arrived. Aside from today, the air always smelled nice, normally infused with something fruity or in the cinnamon category during fall.

The townhouse I used to own was much larger but never as stylish, which was one of the many reasons why I always loved coming here. I'd told Yaz several times that if this cleaning gig of ours made us enough money, she should consider interior decorating on the side. She definitely had a knack for it. The girl stalked every antique dealer, estate and yard sale in town. First-name basis, sort of thing.

We sat at her dinette, a silk winter arrangement at its center and four cloth placemats with snowflakes indicating Yaz hadn't decorated for spring yet, which she did for all the seasons.

She dove into the bag. "Thank you again, Nat. Can I reimburse you for this?" She opened the carton of chicken noodle soup, releasing notes of chicken stock and garlic into the air. I almost wished I had bought myself one as she tore apart a piece of French bread and dipped it into the broth. When she stuffed the bite into her mouth, her eyes rolled back. "Man, that's good."

"No need to pay me back. I also got you that chicken pesto ciabatta you like so much. I wanted to bring you dinner sooner, but I didn't want to get sick." I lowered my chin and gazed up at her. "My bad." I was also shorthanded at work, but that didn't need mentioning.

This time, she waved *me* off. "Oh, hey, I don't friggen blame you. I'd avoid this thing at all costs. When did I catch this?" Her eyes looked upward. "Ten days ago? It's not fun."

"Glad you're feeling human again. You look great, actually."

Knock, knock, knock.

Yaz paused her eating and started to rise.

I made a gesture for her to wait. "You sit and eat. I'll go see who it is."

"It's probably Ross." She spoke around her next bite, which came out muffled. "Thank you."

She was right. Her main squeeze, donning thick black hair, which he kept short, expressive dark-brown eyes, and a beard more stubble than short (only it was always like that), stood in the doorway. Standing at six foot even, Ross had a medium build; his clothes normally coordinated and fashionable, like Yaz's. Not today, though. His canvas gray jacket and yellow vest, bright enough to be classified as fluorescent, indicated he had just come from work. A hint of gasoline clung to his clothing.

"Hey, Ross. Yaz is eating lunch." I realized the time and welcomed him in. "Well, brunch. Come on in."

He smirked as he followed me, carrying a paper bag of his own. "I guess great minds think alike. I brought her some bagels and chive cream cheese."

While still chewing her food, Yaz sprang from her chair. "Hey, babe. What's this?" Her gaze zeroed in on the bag in his hands.

Ross kissed her cheek. "You look much better." He brushed a few loose strands away from her face. I brought you bagels and cream cheese. I got the chive cream cheese we tried a few weeks ago."

Her face lit up. "You guys are gonna make me fat." She patted her belly for emphasis.

Ross gave me a look as I refrained from rolling my eyes.

"Yeah, right. You look like you've lost weight." I scanned her kitchen. "Mind if I make myself a cup of coffee? Do you still have any pods, or are you out of those, too?"

Yaz flung a thumb over her shoulder, her gaze locked on Ross. "Yeah, I've got plenty. Help yourself. You know where everything is."

Giving them a semblance of privacy, I ventured into the kitchen.

"I missed you, hon." Ross kissed the top of Yaz's head. "How are you feeling?"

"Much better, and I missed you, too. But I didn't want to get you sick." She stood back a few inches. "I'm glad the wedding expo was worth it. Are you on lunch?"

"Early lunch. I have to head back soon. Being gone last week, I've got a ton of work to catch up on."

"Do you want to come over later? I don't quite have the energy to go out just yet. But we can watch something on streaming." Her voice grew soft and girly.

"I'd love to, Yazzy, but I have a big project that I need to finish."

"But it's Saturday." Her voice went from girly to whiny as I opened a pod of hazelnut coffee and plunked it into her coffee maker, finding a mug to catch the steaming beverage.

Ross touched the end of her nose with his index finger. "You know that I have to work one weekend a month. This is my weekend. And I was gone last week. Sorry, hon. I can come by tomorrow if you'd like."

I pulled the flavored creamer out of the fridge that Yaz

knew I liked. As I did so, I couldn't help but notice the lag in Ross's voice. Was he not feeling well, either? I hoped not.

"If I'd like? Of course, I want to see you tomorrow." She took a breath. "You, okay?" In my periphery, she ran her fingers through his hair, her tone laced with concern.

"I'm fine. Listen, I gotta get back." He kissed the top of her head again. "Save me a bagel for tomorrow. Love you." He glanced over at me. "See you, Natalie. Thanks for checking on our patient."

The coffee maker sputtered and dropped a cup full of caffeine goodness into my mug. "No problem. I hope work goes by quickly for you." I poured some creamer into my steaming mug and returned it to the fridge.

With the aroma of hazelnut promising a tasty experience, I wandered back to the table to sit with Yaz, who continued to eat but with a little less enthusiasm.

I blew on my coffee. "Everything okay?" I took a steamy sip, the heat warming my throat.

Yaz opened the container holding the sandwich. "Yeah." She didn't sound convinced as she took a bite.

"Are you sure? Is Ross having problems at work or something?"

She nodded and swallowed. "Yeah, he is, and he works crazy hours. I don't know how he keeps everything straight. The plant he works at is in dire need of upgrades. Pipes leak, exposing them to toxic chemicals that management won't do anything about. Last week, while Ross was gone, LNG burned one of his workers."

"What's LNG?"

"Liquefied Natural Gas." She made a face. "Basically, it freezes like liquid nitrogen. The gas has to be *that* cold to liquefy. The man's burns were so bad he had to go to the ER.

His company reported the incident to OSHA. I want Ross to quit. It's not safe there."

I placed my mug on the table. "I don't blame you. That's awful. Doesn't he also work for the county? Plus, it sounds like he's making great progress with the wedding photography, right? Could he just quit and do those jobs?"

Holding half her sandwich in her hands, she pointed. "My sentiments exactly. Ross said he's trying to get steady work with the county, but they aren't hiring right now. The pay is really good at the plant. The wedding photo business doesn't produce much yet, but he's working on it." She took a bite of her sandwich, chewed it quickly, and swallowed. "It's because he doesn't have time to really explore anything else. The expo was rare. These accidents at work worry me. One of these days, I'm afraid Ross is gonna get severely injured. He works with this guy, Vic, who doesn't pay attention to what he's doing. And he's kind of a bully, according to Ross, who is his supervisor. Ross tried to reprimand him a month ago about not tightening up some valves, and the guy got right up in Ross's face about it."

"Jesus. Did Ross report him to management?" Ross wasn't a big man or the aggressive type.

Yaz set her sandwich down and released an audible breath. "He said he's afraid that Vic will go after him. The guy was in prison for assault. This job is part of his work program. Ross spoke to Vic about it. Not sure it did any good." She set her jaw. "I mean, I know the money is good, but is it worth his health and safety?" Her pleading eyes reached out to me for understanding.

I waved my palms subtly. "Hey, I agree. I think he should quit too."

She resumed her eating, silence settling between us. Poor Yaz. Her brow furrowed as she rose from the table, returning promptly with a plate to place her sandwich, which was already half eaten. "Anyway, I'm worried about him."

My mother was worried about Harry. Yaz was worried about Ross. I wasn't sure what was going on with Justin. My brother lived out in LA and wrote screenplays. I should have him write one more titled *Three Women and Their Troubled Men*.

* * *

With a caffeine buzz still coursing through my veins, I left Yaz and called Justin on my way home to await his arrival. His tone didn't sound any cheerier than it had the last time we had spoken. *What is this, bummed-out Saturday?*

"Do you still want to take a drive? It's okay if you don't. I have plenty of paperwork to do, and I need to organize our inventory at the storage unit. I was going to do it on Monday after work, but I can do it today instead."

"Nope. I'm on my way to your place now. Be there in twenty."

* * *

Justin offered to drive, and I let him, ready to sightsee and relax. Meandering along the larger Appalachian range, the Blue Ridge Parkway was a marvel regardless of the time of year. Few roads, mountainous or otherwise, could boast about extending from southern Pennsylvania, through Maryland, Virginia, West Virginia, North Carolina, South Carolina, Tennessee, and Georgia, but the Blue Ridge Parkway could. Hard to believe that such a landmark was only an hour from my home. We didn't plan to go all that far, only about ten miles to bask in the countryside. Some elevations made you feel as though you could fall off the edge of the earth. It was quite magnificent, even without leaves. Given the time of year, fewer sightseers were another benefit. Afterward, we planned to have lunch at a cidery that made the best chicken caprese sandwiches I had ever tasted, homemade chips as a side. A nice day stood before us, somewhat tampered by Justin's hunched shoulders and tight expression. He was practically leaning over the steering wheel as though he wanted to strangle it.

"Do you want to talk about it? Is it something at work?" With my seat belt secured, I turned in my seat to offer him my full attention. I considered taking his hand closest to me, but it remained gripped on the steering wheel, so I thought better of it.

His lips compressed into a thin line. "That dickhead James Logan said he no longer 'requires my services.'" He pinched his face. "We had a twelve-month contract. I was planning on that money!" The grip he had on the wheel turned his knuckles white.

"If you have a contract, he can't—"

"Well, he did! And he has the lawyers to back him up." Looking like he was about to spit venom; he glared over at me. "You want to hear the worst of it?"

I wasn't sure I did.

"He stiffed me for the last two weeks. When I confronted him about it, he said he'd make life very unpleasant for me if I gave him any trouble." If he clenched his jaw any tighter, I feared Justin would crack a tooth. "I just bought a new custom mower and other lawn equipment on credit, planning on that money." A tense breath escaped his lips. "I've had three customers cancel their plans with me this year. Money is tight." He flailed a hand, screaming his words at me. "But this asshole is made of money! He can afford whatever he wants! I fucking hate him!"

I softly touched his forearm. "Do you think it's worth getting a lawyer and fighting him on it?" This man, Logan, was a menace. No one had the right to destroy people's professions like he seemed to think *he* could.

"You're joking, right?" The fire in Justin's eyes told me *he* wasn't. "I just told you I am broke. How am I going to afford a lawyer?"

I knew he wasn't attacking me personally, but it kinda felt that way. *He's just upset. Let him vent.*

"Plus, you think I'm gonna do that after what Harry told us? I don't want him ruining my reputation in this area. I don't have the skills for anything else. I've been mowing lawns and taking care of people's landscaping since I was in high school. And I'm barely making a profit now." Anger and frustration rushed blood into his cheeks. His voice dipped lower. "I'm afraid if I cause a stink, he'll ruin me. I wish the motherfucker would fall over dead!"

"Don't say that, Justin." I leaned closer. "After what Harry said, I don't blame you, though. This man sounds like a horrible person. I can lend you some money if you need it." I didn't have a lot, but I had a few bucks I could spare. The one caveat was the same worry I'd been harboring: not knowing Justin well enough. I had to remind myself that if things didn't work out between us, I might never see whatever money I offered him again. As much as I wanted to help, I decided on a small amount that I would be comfortable with, keeping my thoughts to myself. It would be something we could discuss later.

"I can't take your money. This is something *I* need to fix as a man."

As a man? Oh, brother. Did Justin know which century he was living in?

The day started out tense and quiet, but as the hours passed and the view dazzled our eyes, my boyfriend lightened up. Soon, his hand found my knee, his body relaxing into his seat.

"I used to hike up here with my buds when I was younger. We found some great scenic spots." His eyes took in the vast scenery as he spoke.

"Oh, yeah?" This was something we had in common. *I can work with this*. "I love it up here. Maybe *we* can hike sometime. You know, bring a picnic."

He squeezed my knee. "*You* hike? Aren't you afraid you'll break a nail?" His mocking tone brought my hand up to whack his shoulder.

"You do know what I do for a living, right?" I flipped my hands back and forth in front of his face. "See any long nails here?"

No reply. This was yet another aspect of Justin that bothered me. It was as if he knew me but didn't really *see* me. He was too busy making wise cracks and spouting nicknames that always made me feel a little less than. But we were here, so I did my best to enjoy myself.

We had lunch at the cidery, which I paid for, despite his misgivings.

"You drove and paid for the gas. I got lunch."

We also tried two different ciders, which did wonders for his mood. It just made *me* tired. We strolled around the property holding hands and chatting about the weather and how nice it was, plus the incredible meal we had just eaten.

"Thank you for lunch. I really enjoy being with you, Cupcake. I was in a shit mood before, but I feel much better now." He brought the hand he was holding up to his lips and kissed my knuckles.

There went the pendulum, back into Team Justin territory.

"How cool would it be to own something like this?" He gazed up at the cidery on the hill, the manicured land around it expanding toward a picturesque brook with stone accents. "Beats cutting grass for a living." He nudged me with his shoulder. "Or cleaning everyone's shitter."

I shook my head. "I clean more than 'shitters,' thank you very much."

Justin smirked. "Yeah, you know what I mean."

I inhaled the fresh air. "I do. And it would be nice." I lifted my hand in front of him, rubbing my forefinger and thumb together. "But you need money for something like that. A lot of money."

"Yup. Like my grandpa used to say, 'Spit in one hand, wish in the other, and see which one fills up first.'" Justin stared off as a light breeze sent a shiver down my spine, a thick cloud blocking out the sun. "Only rich assholes get breaks like that." His eyes went vacant as though pondering his life. "I've seen too many people suffer at the hands of . . ." He shook his head. "Never mind. Not worth wasting my breath over."

I wasn't sure what to say. Landscaping was a tough profession. Aside from the exposure to chemicals, the bugs, and the ticks, there were the elements to consider, none of which were forgiving. There was a reason Justin didn't have an ounce of body fat. I was also worried about too much sun exposure, but he didn't need me agitating an already stressful situation.

Another chill crawled up my arms. "Brr. It's getting cold." I wrapped my fleece jacket tighter around my waist.

That seemed to snap Justin out of his thoughts. "Sun will be down soon. We better head back." With our hands intertwined, we headed for his truck.

* * *

"Do you want to come in?" Parked in my mother's driveway, I extended Justin *the look*, the one that said I was ready for more intimacy. We'd been making out for several minutes now, our tongues exploring each other's mouths with new intensity. To check that things were moving in the direction I hoped they were, I allowed my hand to graze the protrusion in his pants casually. I took that as a good sign. I laced my arms around his waist and looked up at him. "Let's go get comfortable in my bed. Mom's playing cards with some friends. She even took Daisy with her." My voice fell into a seductive timbre, imagining our first time together. It had been a long time for me, and my insides were moist and ready.

Until he yawned . . . right in my face. In his defense, the proximity of my face to his didn't allow any other option. *Okay. Let's try this again.* I moved in for another kiss when he yawned again. Was he doing that intentionally? Suddenly, I wasn't as confident in my sexual appeal. The moist heat brewing between my legs turned to ice.

"Can I take a rain check? I'm beat, Cupcake." Justin repositioned himself so he was facing the steering wheel and not me. It felt abrupt, almost as though he was nudging me away from him.

"Are you sure? We can just cuddle. I don't mind if you fall asleep." I wished I hadn't said those words. It only made me sound desperate.

"Not tonight." He started the truck.

And that, as they say, was that. I felt like I was in high school dealing with a boy who didn't know any better. Justin was a grown-ass man. We'd been together long enough that I had to wonder. What was his deal? That was something I stewed over for the next few hours, streaming shows but absorbing nothing. Had I gotten so lonely that I felt the need to throw myself at men now? In some ways, I was glad he had turned me down. It made me realize why I was with him. *Boredom.* Maybe it was time to go it alone. *Again.* At least when I was alone, I didn't have to accept what I knew wasn't right for me.

When Mom came home at 9:30 p.m., I was so glad to see her *and* my baby.

"Where's Justin?" my mother asked. "You had the house to yourself."

"Don't ask."

I didn't see Justin on Sunday. He *claimed* he had a pulled muscle in his back and needed time to rest.

What Justin didn't realize was that the more time I spent away from him, the more I realized what my gut knew deep down. *He isn't right for me.*

Between work and my organization project on Monday, I kept busy. I took Daisy with me after hours so she wouldn't feel neglected. She rested in her doggy bed and watched me work at the storage unit. By ten o'clock I was asleep in my own bed. No word from Justin.

The next morning, I met Mom in the kitchen for breakfast. Her gaze remained glued to the morning news on the small TV tucked away in the corner of the room.

I filled Daisy's water bowl and then her food.

"How was your card game Saturday night? I forgot to ask."

Sitting on her barstool enjoying a bowl of oatmeal, my mother placed her spoon next to her bowl. "I didn't play cards. I got a call from Bea and went to see her."

"Our old neighbor, Bea?"

"Yeah."

"Oh, how is she?"

"Not good. Since the fire, she's been very upset. Nigel fell the other day, and Bea could barely get him up. She's worried he hasn't recovered from the pneumonia he suffered from a few weeks ago. She thinks he needs rehabilitation to get his strength back."

While Daisy chewed on her crunchy food, I poured myself a cup of coffee and stood leaning over the counter, facing my mom, my hands hugging the mug for warmth. "I'm sorry to hear that. Can she get him into a rehab facility that can help him?"

My mother pushed her bowl away. "Not easily. They lost a lot of money in the fire at their gift shop. Bea has been fighting with the insurance company to get *something* back. Money is tight for them right now."

I took a sip of coffee, my throat welcoming the warmth and strength of the vanilla flavoring. "I can't remember. Do they have any kids who can help?" Bea and Nigel moved next door after I had left home, so I never really got to know them. But Mom had. And she enjoyed having them as neighbors. Even though they didn't spend oodles of time together, they looked out for each other. When my mother's rain gutters clogged, Nigel climbed up on his ladder and cleaned them. When Bea's sister died, my mom made food and stayed with her.

My mom shook her head and lifted her palms in a flustered manner. "They have one son, and from what I remember, he's done quite well for himself, but I also remember he's a very selfish person. Barely makes time to see them. I guess he and Nigel had it out years ago, and the boy has washed his hands of his parents ever since." She mumbled under her breath. "I guess he's not a boy anymore." Worry lines bunched around her eyes. "So sad, really. Bea and Nigel are such nice people. They'd do anything for anyone. Bea told me they took in foster kids when they were younger, long before they had moved next door. They had just become empty nesters at the time, and their only son had gone off to college."

"I remember you telling me about that. That's too bad about the son."

My mom hopped off her barstool, took her bowl and utensils in her hands, and headed for the sink. "Downright awful, if you ask me. Apparently, James didn't like them taking in foster kids. Said they were strays, and it made him look bad. That was when he cut ties with them." Her hands got busy scrubbing her bowl, even though there was a dishwasher two feet away that could do the job for her. This was a remnant of the older version of my mother: the frantic cleaning with agitated hands.

"Authorities are investigating a series of fires in the Charlottesville area."

My mother and I stared at the TV.

"A developing story out of Afton right now, where a fire has destroyed the home of a prominent Charlottesville banker. The residents of the home were sleeping when a neighbor spotted smoke in an outbuilding and knocked on the door to warn the occupants." A woman with shoulder-length wavy brown hair and a black V-neck top that highlighted her ample chest reported the story, an image of Charlottesville behind her as a backdrop. "It is an active scene. We now go to Toby Banks, who is live with the breaking details . . . Toby?"

The image switched to a handsome man with short black hair and a clean shave, wearing a white button-down shirt. He stood in front of a mansion of a house, gutted by fire, a spectacular view surrounding it. A large red banner ran across the bottom of the screen with the words *Breaking News* to punctuate the report. "Well, Nicole, it appears the fire started in the attached garage before it spread to the main house. It quickly expanded into the walls and up to the third floor. We're told that the residents were in the home at the time of the blaze. Firefighters, calling it a three-alarm, have reported the house and the attached garage a total loss, estimating damages in the millions. The cause of the fire is still being investigated at this time. Live in Afton, this is Toby Banks. Back to you, Nicole."

Once Toby had pivoted the focus to Nicole, she said, "Thank you, Toby," and switched to a story about a sinkhole near a local high school.

My mother dropped her bowl into the sink, making a small splash from its weight. Her face turned the color of the oatmeal she had just eaten, her mouth gaping open.

"Mom, are you okay?" I came up beside her, touching her upper arm. "What's wrong?"

It took her a minute to respond, which only worried me more. Was she having a relapse?

"That house they showed in the report."

"Yeah? What about it?"

"I think that's Bea's son's home, James. The one I was just telling you about. Oh, my heavens. He's the same person Harry was talking about. I don't know why I didn't put that together before now."

The details of the news report repeated through my memory banks. *Prominent banker*. Bea and Nigel's last name was Logan. Their son had to be James Logan, the man who ruined Harry's reputation and who violated Justin's contract while cheating him on pay. There couldn't possibly be two James Logans who were not only bankers but who lived in Afton. My mother described James as selfish, which also fit his profile. "James Logan is Bea's son? How do you know that's his house?"

My mother placed her hands on the edge of the sink to stabilize herself. "Years back, Bea showed me a picture of it. I think it was when he had first built it. She was so proud of James, even though he wasn't giving her the time of day by then. I remember everything about the house: how it stood on the hill and that incredible view. It's the same house. I'm sure of it." She turned, her gaze wandering the kitchen. "I need to find my phone so I can call Bea. She must be beside herself."

Something else came to mind—Bea's gift shop. Also burned. *Someone is targeting the Logan family!* What about the other properties? Were they tied to Logan as well?

Chapter 9

Wrong Place, Right Time

I saw him yesterday. It was by accident. He was leaving the bank and pulled right out in front of me in his fancy car. I slammed on my brakes, horn blaring, the smell of my brake pads and rotors burning.

I rolled my window down and bellowed, "Watch where you're going, dickhead. I nearly hit you!"

The douchebag flipped me off and went on his way.

Fuck you! My jaw clenched, every muscle in my body tight and angry. This would not stand. Logan had more money and opportunity than 99 percent of this fucking country, and yet, he always wanted more. He lied, cheated, and stole from everyone who knew him.

How did he treat his family? The wife with the expensive tit job and the plastic face, and the kids who never knew loss or envy. Would they grow up to be just like him? People who snubbed their noses at the needy while attending Ivy League schools with hefty bank accounts? The popular kids.

My nostrils flared as I bared my teeth. Lately, my stomach had been fucked too. I was chewing antacids like candy. The son of a bitch was taking his toll. And I *wasn't* having it . . . not for one more goddamn day!

I wasn't planning on making this final score just yet, but I'd barely slept lately and my patience was running thin. I had other debts to settle, but they could wait.

I followed him. All the way to his office. I parked. I waited. Hours passed. Eventually, Logan walked out the front door with two men, all outfitted in expensive suits, laughing and carrying on. Logan slicked his oil-spill-colored hair back, his weak-ass jaw shaved. Hell, I could practically smell his expensive cologne all the way from my truck.

The three stooges climbed into Logan's Audi and drove off with me trailing right behind them. As the sun dipped below the horizon, Logan parked at Wagyu Steakhouse, where a dinner bill cost more than most people's mortgage payments.

I climbed out of my truck and walked past the threesome, catching his eye. He never spoke to me, only smiled, his smugness a nail gun to my pain. Truth be told, he didn't know who I was. Had no idea the pain he had caused in my life. It took everything in me not to crack his arrogant jaw and strangle the life out of him right there on the sidewalk. My fists dangled at my sides.

Doing so would end him, but it would also end me. And I had no intention of spending the rest of my life in jail. Not for a loser like him.

You think you're so fucking smart, don't you? It was then that I decided—he would come next. Maybe with him gone, his kids would stand a chance of becoming decent people.

Maybe someday they'd even thank me.

Chapter 10

Natalie

I awoke to the sensation of a tongue licking my nose and cheek, followed by a few pants of warm breath against my face. If only it were a handsome man doing this to me and not my dog.

Daisy emitted a tiny growl, sending me a message: *Wake up! I gotta go potty*. After months of potty training, I was used to this wake-up call.

I pried my eyes open. The clock next to my bed flashed three-thirty. "Okay, Daisy. You gotta go potty, girl?" I nudged her face away from mine and rolled out of bed, locating my flannel pants on a bench opposite my footboard. Once dressed, socks on my feet, I slid on my comfy slides, the ones I wore around the house, and ventured toward the back door with my little pup in tow, her nails making a *tick, tick, tick* across the hardwoods.

I grabbed my jacket from a small closet and opened the back door, where a late-night blast of cool air confronted us.

Daisy wandered the backyard by the fence bordering Alan's property. I hated it when she did that, but it was late, and what difference did it make? As long as she did her business in a timely fashion, I was fine.

"Okay, go potty, Daisy." Not sure why I had to ask her this. I hoped certain words and phrases would register. During the day, I had taught her to ring a potty-training bell that hung from both the front and back doors of the house. She and I were a work in progress.

I wrapped my jacket around my waist and wiggled my legs for warmth. "Hurry up, Daisy. Go potty, so we can get back to bed."

While the little pup sniffed the ground along the fence line, I waited, my gaze wandering the surrounding area, especially the pitchy woods growing thick out back.

I loved the privacy, but couldn't help but wonder what animals lurked. Especially on a night like this one, when the moon was hiding behind a dense layer of clouds, the darkness so thick, I could barely see my dog.

You forgot to turn on the outside light, genius. Oh, well, this won't take long.

Movement cut through my thoughts, my senses on guard. If a raccoon or a fox came bounding over the fence, I was ready to grab Daisy and whisk her inside.

A shadow appeared on the other side of the fence. *Alan*? Oh, shit. What was he doing out here at this hour? My heart slammed against my ribcage, and I lost my breath. What was it about this dude? He'd been harmless so far. *Rude,* but otherwise benign. Maybe it was those gas cans? His uncanny resemblance to the man in that Netflix show? Or just a sixth sense?

"D-Daisy, w-we gotta go," I whisper-yelled.

At this point, she was in full squat mode, doing her business.

The shadow moved closer as my body trembled and my

lungs strained to accept any semblance of oxygen. I wanted to run, but I stood paralyzed.

The shadow lifted something large. A flick of a lighter followed. All at once, a dragon-sized ball of fire illuminated the night.

All went dark. Alan moved closer. The fire ignited again, and I could see flames escaping Alan's mouth. It was like something out of a circus. The heat flushed my cheeks with its warmth.

Daisy, having finished, backed away from the fence and barked at the wild display.

In an instant, I could see Alan clearly, until the firebomb extinguished, and darkness returned.

Alan lifted the bottle and spat more flames. His head turned slightly, his gaze meeting mine.

Holy shit. What if he spat his flames over here?

I grabbed Daisy, who was barking like crazy. "Come on. It's okay." I wrestled to secure my scared pup in my arms, and I bolted toward the door, evil laughter sending my nerves into a frenzy.

I slammed the back door, locked it, and peered out the back window. Nothing but pitch-black challenged my vision.

"What the hell was that?" I was living next to a lunatic.

Daisy and I slept on the couch, my ears pricked for any noise or sound of entry. I had turned on the back and front outdoor lights, my cell phone waiting to call 911. I almost woke my mother up, but chose to wait. Unless Alan tried to break in or burn our house down, there was no need to rob both of us of a decent night's sleep. I checked the window periodically. No sign of the sicko.

I awoke to Mom watching the news. The press had released James Logan's name as the owner of the house. In addition, the fire had injured him critically. He was in intensive care, suffering from smoke damage to his lungs. A pit developed in my stomach at the thought of it. And the story worsened. Not only did they suspect arson, but the authorities believed it was the same person who had torched that small home in town, Bea's gift shop, and a local warehouse that housed various forms of equipment. This was fire number four. *I was right!*

Since Mom was so worried about Bea, she didn't question why I was sleeping on the recliner couch. I gave her Wednesday off to spend with her friend. It was a rather light workday for me anyway, and Yaz was back up and running again, able to help me work in half the time, her mother always filling in the gaps.

I didn't mention Alan's shenanigans to Mom. She had enough on her mind.

Weird didn't begin to describe my neighbor, but was he dangerous? That part, I wasn't sure of.

Justin hadn't called in the past few days. So, I called him on Wednesday night. It was now April, and our relationship was heading into destinations unknown.

"Hey, stranger. I haven't heard much from you. Is everything okay?" I refrained from what I really wanted to say, which was *I think it's over between us.* I didn't want him to assume it was because he had rejected me sexually. That wasn't it. In fact, I was glad we never went that far. Why complicate a relationship that was already doomed? There were aspects of Justin's personality and attitude that grated on my nerves. Over time, I could see them worsening.

"I told you I would call you. I've been trying to figure some things out. Sooorry." He didn't sound sorry, more apathetic.

"You did?" I didn't remember him saying he'd call. "What are you trying to work out? Can I help?"

A tense voice replied. "What do you mean, what am I

trying to work out? How I'm gonna make ends meet. I told you about all of this!" He exhaled with a grunt.

"I just meant specifically. Never mind. Can I help?"

"I'm good, thanks."

A quiet moment stretched between us.

I tried another subject. "Uh, did you hear about James Logan's house burning down?" I wondered how he felt about it, given the state of his life.

"Yup."

"I read on my newsfeed that they suspect arson."

Should I mention Alan?

"Yeah, well, I doubt they know that much. He probably started it himself for the insurance money. Listen, I gotta run." *Click.* The call disconnected.

The conversation was so short, I found myself staring at my cell phone in disbelief. That was when a new call came in. *Unknown number.*

"Hello?"

A man's voice answered. "Yeah, is this Natalie from Dust Bunnies?"

"Yes, it is. Can I help you?"

"Oh, hey, this is Aaron Marino. I live out in Crozet, and you cleaned for me last week."

My heart leaped into my throat. This time, for a good reason. "Oh, hi, Aaron." I didn't think it was possible to sweat so suddenly, but my armpits sure did. If only my heart rate would calm down. I felt as though someone had just slapped defibrillator paddles onto my chest.

Breathe.

"I hope you don't mind my calling you. I just figured I'd contact you instead of your partner since you've been to my house before. And you left your card." He cleared his throat. "I, uh, wondered if you could clean my house again for me. . . . My company left, and I got a big project I'm working on. . . . I can pay extra for the short notice."

"Let me check my schedule. Can I call you back on this number?"

"Sure. Take your time, thanks." *Click.* My second call ended.

I kept my schedule on my cell, which I quickly perused, all while my pulse raced at the prospect of seeing Aaron again. Given the tepid romance between Justin and me, I didn't even feel guilty about it. Our days were numbered.

Aaron had taken the initiative and called me. Good. He didn't think I was stalking him the other day when he caught me with my mother near his mailbox. What a relief.

As it turned out, my Friday work schedule ended at 2:00 p.m. When that normally happened, I would catch up on emails, do my bookkeeping, and sometimes schedule a much-needed massage. Working for Aaron trumped all of that. I called him immediately and set up a second cleaning for 2:45 on Friday.

I conveyed all of that to my mother over dinner on Thursday evening. She'd made vegetable lasagna, so I constructed a large winter harvest salad as a complement. She'd found the recipes in one of her grocery store flyers.

"Yum, this is delicious, Ma." Our meal offered its support, which I savored. The situation with Alan and the lack of sleep was taking its toll.

"Thank you, Natalie. I agree. And your salad is also pretty great." She tucked a bite of the mixed greens and dried cranberries into her mouth, crunching on the candied walnuts. She quickly dabbed away droplets of vinaigrette made of olive oil, balsamic vinegar, and fig preserves from her mouth with a napkin. "Mmm. So good."

We sat in the dining room for this meal, instead of at the

kitchen island or at the table in the breakfast nook, which was where most of our quick meals took place. Mom had lit a couple of tapers, and we enjoyed our meal for a change with nowhere to be.

"What's Harry up to tonight? I haven't seen him around lately."

My mom lifted one of her brows. "I could say the same about Justin."

Using my fork, I cut myself another bite of lasagna. "Yeah, I know. He's having some issues with work. Mainly, how he's going to afford the equipment he just purchased after that Logan dude fired him." I was about to explain that things weren't working out between us when she spoke.

"Why did you say he fired him again? I can't remember."

"I'm not sure I ever said. But according to Justin, Logan didn't give him a legitimate reason. He just up and canceled their contract, and then he shorted him on past pay." I took a sip of my pinot noir. The balance of fruit and earthy notes presented a nice pairing with the lasagna.

My mother paused her eating. "You're kidding me? I remember Justin telling us he worked for James. What is it with that man? On top of that, Bea is beside herself with grief over what happened at her son's house. She offered to take his wife, Trudy, and the two grandkids to stay with her and Nigel, but they said they preferred to stay at one of their rentals instead. Bea has been at the hospital around the clock, checking on James. Nigel won't discuss it." She palmed the goblet of her wineglass, staring off. For the most part, my mother rarely drank alcohol, but every now and then, she'd enjoy a glass of wine with dinner. Or a margarita at a happy-hour price.

"How is James, by the way? I heard he was in intensive care."

She let go of her wineglass. "Not good. He's on a ventilator.

They're not sure he'll make it. The fire damaged his lungs pretty severely." Her hand returned to her wineglass, only this time, she took a sip. "I'll bring that extra pan of lasagna over for Nigel in the morning. I told Bea I made it for them to have. I'm sure they aren't eating well, and they're no spring chickens. They need to keep their strength up." My mom, always the caretaker.

With my salad devoured, I swallowed my last bite of lasagna, which I washed down with a sip of water. "I've been reading about these fires, Ma. The authorities suspect arson for all four of them. And they also believe it's either the same person or the same group of individuals."

She tilted her head a notch and narrowed her eyes. "Four fires?"

"Yeah, the first one was at a small house, the second one was Bea and Nigel's gift shop, the third at a warehouse in town, and the fourth was James's estate. And the authorities think they are all connected."

"What makes them think that?"

I shrugged. "I'm not sure. They must've found evidence of some sort at all four locations. I mean, James's house must've had top-of-the-line—"

Knock, knock, knock.

I jolted; my nerves still frayed from the spectacle I'd witnessed the night before last. I still hadn't told anyone. Too many other pending issues.

Her eyebrows squishing together, my mother put down her wineglass and pushed her chair back. "Who could that be? I wasn't expecting anyone. You?"

I had already stood. "No, maybe it's Harry or Justin." I wasn't that keen on seeing my new boyfriend. We had a very uncomfortable conversation in our future.

We rushed to the front door to find Bea waiting outside.

"Is it okay that I stopped by? I hope I'm not interrupting dinner." Holding her large brown purse close to her abdomen, Bea stood all of five feet, her gray hair short and unruly, her wool coat something one might see in a 1960s movie. Lines deepened around her gray eyes and mouth, making her seventy-five years (according to my mother) look more like eighty-five.

My mother whisked her friend inside. "Don't be silly. Come on in. Are you hungry?" She kept her hand on Bea's arm.

"No, I don't want to impose."

Before she could object any further, my mother had Bea's coat off, revealing a light-blue button-down top with a pair of olive pants, the kind with a pleat running down the front and an elastic waist. "Have you eaten today?"

Bea was sitting at our table within no time, consuming a plate of lasagna with salad. She declined a glass of pinot and chose a cup of coffee instead. I also set a glass of water next to her coffee, suspecting she probably needed the hydration.

Having finished our meals, we sat across from our old neighbor, ready to listen. Several yawns fought to free themselves from my lungs. I hoped Bea hadn't noticed, thinking I wasn't interested.

Mom leaned into the table; her arms extended toward her friend. "How is James?"

Bea had just swallowed a bite of salad when she placed her fork next to her plate. Her red eyes moistened with tears. "Not well. His lungs sustained too much damage. They don't think he's going to make it. It's awful to see him this way. All those tubes going in and out of my son. I can't imagine what it's like for my poor boy. Trudy came by but didn't bring the kids. She didn't want them to see their father like that." She released a shuddering breath. "I told her I could watch them, but she said they have a nanny." Bea lowered her head. "I don't even know my grandkids. I've barely seen them over the years." With sorrowful eyes, she gazed over at us. "What did I do that was so wrong? I will never know why taking in kids less fortunate would upset my son so. I grew up in foster care; did you know that?" As tears drizzled down her weathered cheeks, I ran to grab her some tissues, returning a moment later.

"Here you go."

"Thank you, dear." Bea wiped her face, her voice defeated and somber. "Nigel won't even talk about it. He was so angry at James for turning his back on us. When I broke my hip, he was even angrier that James never came to see me. I told him not to fuss, but he's a stubborn old goat. When the gift shop burned, we never heard a word." More tears of anguish soaked poor Bea's face. "I just want my family together again. I don't care about what's happened. But Nigel won't budge."

My mother rose and took a seat next to Bea; her arm draped over her friend's hunched shoulders. "I'm sure he'll come around. I remember when you broke your hip and how attentive Nigel was. He's a good man. He's just hurting right now."

Holding her sodden tissue away from her face, Bea said, "He may not have much more time, Rose." That was when the dam broke, Bea releasing cries of heartache onto my mother's supportive shoulder.

I teared up, too. James had parents who tried to set a good example. Paid it forward. Somehow, their attempts backfired; James going in the opposite direction. I'd never met the man, but I knew he was selfish and vindictive. I couldn't imagine what kind of father he was.

When the tears dried up, and more coffee made it into Bea's mug, the conversation pivoted.

"Have the authorities told you anything more about the cause of the fire, Bea?" I asked.

She shook her head. "They haven't said much. *To me.* I'm sure Trudy knows more. She's his wife. I'm just a . . . nobody."

My mother took a firm hold of Bea's hand. "You are *not* a nobody! Now, I don't want to hear that kind of talk out of you anymore."

Trying to steer Bea away from self-deprecation, I continued. "Did you know there have been four fires in the area, and the police suspect arson? I've been reading about them online. One was at a small house on Richardson Road, one was at your gift shop, another was at Mantel Warehouse, and the last was at your son's home. I don't know how they know this, but they believe they are all related. Did your son have anyone who held a grudge against him?"

The minute those words escaped my lips, my mother and I locked gazes. We knew of two people who could fit that bill: Harry and Justin. But Harry and Justin wouldn't torch half the town for no reason. As subtly as I could manage, I shook my head at Mom. *Don't worry, it's not them.*

"It could also be random, Bea, since there were three other properties damaged that had nothing to do with James." *Except for the gift shop,* which I kept to myself.

Bea fiddled with her used tissues. "Did you say Richardson Road?"

I nodded. "Yes, why?"

"James owns a lot of rental properties in that area. Richardson Road is one of them. He also owns that warehouse."

My mother and I exchanged another look. So, all the properties *did* belong to James. Except for one. But I suspected the arsonist knew Bea and Nigel owned that gift shop as well. Now, we had a connection. That was the missing link that the authorities already knew about. Maybe our respective boyfriends weren't completely off the hook.

Something else came to mind. The incident from two nights ago. I still hadn't mentioned it. "I meant to tell you this, Ma, but the other night when I brought Daisy out to pee at 3:30 a.m., our weird neighbor was up."

Bea shifted in her seat, her voice much less emotional. "His yard is a disgrace." She flailed one hand. "Trash cans out front, pallets leaned up against the house, and what's in all those buckets he has stacked by his garage. I'm surprised the HOA allows that."

"He put the buckets out there last week. The HOA has been fighting with him about many things over the past year. He's making it difficult, though, so they may have to fine him. As you know, Bea, our HOA is small, and we don't have the resources to do much." My mother sat back in her seat. "I called the county on him last summer when he refused to cut his grass."

Our conversation was getting off-track. "That's not why I mentioned him. The other day, I caught him loading the trunk of that old sedan of his with empty gas cans. I think they were gas cans. Six of them!" Both Bea's and my mother's eyes grew wide.

"Really? When was this?" My mother stared me down.

"Last Saturday. I had brought Daisy out to pee, and I wanted to grab the mail from the day before. That was a lot of gas cans. I'm assuming they were empty because of the way he carried them. And that's not all."

Both women leaned into my conversation with expectant eyes. It was nice to see Bea perk up from her distress.

"The other night, as I said, I brought Daisy out to pee, and he was out there. I didn't see him at first. I was waiting near the fence between his backyard and ours when I caught movement and heard a noise."

"What sort of noise?" my mother asked.

"I don't know. A lighter sparking. He spat something into the air, and then he lit it as someone would do in the circus. He literally blew fire. Several times." As I thought about it, I could feel the heat from it against my cheeks.

"My god." Bea's hand went to her gaping mouth.

"Why didn't you tell me about this?" My mother was now standing. "We should call the police!"

I rose from my chair and raised a palm. "Nothing happened after that. I grabbed Daisy and went inside. That's why I was on the couch this morning. I was keeping an ear out. But when it happened, I think I heard him laughing at me. He's a strange man, Ma. We need to be careful around him. For all we know, he could be the arsonist. The guy definitely has a fixation with fire." Was it also odd that he lived in Bea and Nigel's old house, yet another connection to James Logan?

Chapter 11

Natalie

I cleaned a bridal salon first thing the next morning, plus the homes of two senior citizens, my mind wandering to my next job that started at 2:45.

Before I left for Crozet, I took a shower and added a moderate amount of makeup. I also changed my clothes into something a little less scrubs-worthy, yet accommodating for cleaning, which turned out to be a flattering pair of black leggings and a form-fitting fuchsia tunic that if soiled, I wouldn't mourn the loss of. Since I'd been doing this type of manual labor for a living, my body had rewarded me with ten less pounds around my hips and waist and a firmer body. I decided that I'd flaunt my new figure.

My behavior was ridiculous, but acknowledging this didn't seem to stop me. I blamed what I felt for Aaron on chemistry and not much else. I knew nothing about him, other than he was a gorgeous fireman who suffered a terrible tragedy years ago. Oh, and he had a nice house. I also couldn't ignore the fact that he liked dogs. Those soft amber eyes, not to mention a body that made it hard to focus on anything else, I wondered why there wasn't a woman living in that big house with him. Images of making love to Aaron in those lonely bedrooms, our cries of ecstasy reverberating off the walls, came unbidden, causing shame to weigh heavily on my heart. Aaron was obviously not interested. He was alone for a reason.

By the time I reached his house, I had talked myself out of canceling the job three times. What was I afraid of? Strange how those same nerves crept into my psyche, the ones I had felt before I had even met Aaron. It was as though I had some sort of premonition that this person was going to have a significant impact on my life. I just hoped it would be a positive impact and not a negative one.

* * *

"Thanks for coming." Wearing a tight gray long-sleeved T-shirt that formed like a second skin over his bulbous arms and pecs, a pair of navy sweatpants paying homage to his muscular legs and butt, Aaron stood before me in all his dreamy goodness. *Jesus, is he even more handsome than I remembered?*

That spark, which in my mind belonged to chemistry more than connection, ramped up my pulse and had my knees slightly weak. If I had a portable fan, I'd have aimed it at my face right now. Or maybe my armpits.

"No problem. How was your visit with your . . . friends? Or was it family?" Did I stutter? I hoped not.

Aaron backed out of my way so I could enter. "Friends. And it was fine."

The table at the center of his foyer was now empty of mail, its only inhabitants a pair of gloves, a folded-up newspaper, and a set of keys, which I assumed belonged to his silver truck, now parked out front.

"Well, even friends can be a handful." I made a face as

though I understood the pressure he was under, which, of course, I didn't. I loved friendly gatherings and even family ones with my brother, aunts, uncles, and cousins. It seemed I was playing a part here: the understanding cleaning lady.

Placing one hand on his hip, Aaron ran his fingers through his thick hair. "So, the house needs pretty much the same things as before. The sheets need to be washed, but don't bother putting them on the beds. If you could fold them and put them back in the hall closet I showed you last time, that would be great. Some of them are in a pile in the laundry room from their air mattresses. Other than that, vacuuming, mopping, washing dishes, or whatever you see needs doing. No need to dust. You already did that last time." He buried both hands in the front pockets of his sweatpants. His voice lightened. "No scrubs today?" His arms flexed, drawing my attention. What would it feel like to have those muscular arms wrapped around me right now?

"I'm sorry, what did you say?"

He pivoted his body in a subtle way back and forth. "Scrubs." He removed one hand from his front pocket and pointed at my outfit. "Not wearing them today."

Blood rushed to my cheeks. "Oh, yeah, right. Ha." Christ, what was wrong with me? "Nope. Laundry day." The way he seemed to size me up with his eyes had my inner thighs yearning for something spectacular to happen. I imagined Aaron taking me into his arms and kissing me like no one had ever kissed me before.

Aaron scratched at his short beard and coughed out the words, "You look nice." He then perked up and pointed toward the door leading to his basement. "Anyway, I'll be working downstairs. Knock if you need anything. I'll check back in a couple of hours." He made a quick exit, leaving me in need of a cold shower.

"Pull yourself together." I mumbled the reprimand, hoping Aaron hadn't overheard me. Yes, it had been a while since I'd been intimate with a man, but I wasn't sure I could blame that *solely* on my raging hormones. Justin never inspired such a reaction, even when we were making out. Justin was attractive. This was far beyond mere attraction. I wasn't sure what this was.

In need of a distraction, I got busy doing my goddamn job. *Remember that? The reason you are here?*

* * *

Two hours passed when Aaron appeared in the kitchen. I was unloading the dishwasher while waiting for a second load of sheets to finish drying. A gentle whirring sound, accented by the tumble of sheets, soothed my ears. I'd vacuumed the first floor, mopped, and straightened. His guests left no evidence behind telling me who they were, other than some dabs of fruity-smelling toothpaste in one of the upstairs bathrooms and pink shampoo drizzled on the floor of the bathtub. A child was here. That was all I knew. Could've been a niece (pink shampoo suggested a girl) or even his own daughter, if he had one.

"How's it going? I hope the place wasn't too much of a mess." This was the friendliest Aaron had ever been to me, other than his moment with Daisy. He came over and started helping unload the dishwasher.

"You don't need to help. That's what you're paying *me* for."

"Oh." Aaron stood back as though not sure what to do with himself. He fidgeted.

"That's fine. You know more about where this stuff goes than I do." I handed him a casserole dish, inviting him to resume his duties.

Once we had the dishwasher unloaded, he helped me fold the sheets in the dryer. "So how did you become a house cleaner?"

After the sheets, I folded a set of hand towels, placing them on the lid of the washer. "Well, I was an accountant, to be honest."

Aaron's head flinched back. "An accountant? How the hell did that turn into this?"

I folded a few mismatched washcloths. "Well, you see, my mother got sick . . ." I stopped and contemplated what I wanted to say. "It kind of goes back farther than that. Um, my dad divorced my mom when I was a teenager, about twenty years ago. Cheater. Found a new, *younger* wife a little too quickly, if you know what I mean." Anger ground my teeth together. "It really hit my mom hard. We all sort of went our own ways after that for a while. I remember my little brother, Jack, always busy with lacrosse and spending time with his buds. I had the *mathletes* and hung out with friends like Yaz. You spoke to her."

Aaron nodded. "I remember."

"She's also my best friend. Mom was a stay-at-home parent and worked as a bookkeeper for crap pay after the divorce. We *all* worked back then. I had a part-time job after school and on the weekends. My mother didn't have much to give us for allowance or personal expenses." The muscles in my jaw grew tired of clenching as I stacked the washcloths on top of the hand towels. "My dad paid for my education. Not all of it, but enough." I almost hated to admit that. He'd done the same for my brother, who chose a theater major. (Pause for an eye roll from my dad.)

"Anyway, my mom became obsessive about cleaning. It was a control thing. On top of that, the woman barely ate anything. She got really thin. That was when I finally had to do something. In a lot of ways, I felt like the parent for her and my little brother. I did the grocery shopping and made a lot of the meals. Paid the bills. At least I didn't have to clean, right?" My feeble attempt at humor did nothing to lighten my heavy heart. Most sixteen-year-olds were out partying and pushing the limits of their freedom. Not me. I was too worried I'd lose the one parent who hadn't deserted us.

"I had to ride her ass about taking a break and eating more. My brother's job was to mow the lawn in the summer, shovel the walkway and driveway in the winter, and take out the trash." As I talked, I pulled more linens from the dryer and folded them, the fresh scent of the dryer sheet reaching my nose. "It was funny. How many kids could say their big sister was the person who paid their allowance? But that was how it went. Mom continued to clean our house, even though it wasn't dirty." As I spoke, it almost felt as though I was talking about some other family. Our lives had changed so much since then.

I piled all the clean linens into the basket, ready to carry it upstairs.

Taking the basket from my hands, Aaron led the way.

Why haven't you excused yourself to leave? There was no need for him to pretend he was interested.

"What happened next?" Not pretending. He *was* interested. I took comfort in knowing this. No previous boyfriends had ever asked me anything about my life, other than superficial stuff. Justin included.

"When I left for college, I felt better knowing that my mom could stay where she was since my dad had left her the house, mortgage paid. And I didn't go far, so I could come home anytime she needed me. Dad also paid her alimony for half the number of years they had been married—fifteen to be precise—and not a *day* longer."

"Ma kept her married name, Dugan, so she matched my brother and me." I sighed, knowing this next part would be difficult to explain. "Around two years ago, she started getting sick." A lump formed in my throat. "The woman who never stopped cleaning, lost all her energy. She had to let the cleaning go. And man, did *that* stress her out. I remember her saying once, 'My house is falling apart. I can't take much more of this.' To be honest, the house wasn't *that* messy, not compared to most homes I'd been inside. But for her, the situation was awful. I knew she was losing it. And if I didn't do something about it, I'd lose *her* in the process. I couldn't let that happen, Aaron. I tried to help, but I worked impossible hours as a CPA." My tone slumped, right along with my shoulders. I felt so trapped back then, as though I had few options.

"It was a tough time. I did what I could to support Mom, consulting with her doctor on my lunch break and trying to help organize the details of her life—a slew of insurance papers and other documents. What I couldn't get done during my lunch, I worked on at night, which wasn't easy since no one was open late. Weekends weren't an option, either. I worked most of them."

"What was wrong with her?" Aaron's brow tensed as he listened.

We'd returned to the laundry room, where I emptied the last load from the washer into the dryer. I released a heavy sigh filled with years of anguish. "It turned out she had lupus. And it got worse. All of a sudden, she didn't want to drive, so I had to find neighbors and friends to bring her to and from her appointments. She had also let her license expire. My little brother moved away years ago. He's thirty-three and single. No obligations. Other than food and shelter. And the man has four roommates. But given his limited income, it was totally up to me to help Mom. *Again.*"

I paused to glance at Aaron.

He held me in his gaze, concern narrowing his eyes. "Wow,

that's rough. She's lucky she had you there." He expelled a tense breath himself.

"Yeah, well. She had the house and a small nest egg." My voice lowered. "As far as my mom went, I knew how situations like this could go. Like flash paper, her assets could all disappear in a puff of smoke." My chest constricted. "I'd heard stories about people who were doing just fine until they became ill, and how the medical costs had forced them to sell their homes, some destitute and homeless." The anxiety of it stirred a pool of acid into my gut. I pushed on my breastbone to stave off heartburn.

"Are you okay?" Aaron touched my arm. His cheeks flushed, the corners of his mouth crimped downward.

"Yeah. I'm fine. It's hard to talk about."

"You don't have to—"

I waved him off. "No, it's okay. You asked how I got here." I inhaled and released a calming breath. "During all this, I'd hired a few people to clean her house, and the prices were outrageous, and they didn't even do a good job. So, one night when I was complaining to Yaz, we decided to start our own business. I sold my place and moved in with my mom. She has a ranch-style home. Nothing fancy." I gestured toward his kitchen. "No granite countertops or marble floors like you have."

It didn't matter to me how fancy her house was. I appreciated everything about it, from the flowered wallpaper in the kitchen to the white cabinets with wood trim, and even the green stove and fridge that outlived anything one could purchase today. The air always smelled fresh. The walls adorned with images of me and my brother growing up. It was like living inside a big hug. "Anyway, she seemed happy to have company again." I raised my brow, trying to lighten the mood. "Until she met her new man, but we've managed to coexist without stepping on each other's toes *too much.*" With the dryer working on its final load, I wandered into the kitchen. "Sorry, I didn't mean to monopolize the conversation." I was flustered, offering so much information about my life. And yet, it was a relief in a freeing sort of way. I had stepped up when my family needed me. I took comfort in that.

Unexpectedly, Aaron wrapped his strong arms around me.

I was floored. The hug was brief. The impact was immense. The minute he pulled away, I missed the warmth of his body so close to mine. I yearned for it.

"You didn't monopolize anything. I asked, remember?" He kept a close watch on me.

Feeling heat reach my cheeks, and trying to avoid crying, I stepped away, the kindness from his gesture still touching my soul. "Thanks for listening."

A silent moment rested between us.

"Other than the load in the dryer, that about does it for cleaning. Thanks again for listening to my rambling." I ran a hand across my tacky forehead.

"Of course. And I can take care of that last load. House looks nice." He gazed around, then took a breath as though allowing himself a reset. "Hey, you got time for a cup of coffee . . . or a beer?" A splash of pink flooded his cheeks this time. "Or, if you're busy—" He fidgeted in place.

"No! I mean, yes, I've got a few minutes." I quickly checked my cell to see several texts and missed calls from Justin.

> Sorry, I've been so preoccupied, Cupcake. Work shit is stressing me out. Want to get together tonight? I seem to remember we had some unfinished business. I'm game if you are.

When I hadn't replied in a timely manner, more texts crowded my small screen.

Are you pissed off at me? Even if you're busy, shoot me a text and let me know you're not mad.

Geez, when had Justin become so needy?

I sent a quick reply.

Not mad. Just busy. I'll call later. Can't make dinner. I had a last-minute job come up.

I followed Aaron to the center of the kitchen, doing my absolute best not to gawk at his ass. Before he reached the fridge, he took out his wallet and paid me in cash. "I hope that's enough. If it's not, I can pay by credit card."

"I'm sure it's fine." I started to put the cash in my purse, now sitting on the kitchen table, when Aaron spoke.

"Make sure you count it. I'm not offended. You did this job at the last minute, and I want to compensate you." He crossed his arms and widened his stance as though not willing to move an inch until I conceded.

I waved a hand in the air. "Okay, okay." I sat at the table and counted what came out to be two hundred dollars. "Wait! This is way too much." I put half on the table.

Aaron had just snagged two beers from the fridge. He opened them, creating a small *hiss* from the release of carbonation, and dropped the caps on the counter with a *ting*. "Keep it. Like I said, you did this job at the last minute. Consider it a priority bonus." A small smirk spread across his face as he approached the table and took a seat across from me, sliding one of the opened beers my way to enjoy.

"Thanks for the beer. But the bonus is not—"

He made a sound in his throat, raising one palm. "I insist."

"Oookaaay." I put the money in my wallet. "Thank you."

Aaron took a sip of his beer. He placed it on the table and cupped his hands around it. "That sucks about your dad. He sounds like a real piece of work. Do you have any contact with him now?" He pulled from his beer again.

I took a sip, enjoying the cold hops against my parched throat. "Nope. I don't hear from him anymore, and that's fine by me. He's a jerk. I know that's a mean thing to say—"

"No, no, I get it." Keeping his forearms on the table, Aaron clasped his hands loosely. "What he did was not cool to your family. And what happened to your mother sucks too. Sounds like your family has been through a lot. Hold on a second."

Aaron rose from the table and left the room for a brief moment, returning with a canvas shopping bag. "Remember when I told you I used to have a dog?"

"I do. CB. Cotton ball, right?"

Aaron's face lit up. "Good memory. Yes, well, I found this stuff in the attic, and I thought Daisy might enjoy them."

I placed my beer on the table. "Good memory yourself. Thanks, what is it?"

Aaron returned to his seat and pushed the bag across the table. "It's just some toys. I took out the ones that are too big for her. I believe there's a few chew toys in there I never opened." He made a dismissive gesture while one shoulder rose and fell. "It's fine if you don't think she'll like them. They were just sitting around gathering dust." He drank from his beer again.

I peered into the bag, where a few soft toys stared up at me, some with tags still on them. The touch of an orange and furry octopus produced a nice *squeak* that I was sure Daisy would go crazy over. "Wow, this is great. She'll love them. Are you sure you won't need them?"

"I have no need for them . . . anymore." His voice went stony, a tone I had grown accustomed to.

Had Cotton Ball died? I assumed so. That was one aspect of owning a pet that I had to grapple with: outliving them. I'd only had Daisy for less than a year, and I already loved her more than I ever thought possible. She was part of my family. "I'm sorry. Did Cotton Ball pass?" The moment the words escaped my lips, I regretted them. It was none of my business what had happened to Cotton Ball. I had willingly told him about my life. I couldn't expect him to do the same. I prepared myself for the It's-none-of-your-business reply.

Very atypical of Aaron, he caught my worried gaze. "He's not dead. He lives with my ex . . . fiancée."

Okay, that sent my mind down another rabbit hole. *Fiancée?* Who was this woman, and why was she an ex? *Calm down. Don't push too hard.* Listening to my inner voice, I closed the bag and relaxed back into my chair. "Thank you for the dog toys. And I wanted to say sorry about driving by the other day. I had told my mother how nice your house was, and since we had a few minutes to kill, she asked me to show it to her."

"It wasn't a big deal . . . I just had to get back. I didn't mean to come off rude." Aaron stretched his legs out over a neighboring chair to his right, making himself comfortable. "Considering what she's been through, your mom looked well. How is she doing now?"

It was so strange to have this type of conversation with Aaron, the man who barely spoke the first *and* the second time I'd seen him. I was worried my mother's question had offended him the other day. Apparently, not.

"She's doing well. She's in remission now. And she works for me." I made a face. "My mother is a neat freak like you wouldn't believe."

Aaron's amber eyes twinkled, a slow smile spreading across his lips. "Really? Well, that's . . . great. Like mother, like daughter." His gaze scanned the kitchen and the sapphire-blue granite countertops that gleamed under the recessed lighting from above. "You're thorough. I'll give you that."

I wanted to know so much more about this man. But how could I breach that topic when I'd seen one general question from my mother cause him to shut down.

"So, you said you had friends here last weekend. How did that go?" While I awaited his answer, Aaron stared down at the bottle of beer in his hands.

Was my question a bridge too far? Was he going to excuse himself quickly and leave?

"It was my two best friends, Rodney and Chuck, and their families."

Phew. I was holding my breath.

"Rodney moved to Chicago a few years back, and we haven't seen each other for a while. I kept putting off their visit, but I was running out of excuses." He scratched his forehead. "They weren't taking no for an answer, if you catch my drift."

"I do." I'd had a few friends over the years who were like that.

"Both married with one kid each." Aaron took a final sip of his beer and set the empty bottle down on the table. "A five- and a seven-year-old. Endless energy." His eyes widened as he blew out his lips. "I told them I'd take them camping when the weather gets warmer."

That perked me up. I leaned my forearms on the table. "I love camping. Do you prefer going in a tent or a camper?"

"I have a small camper out back."

"Cool. I bet that's fun." I smiled, and so did he.

He lowered his chin and stared up at me. "So . . . *you* like to camp?" What an improvement from *Aren't you afraid you'll break a nail?*

"I *love* to camp. I just can't ever find anyone to go camping with me."

Aaron rubbed the back of his neck. "Your . . . boyfriend or husband doesn't take you?" His eyes grew almost sheepish, and I loved it. He was fishing for information, just like I was.

And then I said something that I probably shouldn't have. "I don't have a boyfriend or a husband." Why was I lying? Two reasons came to mind: If I told Aaron that I was in a relationship, I feared he'd lose interest in me. It didn't hurt matters that I had already come to the conclusion that Justin wasn't for me anyway. What I hadn't done was tell Justin that yet.

"Been too busy getting your business off the ground, huh?" Aaron seemed to study me as he crossed his relaxed arms over his chest.

Caught up in my own thoughts, I almost missed his question.

"Well, I don't exactly have men banging down my door lately." I wasn't a fan of self-deprecation, mainly because I'd watched my mother do it for years, but that wasn't why I had said those words. I was curious what Aaron thought about me, and this seemed like an indirect way to find out.

If he said nothing to counter my comment, then he agreed; I wasn't worth the bother. *Maybe*. It wasn't an exact science.

His intense gaze excited every cell in my body. "Nah, your door is definitely worth banging down." A flirtatious grin flitted across his handsome face.

He likes me. I was giddy and rather pathetic at the same time. My cheeks heated bashfully. "Well, thank you. And I would imagine a man like yourself could certainly bang down a few doors, given your profession."

Something shifted in Aaron's aura, a protective layer muting his brilliance. I noticed it immediately. "I'm sorry. I didn't mean to make light of your situation."

His brow furrowed. "My situation?" Skepticism forced his jaw upward.

Damn. Now I'd stepped in it. Suddenly, I noticed the time. It was after six o'clock. "You know, it's getting late." I rose from my chair. "I need to head home."

Aaron stood and faced me. "Why? Is it Daisy?"

Dumbfounded, I said, "Um, no, not really. I mean, I'd like to see her, but my mom is home. I had made arrangements for her to feed Daisy and stay with her until I get there."

This beautiful and mysterious man closed the gap between us. His presence nearly knocked me off my feet. "Then why don't you stay . . . for a little bit longer?"

Chapter 12

Natalie

Faced with a decision, my cell phone vibrated from my purse draped over the back of the chair I had been inhabiting. I suspected it was Justin trying to reach me again. Or maybe Mom.

"I'll agree to stay for a little longer under two conditions."

Towering over me, his musky scent dizzying my brain, Aaron rubbed his beard with one hand. "And what might that be?" His voice grew all throaty, his gaze intensifying. "You want me to talk about being a firefighter, don't you?"

Apparently, my mother's question *did* still resonate with him.

"Nope. That's your business. If you want to talk about that or anything else, that's up to you." Feeling the potency of his attention, I had to look away to keep my thoughts intact. "First of all, I need to make a couple of phone calls to make sure my mom and Daisy are all set, and to check-in with my partner, Yaz." In this little white lie of mine, Yaz was playing the part of Justin.

My stomach growled like a grizzly before I could say more. I was sure Aaron had heard it too.

"Secondly. I'm starving. Can we order takeout or make something to eat here? If my blood sugar gets any lower, I'm gonna pass out. I've been cleaning all day, and I'm not just hungry, I'm hangry." A loud growl from my abdomen supported my argument.

The corners of Aaron's lips curved upward. "Hangry, huh?" He nodded, his gaze wandering the kitchen. "I think we can make that happen."

* * *

I conducted my calls outside, away from prying ears. My mother was happy to watch Daisy, and a little curious about why I wanted to stay. When I told her I was getting to know Aaron a little better, she said something that surprised me. "I knew it!"

"You knew what, exactly?"

Confidence boomed from her voice. "I could feel the chemistry between you two. What about Justin? I have to admit, he's not who I would choose for you."

"Oh, Ma. There is nothing going on between Aaron and me, other than a budding friendship. Who knows, maybe I can bring up Harry at some point."

That prompted an *Ooh* from her on the other end of the line.

"As far as Justin goes, I'm planning on ending it. He's a nice guy and all, but we don't really have anything in common."

"And you feel safe being all the way out there in Crozet with Aaron?"

"He's a firefighter, Ma. Or he was. Yeah, I think I'm safe." Before I ended the call, I made sure to cover one thing. "Hey, if

Justin stops by, can you *not* tell him where I am? Just say that I'm working late or something."

She made a *tsking* sound.

"It's not what you think. It's just that I don't want to stir up trouble before I have a chance to end things."

"Fine. Just be careful."

My next call was to the man in question.

"Hey, Cupcake. You had me worried. I was about to send out a search party for you. Where are you?"

I took a breath. "I'm still working on a job in Charlottesville, and it's running late. I can't get together tonight."

"Got more toilets to clean, huh?" He chuckled.

I grumbled to myself. "I do more than clean toilets, Justin." My tone wasn't pleased. *I have a degree in accounting, you know.*

"Only kidding, Cupcake. How about tomorrow night? I'll take you out to dinner to make up for the last several days." His voice lifted out of the doldrums of the past few days.

"You sound better. Were you able to work things out with your finances?"

"Shit, yeah. It's all good. What time can I pick you up tomorrow?"

"I should be done by five. Let's hold off on dinner, though. There's something I need to discuss with you." Knowing Aaron was waiting for me inside, I felt the need to get this ball rolling as soon as possible.

"What sort of things? Should I be worried?"

"Listen, I've gotta get back to work. Why don't you stop by tomorrow around six, and we can talk then."

"*Stop by?* What the fuck is this?" There was that tone. Was Justin an abusive man? Sometimes I wondered. "Are you planning on dumping me already? Jesus Christ, can't a guy have a few days off?" He was riling himself up.

"Look, I can't talk about this right now. See you tomorrow." *Click.* I ended the call.

* * *

When I reentered Aaron's house, the scent of garlic confronted my senses, a sizzling sound accompanying it. I found him bent over his gas stove, pushing garlic and onions across a skillet with a spatula.

"Oh, hey. I found some jarred marinara that my buddy's wife left in my pantry. I thought I'd embellish the sauce a little. We're Italian, so I can't eat jarred sauce alone, even if it's homemade." He raised his gaze toward the heavens. "God would strike me down, right along with my grandmother." His face brightened, clearly amused by his declaration.

"Oh, so you're Italian, huh? I guess I should have known by your last name. That's cool. I bet you have a lot of good cooks in your family?"

I imagined his boisterous mother yelling at him to *eat, eat, eat*!

Something in Aaron's stature dwindled. Had I struck a nerve? Were his parents deceased? "Something like that."

Change the subject.

I inhaled with gusto. "Smells yummy. Got any bread I can eat to tide me over?" That was probably rude of me. I should have offered to help, but I was running on empty, and my energy and mood were suffering the effects.

Aaron guided me over to the same chair where I had been sitting earlier. He approached the island, where a baguette sat on a wooden cutting board. Using a bread knife, he cut the bread into bite-sized pieces. My mouth was already watering with anticipation. But he didn't stop there. Showing me his creative side, he placed several types of cheeses as well as a few pats of butter next to the bread, transforming the cutting board into a tray of snackful selections.

"Help yourself." He placed the small buffet in front of me, then grabbed another beer from the fridge to replace my empty one. "Sorry, I'm not much of a wine drinker. Not cool for an Italian. I've got bourbon if you're interested." A butter knife, a small plate, and a napkin arrived a moment later.

I felt like a slug not helping him with this, but I was weak; my lunch long since digested. "Beer is fine." I filled my mouth with a small chunk of sharp cheddar and bread, savoring the bold tangy and nutty flavors. "Would you mind if I grabbed a glass of water?" My parched throat needed hydration.

Before I could stand, a glass full of H2O landed in front of me.

"Thank you." I'd never seen a man behave so attentively before. And I would never have guessed Aaron to be *that* type of guy.

Once I had satisfied the hunger sharks, I decided to help, although the way Aaron dashed around the kitchen grabbing this spice or that pepper, I found myself at a loss.

"Tell you what? You cook. I'll clean up afterward."

Aaron gave me a look. "You clean for a living. No, I'll cook, and I'll clean up my own mess. You just sit there and keep me company."

* * *

Since Aaron didn't have any dining room furniture to speak of, we sat at his kitchen table, ready to savor our meal. I thought about our common interest. I rose from the table and rushed over to peer out his kitchen window. "Oh, so there's your camper. It's bigger than I expected." The backyard presented a small patio that reached out toward his lush lawn, everything bare except for his camper parked on a large patch of blacktop that circled around the left side of the house. The roof of what I assumed was a large shed or a detached garage rose slightly above the camper, the main structure hidden from view. A cluster of tall oak and maple trees, supplemented by various pine and firs, filled a small forest off in the distance, allowing the house a secluded setting.

Tranquil came to mind.

I returned to my seat. "Do you take your camper out much?" I took my first bite of food. "Oh, my god. This is amazing!" My eyes were rolling back in my head. "How did you learn to cook like this?" The herbs and spices were beyond anything my simple tongue had ever tasted, the combination of spicy and sweet uncanny.

Aaron used a large spoon and a fork to spool his angel hair pasta, which he eased into his mouth as soon as it was nice and plump. "I told you. We're Italian. When I was younger, my aunt was always trying to fatten me up."

Still, no mention of Mom and Dad. I found it alarming, but only because I hoped they were still around. A sudden thought hit me: Were his parents the ones who perished in the fire? Did Aaron try to save them, injuring himself? But he'd implied he wasn't from here, nor was his family.

Regardless, this wasn't some recluse who hid himself away in shame. This was a normal, red-blooded male who had family and friends who loved him. *Wasn't he?*

I struggled to keep my thoughts straight. A question rose in my mind that could help answer my previous theory. "Didn't you say your family wasn't from here?" It was a stretch. He'd basically shaken his head at my direct question from the first time we'd met.

I raised a palm. "Sorry. I said I wouldn't pry."

My dinner companion swallowed his next bite, which he

washed down with a gulp of water. "No, it's fine. It's been a long time since I've talked about myself. My family is from Florida, Cocoa Beach."

"Does your family still live there? Do they come to visit?" *Were they burned in that apartment fire?*

"Yes, and no, they don't come to visit. My grandfather worked for the Kennedy Space Center back in the late sixties, so he moved there with my grandmother. My dad and uncle were kids at the time. They were from Vermont."

"Wow. So, you're not from Virginia?"

"No."

"What brought you here?"

"Paula."

Again, not wanting to pry, I left it there, hoping Aaron would fill in the gaps. It was a relief that he was from Florida and likely that his parents didn't live here. It was sad, however, that they also didn't come to visit, which could also mean one or both were deceased.

"I always knew I wanted to be a firefighter. My father was one, and so was my Uncle Ed. Both men were larger than life in my eyes, always helping where they could. Not sure what good it did them."

My father was one? What did that mean? Did *was* indicate he was retired? I hoped that was the case.

Aaron grew quiet for a moment until he found his words again.

It was clear to me that he wasn't used to sharing like this. He had no idea how much I appreciated his trying.

"When I was in training, I met Paula at the fire academy. She was originally from Virginia. She said she wanted to try living in Florida for a while. You know, enjoy the palm trees and the surf. When things became serious between us, I proposed. She said she'd marry me, but she wanted to move back home. And so, I agreed to go with her. The station in Charlottesville offered better benefits and more opportunities for growth. I wanted to become a captain."

A gorgeous man traveled the eastern seaboard to be with his love. What could be more romantic than that? I doubted any man would travel to the next town for me. Where was Paula now? Did she mourn the loss of Aaron? I knew I would.

"That sounds nice. Are you glad you came? Do you think you'll ever return to Florida?"

Aaron thought for a moment, his posture stooping. "It *was* nice . . . until I fucked it up." He took his beer in his hand, lifted it, and held it near his mouth. "Am I glad I came? I wasn't . . . for a long time. And no, I don't have any plans to return to Florida. I'm more of a mountain man than a beach dude. Getting too crowded down south."

Do you still see Paula? Does she live nearby? What did I really want to know? *Do you still love her?* I knew I couldn't ask any of those things as much as I wanted to.

"I get that. I like Virginia myself. But I was born and raised here."

A pause cropped up and lingered. I understood why. We didn't know each other. And yet, despite Aaron's guarded personality, I felt more at ease with him than I had with any other man in a long while, including Justin. *Especially Justin.*

"Does your dad still live nearby, or your brother?" As he asked this question, Aaron let his gaze fall to his beer again.

Was he as nervous about asking me personal questions as I was about asking him? It seemed we were both treading lightly with each other.

"My dad moved to North Carolina to work for the power company there. My brother lives out in LA. He's trying to make it in the movie industry."

That piqued his interest. "An actor, huh?"

"No. He wants to be a producer. So far, he's only been able to snag entry-level positions. And he's a great writer. He's written screenplays for six movies. According to him, no one is interested in reading any of them. He's got talent." I smirked. "Unlike his sister, who works with numbers, not stories."

"You seem to be doing pretty well for yourself. You've got your own business. That's more than most people can say." His eyes shone, the compliment softening my heart.

"I guess. I'm just a cleaning lady. It's not rocket science." Why I felt the need to downplay my profession was beyond me. Running a business of any nature took skill, dedication, and hours of hard work.

Aaron pushed his plate back and sat forward, his forearms resting on the table. "You're a lot more than that." He sized me up. "Anyone with a brain can see as much."

Goosebumps ran down my arms.

How refreshing. A man who actually got me. And yet, I found it difficult to respond. My focus shifted toward my paper napkin, which I played with for no apparent reason. "You don't know me." *Nice job stating the obvious.* "And I don't know you." Now, I was redundant.

He watched me for a moment. What was he thinking?

"That's true. But isn't that what we're doing here? Getting to know each other?" Aaron stood and collected his plate.

Was that what we were doing?

I followed his lead, taking my plate before he could do it for me and followed him to the sink. "I said I'd clean—"

"Yeah, I heard you. But I'm not one to take advantage." Standing next to his rather tall and robust self, I nudged him with my shoulder. "Besides, if you let me help, maybe you'll ask me back." Disgust had me shaking my head at myself.

"I'd like that."

So would I.

What didn't fit in the dishwasher, we took care of by hand. Aaron scrubbed and rinsed, and I dried, a large towel placed on the counter to soak up the extra drops from the pots and pans until Aaron could put them away. The window over the sink brought his camper back to mind, although it was too dark to see it now. I realized he had never answered my question from earlier. "So, do you take the camper out a lot?"

Aaron handed me a large stainless-steel pot. "I do. How often do *you* go camping?"

His question snagged a distant memory from my memory banks. "Not often enough . . . I used to love going when I was younger. Before my dad left my mom. Oh, gosh, I must've been nine or so. Jack was only six." I placed the dried pot onto the toweled surface. "Anyway, my dad found some great deal on a pop-up camper." I tipped my chin toward his unit, waiting out in the darkness, which I was pretty sure was a Class C, with the cab of a truck attached. "Nothing as nice as what you have. Ours had canvas walls and barely enough room to sleep, much less entertain, but that year, he took us all over Virginia in that camper. We saw the ocean and the mountains. At night, we sat out under the stars, and he'd tell us stories. My mother did too." My heart lifted. "I'd never seen my parents happier. We played games, we fished, and we hiked. If we were at the beach, we made sandcastles and threw the Frisbee. If it rained, we went to a movie or an arcade. It was probably one of the best memories of my parents when they were happy. Jack and I walked on the beach looking for shark's teeth." My voice filled with pride. "My mother was a pro at finding them, you know. I remember walking behind them as they held hands." A lungful of air released itself, the memory so precious in my heart. "I just remember feeling like everything in my world was good. We were happy." When I realized that Aaron had stopped working, I turned to face him.

And that was when he used his clean index finger to mop a single tear that had fallen down my cheek unbeknownst, the scent of dishwashing liquid fresh on his skin.

"Anyway, it was a lot of fun." My tone changed, as did my mood. "He sold the camper the following year, and that . . . was that." I always wondered what had motivated my father to give us that gift. Did he know by then that he'd be leaving us soon? Was he trying to make up for things that hadn't occurred yet?

I gazed up at the clock on the wall. "Wow, it's ten o'clock! I better get home."

* * *

Justin never showed up the following night. I waited until seven before I texted Yaz to see if she wanted any company. Ross was there, but she told me to come over anyway. They were having cocktails to enjoy with takeout pizza. She also told me to bring Daisy, which sealed the deal. Mom was out with Harry for the evening, something about a concert at a local venue.

"I'll bring chips and salsa."

I was there in no time. I really wanted to tell Yaz about my dinner with Aaron, but having Ross around held me back. It was fine. It gave us a chance to be together and talk about light-hearted topics such as the ever-changing April weather and what the dogs were up to these days. The pups kept us pretty busy as they ran *zoomies* around the house. I'd never seen dogs run faster. I was afraid they were going to smack head-first into a wall, which, somehow, they managed to avoid.

"What's Justin up to tonight?" After devouring four slices of New York-style pepperoni pizza, Ross had just plopped himself down on Yaz's comfy sofa with a rum and coke clutched in his hand. He stretched his feet out over her matching ottoman as I took the chair perpendicular to him and Yaz, who had snuggled up next to her man.

I chose vodka, lemonade, and cranberry for my cocktail; Yaz went with a White Russian.

Returning to Ross's question, I sighed, my tummy full of pizza, and my heart uncertain. "I'm not sure where he is. He was supposed to stop by earlier but was a no-show." I took a sip of my drink, enjoying the burst of fruit flavors on my tongue.

"Maybe he got tied up at work." Ross turned on the TV. "Anyone up for a movie?"

"Sure. I'd be down." I checked my cell to see if any texts had arrived from Justin. So far, nothing. I hadn't heard from Aaron either.

Daisy and Sadie came zooming past, full of unrestrained energy. I reached out to try to pet my girl, but she was too fast for me.

Ross and Yaz scrolled through the movie selections while I thought about Aaron and our time together. He had my phone number, yet he hadn't called or texted me since last night. It had only been twenty-four hours since our dinner, but I was eager to reconnect with him. Aaron wasn't a man who flaunted what he had, nor was he one to share or show much emotion. It was when he allowed those barriers, which he'd done such a good job building around him, to lower that I got to witness who he was or who he could be. He'd been engaged once until, as he so eloquently had put it, *fucked it up*.

How had he fucked it up? He also spoke about his father and his uncle in the past tense. Or maybe it was their profession that he was referring to, not so much them. His aunt cooked for him, not his mother. I just hoped his father and uncle were retired and hadn't perished on the job. The status of his mother added more mystery.

Whatever the reason, when things with Paula fell apart,

why had Aaron stayed here? He said he liked the mountains, but was there more to it? It would be difficult for me to leave my mom, but not everyone felt like I did. Jack moved all the way across the country.

I thought about the apartment fire that had injured Aaron and had cost two innocent lives. A man and a woman. Something else lingered in my thoughts: could someone from Paula's family have perished in that fire? She was from this area. If so, that would certainly create a strain between them. I realized that most of my theories were way off. That didn't stop my mind from racing in one direction or another. I blamed my mother.

Aaron didn't move around like an injured man. He always wore long sleeves, though. What did those shirts hide from prying eyes? Aaron's life was a Pandora's box of sad stories. And I wanted to hear about every one of them, including the fiancée who had left him. I'd never been more interested in my life.

Was it because he was the first person in a long while to make me dinner? He even brought me appetizers to appease my hunger. He doted. No one had ever doted before. And he complimented me regarding my business ventures. More importantly, he listened. What he didn't do was think up lame nicknames like Cupcake or Cleaning Lady. Or sum my workday up with *cleaning shitters*.

Bang, bang, bang.

The sound of the door had both pups scrambling near the entrance, barking and carrying on, a cacophony of canine distress.

Ross and Yaz both stopped their streaming search and stared over at the door.

"Is your mom coming over?" Ross looked to Yaz for an answer, who shook her head.

"Not that I know of."

The banging grew louder. "Hey! It's Justin. I know Natalie's in there. Her car is out front!"

Justin had met both Yaz and Ross, not that his tone indicated as much. The angry voice that boomed through the door behaved as though I were being held hostage. *Open up, or else.* He didn't say those words, but his loud bangs and crisp tone inferred as much.

What did he want? He'd basically blown me off earlier.

"I want to speak to Natalie!"

Ross and Yaz stared over at me with wide eyes. "Everything okay between you two?" Ross slowly rose from the couch, Yaz right behind him.

At that moment, I wasn't sure.

Chapter 13

Natalie

"I'll get it. You two continue your search." I set my drink on the side table next to me and headed for the door as Ross and Yaz returned to their seats on the couch. "Okay, okay. It's only Justin, calm down, you two." Neither pup listened to my reassuring words as I stepped over them. Instead, they jumped around like popcorn on a hot skillet. And when I got the door open, they both tried to make a mad dash outside. Whatever one pup did, the other just *had* to mimic, which included the barking that was loud enough to shatter my eardrums.

"Hey, get back in here!" I pulled them both back, which wasn't easy. "Can you hurry up and get in here, Justin?"

It had been cloudy all day with the threat of rain. Mother Nature was making good on her threat. A steady stream fell from the sky.

My soon-to-be ex-boyfriend abided. His breath and body reeked of alcohol, along with something else . . . *gasoline?* Some chemical? Disheveled, Justin wore a loose-fitting T-shirt and baggy jeans. His five-o'clock shadow headed toward midnight.

If I hadn't known any better, I would have sworn he had just woken up. He was drunk. Showing up at my best friend's apartment in this condition only reinforced the fact that I had made the right decision about ending this so-called relationship with him.

The dogs ran around Justin's legs, stopping only to jump up with their tiny tails wagging wildly. When Justin didn't acknowledge either of them, I shot Yaz a look that said, *Help!* I hadn't even had time to update my friend on what was going on between Justin and me, but something told me she knew.

Message received, she rushed over and ushered the dogs into her bedroom, the words, "Hey Justin," trailing behind her.

"Hey, dude. I was just asking Natalie where you were." Ross approached, his hand extended.

The two of them had only met a couple of times: once for a movie, and once when I stopped by Yaz's place with Justin to drop off some paperwork.

Justin shook Ross's hand. "Yeah, hey, mind if I talk to Natalie alone for a minute?"

My jaw clenched. Did he have the actual nerve to ask Ross to leave the room? Wasn't happening.

I grabbed my slicker from a small coat tree near the door and slid my feet into my sneakers, tying them up quickly. "No worries, Ross, we'll go outside." I grabbed my cell and stuffed it into my jacket pocket. "I've got my cell if you need to reach me." I wouldn't be far, but they had my dog in their care, and at Daisy's young, impetuous age, anything could happen. She'd sprained her leg last week from jumping off the couch.

Outside, the April night sky shed a few more sprinkles that, according to my weather app, would transform into heavy rain before morning. The dampness in the air seemed to make the upper sixties feel more like the lower sixties. I wrapped my coat tighter around my waist, wishing I had drunk more of my cocktail to heat my insides.

"What's this about, Justin?" I approached my minivan and leaned my back against it. "I waited for nearly an hour for you earlier, and you never showed up . . . or called . . . or texted." I flailed one hand. "Have you been drinking?" Stupid question, but sometimes, stupid questions had a place. Plus, starting an argument seemed like the perfect segue for a breakup.

Justin rubbed his bloodshot eyes. "Maybe I didn't want to hear your *Dear John* speech." He coated his voice with self-pity.

I wasn't falling for it. "Look, this can't be a big deal to you. We've only been seeing each other for a few weeks"—I didn't count the week we hadn't seen each other at all—"We just don't have a lot in common. But I'd love to be friends."

There it was. It was such a relief to get that off my chest.

"Why? What did I do wrong?" Justin took a step closer, his glassy eyes reaching out to my sympathetic side.

"You didn't do anything wrong. It's not working for me. But, like I said, I'd be happy to be friends." Total bullshit. I'd never been friends with an ex, and there was a reason for that. Once the attraction fizzled, there wasn't much else to keep us together as friends or otherwise.

"Is this because I wouldn't fuck you the other night? I wanted to. Believe me. I had shit to take care of. I've had a lot on my mind."

It was then that I noticed a cut on his hand.

"What happened?" I gazed at the injury, wrapped in white gauze; the blood seeping through now dried and crusty.

"It's nothing. Doing maintenance. I was cleaning the blade on my mower." He buried said hand in the pocket of his jeans.

Doesn't that hurt?

"Listen, let me make this up to you." He pushed himself

against me, his erection *hard* to ignore. "We can pick up where we were. There's nothing I'd like more than to make you cum, and trust me, I *will* make you cum."

In the time we'd been together, he'd never spoken to me this way. Never even tried to move things in that direction. And I had to admit, if he had offered last week, I might have taken him up on it. Only because I was lonely. Things had changed. I'd gotten to know Aaron, a man who made me dinner and brought me snacks to satisfy my hungry belly. What Aaron had done, really, was show me a man capable of being attentive and caring, all qualities I could use in my life. I'd been going it alone for a long time, taking care of Mom, making sure I had Jack settled. I realized how much I missed having someone take care of *me*. Yes, my mother made meals, but this wasn't the same thing. Aaron was a romantic interest, not a parent. At this point, no matter what Justin said or did, he would never measure up. And my neck was suffering whiplash from his mood swings.

I pushed him away, but I also made sure to be gentle. "That's not it, Justin."

He stood back, his face contorted and tight. "Is there someone else? You been two-timing me?" Angry Justin had returned. I imagined watching a tennis match between angry Justin and happy Justin.

I shook my head and stared at the ground, doing my absolute best to be sincere. I met his gaze. "No, Justin, there isn't anyone else." I lifted a hand and let it drop, slapping against my thigh. "Where in the hell would I have met someone in just a few days?"

That seemed to satiate his anger until my cell phone rang from my pocket. I took it out to see Aaron's name illuminated on the screen. *It's him!* He called. If Justin hadn't been standing there, I would have jumped up and down, my heart racing like a greyhound.

The asshole snatched the phone from my grip before I could silence the call, which was what I was planning to do.

He held the phone up in my face. "Who the fuck is *Hot* Aaron?"

Oh, shit. I'd forgotten I'd added "Hot" to Aaron's name in my contact list.

He answered the call. "This is Natalie's phone, and I'm her boyfriend. Who the fuck are you, and what do you want?" Justin's voice was harsh and unforgiving. He pulled the phone away from his mouth. "Big surprise, he hung up."

Damn it. I had told Aaron I wasn't seeing anyone. Justin had now proven I'd lied. Did he recognize the name from our discussion with Mom and Harry? It didn't appear so.

"So, you *were* whoring around behind my back." Justin closed in, his eyes reflecting anything but kindness.

This time, I shoved him away with a little more effort. "Screw you, Justin! We haven't been together long enough for you to behave this way. We barely know each other. You have no right to speak to me like that! Aaron is just a friend. Not even a friend. He's a client. Yes, he's hot, but we are *not* seeing each other." I reached for my phone, but Justin whipped it away. "Look! I just met him last week and don't even know him. I'm sorry I put *hot* in front of his name, but I'm sure you've met hot women on the job. That's all this is."

I'd noticed Justin's wandering eye on more than one occasion, mostly with servers or passersby when we were out and about. I chalked it up to what most people did. It was hard for anyone to look away when someone beautiful, male or female, passed by. And I'd never been one to worry about such things. Yes, I'd had men cheat, but by that point in our relationship, I hadn't cared all that much. In fact, it gave me an out, just like

Justin was doing right now, only for a different reason. Justin was unstable. I should have noticed before.

I tried to grab my phone again. "I need my phone, Justin! Give it to me. Right now!" I felt like a schoolgirl being teased by a bully. "I mean it. Give it back!"

Justin lifted my phone above his head. "Tell you what"—he threw it like a pitcher would on a mound toward the front lawn, where it landed with a soft thud somewhere in the dark—"go fetch."

I was so angry. Rain had started to fall much heavier, and I needed that phone. It had all my client contacts. When I went to dash off to find it, Justin grabbed me around the waist. "Forget your phone. It's not going anywhere. It will be fine. Come on, I was only kidding. Let's get back to what we were doing the other night. I know you want to."

Is he serious? We'd gone way past patching things up. Who the hell was this guy? What a mistake I'd made dating him.

"Let go of me, Justin. I need to find my phone."

He pushed his lips onto mine, making me wince and muffling any attempt I made to scream. His breath was rancid, and I struggled to identify a single reason why I had ever considered him romantically. I had to free myself. His lips were crushing mine. And then, his icy hands began to grope roughly.

Oh, no, this isn't happening. Remembering his wound, I grabbed his hand and dug my fingernails under the bandage, hoping to jar him.

"Ouch!" He took a step away. "You bitch!"

I raised a palm. "Stop right there, Justin. If you touch me again, I'll have you arrested. Do you hear me? I won't hesitate."

He started toward me as a voice stopped him in his tracks.

"Everything okay out here?" Ross stood outside the front door with Yaz, the patio light exposing their wide eyes and raised brows.

Justin paused for a moment, probably trying to decide what to do next. We weren't alone anymore. Thank god. "Yeah, everything's okay if you call dating a two-timing bitch-whore, okay." He got up in my face again and pointed, his cheeks unusually red. "This isn't over!" He rushed over to his truck and climbed in, slamming the door shut. He fired up the engine and spun his tires out of the driveway, loose rocks flying everywhere, nearly hitting me in the face.

What the hell just happened? How did I not see this coming?

From this point forward, I *had* to pay more attention to those warning flags. And I'd seen a few with Justin. As upset as I was about the altercation, I was more stressed about Aaron discovering that I was a liar. I should have been honest with him. I should have stated that I *was* seeing someone, but it wasn't working out. What an understatement. Filled with conflicting thoughts about what to do, I set off in search of my phone.

* * *

"Wow, I didn't realize that Justin was so abusive." Yaz had just handed me a glass of water as we stood in her kitchen. I'd found my phone, which was undamaged, other than a few smudges of dirt on the screen.

I swallowed a large sip of water, my body in need of replenishment. Tremors still lurked in my bones from the fear I felt, especially when Justin had forced that kiss. His phantom hands lingered on my body. I shivered. I wasn't used to that type of behavior. "I didn't know myself. This was the first time he's behaved this way. He's been upset about that banker, James Logan, who screwed him on a contract and some back pay." I guzzled more water. "That doesn't excuse his behavior."

Ross entered the room. "Who did you say screwed him?" He had been standing at the living room window, keeping an eye out for Justin's return. If that happened, we were definitely calling the police.

"James Logan. He lived in Afton in a big house. And he'd signed a contract with Justin for the year. He reneged on the contract and refused to pay him what he owed."

Ross leaned against the sink; his arms crossed over his chest. "Didn't his place just burn down? I heard something on the news about him being in critical condition. Same guy?"

"Same guy."

Ross made a face, eyebrows raised. "From what I read, they suspect arson, you know. Do you think Justin could have anything to do with it? That dude seems unhinged."

This wasn't the first time that thought had come to mind. I recalled his bandaged hand. What had caused the injury? And he *was* angry at James for cheating him—so angry, he'd been a ghost the past few days. If Ross had asked me this last week, I would have said, no way. But now? After what Justin had just done? I wasn't sure.

My bizarre evening continued when I returned home from Yaz's place. Mom and Harry sat nestled on the couch watching a prerecorded *Jeopardy*. My mother loved testing her knowledge against that show, often doing as well as some of the contestants. When she was on her own, it became a staple in her life.

"Hey, honey, how was your night?" Mom peeled back the mint-colored throw blanket keeping her and Harry warm and sat forward on the couch.

"Well. Not so good, actually."

My mother grabbed the remote off the side table and paused the show. "Why? What happened?"

I told her the goings-on, including Justin's threat before he had left. I even admitted I had written *hot* Aaron on my phone and why.

My mother's hand went to her mouth, her eyes bugging out of her head. She rose and rushed over to me. "Are you okay? Did he hurt you?"

Harry came up behind her. "That's unbelievable. Justin did *that*?"

"He sure did. And I didn't mean anything by putting *hot* in front of Aaron's name. It's just something I do for fun. Aaron and I are only friends."

My mother caressed my back as Harry closed in.

"Is that the same Aaron who I told you about last week? I remember you telling me you were working for him."

I slid my arms out of my rain slicker and draped it over my arm, prepared to hang it in the closet off the kitchen. "Yeah. Same man. He's actually a nice person." I waved a palm. "And I am *not* seeing him romantically." *Even if I wish I were.*

Harry raised his own palm. "Young lady, I wasn't going to ask." His eyes filled with good humor. "That is none of my business, anyway."

I sighed, trying to lighten up myself. "Sorry. It's been a night. Oh, hey, if Aaron is still speaking to me after Justin was so rude to him, I plan to ask him about that fire you told us about, Harry. Maybe he'd be willing to testify—"

"I never asked you to do that!" A pair of angry eyes glared at me, enough that my mother bent her head back to confirm it was in fact Harry who had spoken.

"She's just trying to help, Harry."

Backing away, Harry shook his head, his hands placed on his hips. "I didn't ask for her help, Rose! I told you I didn't want to pursue this." He jabbed at the air with his index finger. "The man's house just burned down. He's in the hospital, clinging to life. Do you think I want any of that attention falling back on me?" A sheen of sweat formed on his brow, which he wiped away with a distressed hand.

I stood there, stunned. "But, Harry, what happened was so long ago."

He clenched his jaw. "Do you think that matters now? If they start looking for suspects, don't you think they're gonna find a way to question the Black man who had a falling out with him?"

"What?" I took a step toward him. "No, I didn't mean to—"

"I don't much care what you meant to do. This is serious! I told you both that I did *not* want to pursue this matter any further. It's finally behind me. And I thank you to stay out of my business in the future." With that, Harry stormed into the kitchen where he grabbed his jacket, draped over the back of a barstool, and rushed out the door.

From the living room, I exchanged a look of shock with my mother. "I'm sorry, Ma. I didn't mean to—"

"Don't be. I'm the one who asked you to do it." She gazed through the kitchen at the front door as though she expected Harry to come bursting back in, apologizing for his outrage. Only Harry never returned, leaving us wondering why in the world he would think the authorities would suspect him of something as serious as setting fires around town and nearly killing James Logan. Was there more to his story than he was letting on?

Chapter 14

Dream a Little Dream

I had a dream last night. I looked into the eyes of the beast as it engulfed the roof of a building I hadn't seen before. And yet, the structure felt familiar. I could almost hear its fiery breath, consuming everything in its path, a gargle of flames. It called out to me from the depths of the void. *You know what to do.*

I was inside now, voices crying out for me to save them. And I tried, but every room I entered stretched into another. Their voices were so close they boomed in my ears, yet far enough that I couldn't see or reach them. A swirl of torment wrapped around me. A cyclone pinning me in place.

What is this?

"Help us!"

My efforts did nothing but pull me farther away from the needy. I fought against a force so strong it exhausted every limb.

The voices had to know I was helpless.

"I'll get to you. I'm coming."

It was as if I were trudging through dark water, every limb weighing astronomically, pushing my resolve to its limits.

My legs couldn't fight anymore. Exhaustion overwhelmed.

"Help us!"

The price was too high. I had to keep going. My feet stuck to the floor, my soles melting into liquid as thick as taffy. Hands reached up from the depths, grabbing at my ankles. Desperate hands. I kicked them away. *Get off me.*

"Save us!"

Fire came slithering through the door, ready to destroy everything in its path. *Burn them.* I kicked my feet away from flailing hands, the ones desperate to drag me under.

"Save us!"

"Let go of me." Flames came from my mouth. I blew down upon the desperate hands. They thrashed and withered, the skin charred to bone, crumbling into ash.

"Help us!"

A realization sat like lead in my chest. A reality that my mind struggled to accept.

I can't! I won't. I want you to die!

Bolting up in bed, sweat dripped down my temples, and my heart beat so hard it hurt. I took several breaths, trying to orient myself. I panted, tears threatening to spill. I hated who James Logan had turned me into. In the fetal position, I remained for hours, tormented by images still haunting my thoughts.

All at once, a new reality settled, a truth so potent that it chased my nightmares away. The beast in my dream wasn't me at all.

It was him. It was *always* him.

"Rot in hell, motherfucker!"

Chapter 15

Natalie

I awoke the next morning with a new mission in mind. No more toxic people. A lifetime had taught me that good people had a way of filling you up. For years (decades, really), I had done that for my mother. Yaz had done it for me. Toxic people, on the other hand, did nothing but tear you down.

My father was the king of toxicity. Not only had he neglected my mother, Jack, and me; he tried to pin the blame on us. *We weren't supportive enough. We didn't appreciate anything he was trying to do for us.* Thinking back, that unresolved father-daughter connection sparked many unsuccessful relationships for me moving forward.

I could see it all as clear as day. What Justin had taught me was to believe in my gut instincts and to stop pushing my better judgment aside for the sake of romance.

Aaron was another story. I never suspected toxicity in his heart. Wounded, yes. Toxic, no. In fact, I sensed Aaron had a lot to give by the way he jumped into action to serve me dinner and take care of my ravenous stomach. The way he asked me about my life and listened as though what I had to say held importance. His generosity toward Daisy. The nuances of his demeanor spoke volumes. I liked him. But did he now see *me* as the toxic one? The woman who had told him she was single when she technically wasn't?

I stayed in bed a little longer, allowing my mind to process things and my body to rest. Daisy was happy to continue cuddling as we watched TV. Most days, my poor pup was either left on her own or carted around to various jobs to watch me clean. Thank god I had my mother to co-parent.

I hadn't heard a word from Justin, and that was fine by me. I hoped he came to his senses and realized that threatening a woman he'd only been dating for a short time was dangerous territory that could very well land his ass in prison. Had he done that sort of thing before? I'd dated my share of losers, but never anyone who had threatened me. And we hadn't even been intimate. I could only imagine the so-called rights he'd have claimed over me *had* we gone that far.

One more thought left an unsettling prickle under my skin: if Justin had anything to do with James Logan's situation, that meant he was a lot more dangerous than I had ever imagined. And if that were a possibility, I'd have to keep my wits about me, including canceling the client whose house I cleaned and for whom Justin landscaped. The Robinsons were nice people, but I couldn't risk running into that maniac again.

I took a shower, made breakfast (which was now lunch), and played with Daisy on the living room floor for a little while, which seemed to brighten my mood. With an exerted growl, Daisy tugged on the end of a large, braided rope while I tugged on the other end, my mind lost in Aaron-land. I'd felt a genuine connection with him I hadn't felt in a long time—something beyond physical attraction—although that was certainly part of it. For a brief moment in time, I was content to the point of complete. We washed the dishes and cleaned the kitchen from the extraordinary meal he'd created, as I envisioned our lives together. Was I losing it? Or was something else going on? Somehow, Aaron felt like that perfect shoe that fit my awkward-sized foot—the foot being my personality in this scenario. The air felt calm when I was in his presence, making the world more tolerable.

I had to confront Aaron at some point but hadn't decided how. I could text, but that felt too impersonal, especially with such a heavy topic. I could call him, but even that felt too easy since I'd already taken the easy route. This time, I needed to *show* him who I was.

I finished my second cup of coffee and brought Daisy out to pee. An April mist permeated the air, the temperature riding the mid-sixties. *Great.* Mist never cooperated well with my wavy hair. When I brought Daisy back inside, my mother was just driving in with a load of groceries. I met her at the door.

"Ma, would you mind watching Daisy for me for an hour or two?"

She plunked her reusable canvas bag along with her purse on the counter and released a heavy breath. "Sure. Is everything okay?"

"Yeah, I wanted to take a run over to Aaron's place and speak to him." I proceeded toward the counter where she stood to help her unpack. "Do you have anything else that needs to be brought in from the car?"

"No, this is it." She pulled a box of oats from the bag and placed it in her small pantry closet. "Do you think it's a good idea to go all the way out there? Can't you just call him?" Worry heightened her tone.

I stood outside the pantry, handing her canned goods and a box of pasta. "I think I need to face him for this one. Calling doesn't feel right. I just need to fix my hair and change. Are you sure it's okay?"

At the counter, she folded her bag and placed it in a lower cabinet on the inner side of the island. Then she removed her raincoat and hung it in a closet next to the door. "It's fine with me. But if he gets nasty with you, come home!"

I approached the open entryway to the living room; my hand braced on the casing. "You're confusing Aaron with Justin, Ma. I would never go see Justin. Not now. But Aaron was a firefighter. And I've never gotten that vibe from him." I smirked at her. "But I promise to be careful."

* * *

Forty-five minutes later, I arrived at Aaron's house. I debated calling him in advance but worried that he'd tell me not to make the trip. I *had* to do this. Even if he told me he never wanted to see me again. This wasn't about Aaron as much as it was about me.

I am not my father!

Wearing my thick raincoat with a jersey-knit black tunic underneath and charcoal leggings, my comfortable loafers cushioning my feet, I approached his door and rang the bell.

No shadows or footfalls made me fear he was in the basement or away, although his truck, with its gas cans and tools in their usual places, was there. I rang the bell again and knocked for emphasis. If he didn't come to the door, I'd try calling. I hadn't driven all this way to return home unsuccessful.

And then I heard footsteps and saw the shadow of a figure through the beveled glass sidelights. The door opened, Aaron standing there in his typical long-sleeved T-shirt—navy this time—and faded jeans. Confusion forced his brow lower, his eyes narrowing.

"Uh." He rubbed his short beard. He didn't say, *What are you doing here*, but his eyes filled with questions.

"Hi, Aaron. I'm sorry to bother you. I hope I haven't caught you at a bad time. . . . I can come back if you wish. . . . I wanted to explain what happened last night. . . . I'm sure you must think the worst of me. . . . I just feel like I need to explain myself." My cheeks were on fire, my hands flailing this way and that, sweat gathering on my upper lip.

He offered a subtle nod. "Nope. It's fine." He stepped back to allow me entry. Relaxed shoulders, kind eyes. Nothing in his demeanor spoke of anger or disappointment. Somehow, that felt worse. Apathy could only mean he didn't care enough to be bothered.

Oh, well, you're here. Get on with it.

I stood in the foyer, my heart racing and my mouth as dry as a desert. Not my pits, though, which were starting to sweat. I forced a tense breath into my lungs.

"Can I take your jacket?" He reached his hand out.

"No, that's okay. I'm not planning on staying. So, I, um, wanted to apologize for last night. I had already broken up with Justin when you called." *If you want this to work, whatever this is, you have to come clean.* "I mean, I hadn't broken up with him when I was here last. I'm sorry for lying to you. I knew Justin and I weren't going anywhere." I scoffed. "And from his behavior last night, I am absolutely certain I made the right decision." Man, was that true. "I was at my friend Yaz's house, and he just showed up. When you called, he made an assumption, even though I told him we were only friends."

We are friends, right? Or had I blown that too.

No response. Aaron stood there watching me, his expression hard to pinpoint. Did he think I was delusional?

Oh god! All of a sudden, I realized that I could have been reading all the wrong signals here. If Aaron wasn't interested in the first place, I was making a complete and utter fool of myself.

What was I supposed to say now? "We'd only been dating for a few weeks. I didn't really know Justin all that well. It's been pretty casual. He surprised me when he'd gotten so angry when I told him things weren't working out."

"Huh." Aaron rubbed his jaw again. "You'd only been together for a few weeks?" His brow rose and fell. "He seemed pretty angry for such a short time."

"About a month. But we hadn't even seen each other over the last week. And his behavior surprised me too. But it wasn't serious between us. Cross my heart." I made the motion of crossing my heart and felt even more foolish for doing so.

Aaron cleared his throat, letting his hand fall away from his face. "I can understand why he was upset."

"I told him you and I were just friends. And that you are one of my clients. He had no right to speak to you that way. I promise you, I never implied we had anything other than friendship happening between us." At least, that was true. I may have lied to Aaron about Justin, but I hadn't lied to Justin about Aaron. And I hadn't cheated on him, either. Using the word *friendship* allowed me to show Aaron I wasn't implying we had anything more between us.

"That's not what I meant."

"Oh?" I wasn't sure what to say, so I let Aaron do the talking for a change.

"I just meant that I could understand why he would be upset about losing you." His amber eyes softened, his cheeks flushing. It was adorable. "What man wouldn't be?"

Many. I could give you a list.

That was what my brain had to say. My tongue, on the other hand, had tied itself into a knot, words refusing to form.

"Do you have any jobs scheduled for late afternoon or evening this Friday?"

I stood there like a dazed idiot, still processing his last compliment. *Think.* What was my schedule?

"Um, I'll have to check, but I think I finish up by four on Friday." I pulled my cell phone out of my jacket pocket. "Oh. I actually start my last job at one, but it's at a home, not a business, so I usually finish up within a few hours." Did he notice my hands were literally shaking as I tried *not* to let my cell phone slip from my sweaty fingers? I felt like I was in high school and the hot guy was asking me to prom.

"Great. Do you think your mother could watch Daisy for a few hours? I have something I'd like to show you."

Show me?

"What is it?"

The corners of his eyes crinkled at the edges. "I can't tell you that. It's a surprise." Aaron's voice filled with fun-loving vibes, his aura welcoming.

Christ on a cracker. He had a surprise for me? It took everything in me to stop from clapping my hands together like a six-year-old. The last person who surprised me with something *nice* was Mom when she found out she was in remission.

"I'll ask her."

He stepped forward and leaned in, placing a tender kiss against my cheek. "See you Friday." His voice was a mere whisper.

The close proximity of his body to mine had my insides firing up with all sorts of emotions and sensations. I was grateful my legs held firm. He smelled of cedar from his work or his body wash; I wasn't sure which. His breath suggested a cup of coffee in his recent past, the kind that had me craving one for myself. And the size of him dwarfed my five-foot, eight-inch frame, but in a good way. He commanded the space around him, and in that moment, I wanted to be commanded. Big time.

He pulled back and smiled again. "Thanks for coming out here. You saved me a phone call."

As I drove home, I struggled to remember what I had said after that. *See you Friday? Looking forward to Friday?* Who the hell knew? All I recalled specifically doing was turning and leaving, saying a few words on my way out.

An interesting week followed. I showed up at two jobs on the wrong days. I left my wallet at the grocery store. (Thank god they called and returned it to me.) And I barely slept. I hadn't been on the receiving end of a surprise in a long time, not a good surprise. Most men surprised me with weird wedding proposals or, in one case, a strange fixation with my toes.

I wanted to call Aaron several times and pepper him with questions, but I didn't. And he never called me either. Was he trying to drive me crazy?

Finally, on Thursday, a text arrived.

We still on for tomorrow?

I put the phone down and left the room for thirty minutes. I didn't want to seem too eager. It appeared high school insecurities were still alive and well in my thirty-something head.

Yes, can't wait.

Once I told her about my date, Yaz took my Friday afternoon job, allowing me plenty of time to shower and primp. "You covered for me when I was sick. I've got *you* covered now, sis." Her mom went with her.

That was when I realized I had no idea how to dress for Aaron's surprise, which required one more text.

What should I wear?

Something comfortable. And warm.

The calendar was pushing the middle of April, inspiring birds to chirp from trees sprouting either blossoms or new leaves. On a sunny day, the temperatures would creep into the high sixties to low seventies, but as nighttime fell, those warmer days transformed into much cooler nights. It had rained on Tuesday and Wednesday, causing the ground to soften and a chill to set into my bones. At one point, I worried I was getting sick. *Not now. Please.* I pleaded with the universe to spare me. And it had. By Thursday, the sun had returned with a forecast of high sixties on Friday that might even reach seventy.

I finished my job in the morning and went home to feed and let Daisy out. With plenty of time to kill, I played with my pup, made myself some lunch, and caught up on some paperwork. In addition to Aaron, we'd signed two new clients as of late, crowding our already busy schedules. I planned to meet with Yaz about the possibility of hiring someone new. What I learned about jobs such as these was that you got what you paid for. If we hired someone offering little pay, we'd most likely receive shoddy work. Our goal was to pay well, which would hopefully attract someone who would complement our Dust Bunnies family. Mrs. Mounivong had mentioned a friend who was looking for work, so we'd follow up with her.

I spent the better part of an hour-and-a-half showering, putting on makeup, and blow-drying my hair. Of course, I also tried on a bunch of different outfits. I'd been to several stores, taking advantage of spring sales.

Comfortable and warm. That was what Aaron had advised.

Comfortable and warm for me meant flannel pants and an oversized sweatshirt. Not flattering and not happening. Given the promising forecast, I chose a new pair of boyfriend jeans with a rolled cuff, which accented my long legs—a pair of tan leather loafers on my feet—and a white form-fitting top with three-quarter length sleeves that molded well to my thinner frame. A few spritzes of perfume, and I was ready to go.

I found Mom in the kitchen, fixing herself a cup of coffee.

"Well, don't you look nice." She gave me a once-over, her smile offering her approval.

"Thanks, Ma. I got this last week on sale." I did a little turn, my hands brushing down the sides of my waist.

With her coffee mug in hand, my mother leaned against the sink, facing me, her grin stretched wide. "I don't think I've ever seen you this excited before."

I gave her a look that said, *What are you talking about?* "Aw, Ma." She must've noticed I'd put a little extra effort into my hair and makeup.

She approached, setting her mug on the breakfast bar as she passed by. "You look great, honey." She paused and placed her hands on my upper arms. "After what Justin did, I'm happy to see you moving on." She spoke with earnest. "As you are well aware, I'm not a fan of your father, but he was a handsome man. You have his strong jaw and high cheekbones. The rest you got from me, including our blue eyes with the golden sphere encircling the pupil. People used to comment about my eyes all the time and how unusual they were. You know, whenever I feel down or discouraged about growing old or looking unattractive these days, I remind myself that I made *you*, an absolutely stunning daughter, and I couldn't be prouder of that achievement. You've got such a good heart, too, and you deserve someone who'll treat you special."

I basked in her adoration. "Thanks, Ma. I appreciate that.

Yeah, Justin was a real piece of work. I'm glad I found out about him." My stomach tightened. "Do you think Justin could have caused the fire at Mr. Logan's house? He had a cut on his hand. A pretty big cut, judging by the bandage. Ross also said something about it, and I haven't been able to stop thinking about it since."

My mother slid onto the nearest barstool, taking her mug in her hands. "I don't know. You had said he was pretty upset about what Mr. Logan had done to him. And from what Harry had told us, that man is not to be reckoned with." My mother blew out a breath. "Speaking of which, I still don't understand why Harry got so upset last weekend? I'm worried he doesn't want to see me anymore." Her voice shook as her face fell into a definite frown.

"Has he said anything about it since? I hope he's not mad at me." I liked Harry, and I especially liked how happy he had made my mother.

She took a long sip of coffee and set her mug down. Her barstool swiveled to face me. "He has no reason to be, but I haven't spoken to him." She hooked a few strands of hair behind her right ear. (It had grown just long enough to reach.) "I'm very fond of Harry, but if we have any hope for a future together, he's going to have to open up and trust me. And I won't call him first! I did nothing wrong." Shoulders back; she firmed her jaw. "I was married to a man who told me nothing." She shook her head, her hands fisted on her lap. "I won't go through that again." Her lips pursed. "I won't!"

I wrapped my arms around her thin shoulders. "I know, Ma. Give him a little more time. If he's not who you think he is, you'll know. Look at Justin. It didn't take long for him to show his true colors. And even though Harry was upset the other night, he never showed any sign of anger or violence. Give it a little more time. And then see how things look."

I hoped my advice was sound. In all honesty, I wasn't sure what motivated the men around me, including my creepy neighbor. The thought that someone I knew could be involved in heinous crimes kept me on edge.

* * *

The warm Friday afternoon brought out motorcyclists, cars with convertible roofs, bicyclists, and walkers of all sorts. It felt like a celebration of nature. I lowered the windows of my minivan to allow a cross breeze to freshen the cabin. Not too much, though; I did have hair to consider. Virginia humidity could be brutal, but that was a problem for July, not April. In fact, the only aspect of spring that I didn't enjoy was the pollen, which covered everything exposed to Mother Nature. The recent rain had washed away the latest dousing, leaving the air unusually clear, the sky a vibrant blue.

Aside from the weather, the ride to Aaron's house was both long and way too short. My stomach felt like I was free-falling from a ledge, knowing I had no safety net. I'd already established in my mind that Aaron was by far the most attractive man I had ever spent time with, but there was something else about him I found intriguing and almost addictive.

I stopped off and picked up a bottle of wine and a six-pack of beer; the brand Aaron had offered me the last time I was there. The wine was for me. I liked beer, but it made me bloat, and that was the last thing I wanted to do in Aaron's company.

When I arrived at his house, I parked next to his silver truck and did one last check in the mirror. My hair grew well below my shoulders, a slight wave to it, so I pulled up the sides with a barrette and let a few tendrils frame my face (my go-to hairstyle), which today, was doing as I had intended.

The blue eyes with tiny gold spheres staring back at me

reminded me of how much my mother and I resembled each other. Considering how much I admired her; I'd take that win. The copper, bronze, and gold eyeshadow I had purchased enhanced the color scheme.

As I approached Aaron's front door, the scent of smoke reached my nose. If I weren't mistaken, the aroma belonged to a campfire. I knocked on the door, determined to stand firm and not allow my legs to wobble or my pulse to inflict dizziness.

The door opened. Aaron dressed in his standard garb: a thin, gray long-sleeved T-shirt and jeans, loafers on his socked feet. We all had our go-tos. Comfortable clothes seemed to be his vibe, which I could easily embrace. His musky scent did a great job of competing with the campfire smoke encircling the house.

"I found your favorite beer." I lifted the six-pack, which he took from my grip.

"Thank you. You didn't have to do that." His gaze landed on the bottle of wine in my other hand. "I see you brought something for yourself as well?" He moved his face closer, then hesitated before closing in again to plant a soft kiss on my cheek.

Awkward.

"It's good to see you."

I followed him inside. His house was as clean as it had been when I had last left it.

"I've got us set up out back, but I'll open the wine and get you a glass first." He led me into his kitchen where a few of the open cupboards boasted doors from new construction. Several, in fact.

"Looks like someone's been busy."

Aaron crossed the room to place his beer in the stainless-steel fridge. "You noticed. Yeah, I got a little industrious this week." He took a beer from his own inventory, opened the bottle—the cap going into a nearby trash can—and placed it on the counter. He took the wine from my hands. "I figured now was as good a time as any to get this house finished." His lips formed the shape of a small crescent moon. "You made the house look nice again. You shamed me into it, so it's your fault." He winked, his amber eyes hard to resist. He located a stemless goblet in one of the upper cabinets and uncorked the wine with a corkscrew he'd pulled from his utensil drawer.

"Oh, it's my fault, is it?" I asked, placing a hand on my hip for effect.

Keeping his focus off me and on his duties, he said, "Yup. You look nice, by the way."

Once he'd filled my glass, he handed it to me and then lifted my purse strap from my shoulder, placing the purse onto the counter. He didn't offer more than that since I wasn't wearing a coat. (I had a thick jacket stored in my minivan, just in case.)

He inhaled a deep breath and released it. "Are you ready to see your surprise yet?" Taking his beer in his hand, he guided me through the kitchen to a back door where a mudroom connected the house to the two-car garage. (I knew that from when I had cleaned the place, checking every door I could find.) Perpendicular to the garage, an additional door with a window allowed us entry to the backyard.

We stepped down onto a patio made of brick pavers, the sun drifting westward but still doing its best to remain warm and bright. The pavers did an adequate job radiating the solar heat upward as they extended twenty feet, providing a place for his rectangular patio set, the table made of beveled glass, the chairs a fine woven material, none of which were here before. That wasn't what caught my eye, though.

A bit farther away and off to my left, an array of flat rocks arranged in staggered patterns encircled a small firepit.

Crushed stone blanketed the outer circle, home to four white Adirondack chairs that watched over the firepit like attentive parents. *Where did that come from?* My eyes took in the camper's front door, which remained open.

The blue-and-tan striped awning, reaching out over a picnic table, and an outdoor rug with a similar color scheme created a perfect sanctuary for outdoor living. It was something out of an L.L. Bean catalog.

The string of patio lights that hung in a crisscross pattern under and along the outer edges of the awning told me that Aaron had thought of everything. A small lantern provided a centerpiece for the picnic table, which also included two place settings already arranged, a red-and-white checkered tablecloth offering a splash of country charm. I set my wineglass on a small white table near the door, astonished.

It was beautiful. Was this all for me?

Aaron snatched my wine goblet, the table teetering slightly. "You may not want to put it down there. That table is on its last leg." Holding my glass and his beer, he gazed out at his work. "When you told me about your memories of camping with your family, I had this idea. It's not in a state park or at the beach, but I figured this would do." He didn't look at me, but something told me he was paying a lot more attention to my reaction than he was letting on.

With nothing holding my hands back, I let them fly to my mouth. "This is beautiful. I can't believe you did all this. Wow. Did you build that fire pit since I was here last?" I knew he had, or he'd hired someone. Either option was remarkable.

"I did. I had all the stones behind my shed. You like it?"

"Like it? I'm speechless."

His posture inflated as he handed me back my wine. "Speechless is good, right?"

"Better than good. Amazing. Remarkable." I took a sip,

needing to calm my racing pulse. This time, it was racing out of excitement. Pure, unadulterated joy.

As he took a swig of his beer, tears stung my overwhelmed eyes. I couldn't remember the last time someone had done something so extravagant. It occurred to me that *no one* had ever gone to such lengths.

He nodded simply, his voice pleased. "It should work just fine . . . for an evening, anyway." He tipped his chin toward a small gas grill. "I bought steaks to grill, and potatoes are already in the oven." He touched my arm. "Let me show you around."

"Sure, I'm sorry. I-I'm overwhelmed, Aaron. This is . . ."

The smile that widened his lips told me he was happy with my response.

Carrying my wine goblet, I followed him into the camper that smelled of linens and a familiar musty camping smell, the one I adored. The space was modest, but organized and clean. On a small counter sat two filets, both rubbed with herbs and something garlicky, if my nose was correct. The table came with a cushioned bench on both sides, an appropriately sized TV hiked high on an opposing wall. Neighboring the humble dining area, two recliners sat built-in for comfort, facing the TV. When we moved this way or that, the camper responded with its own creaks and slight sways.

"It's such a nice camper, Aaron. Wow, you even have recliners?"

"Yeah, I like to get comfortable when I want to."

I took a sip of wine to wash down the emotions that threatened to bubble up and blather. I wasn't just surprised; it touched me that a man with Aaron's obvious struggles had gone to such lengths.

"This is beautiful, Aaron. I can't believe you did all of this for me." Standing near the open door, I fanned one hand out at the picnic table and the chairs around the newly constructed fire pit. Two questions shot from my mouth: "How? Why?"

Aaron took the wineglass from my hand and placed it, along with his beer, on a miniature counter on the opposite side of the sink. "The *how* was easy. I had most of the stuff in my shed or behind it. As for the *why*, your story touched me. And that you trusted me enough to tell me about it. I wanted to bring back some of those memories for you."

He brushed a few strands of hair away from my face as his voice grew soft and throaty. "And I haven't wanted to do something like this for someone in a *very* long time." Those amber eyes stared down at me, leaving me not only speechless but breathless as well. The attraction I felt for Aaron was so powerful that I could barely hold myself together.

"Would I be pushing it if I kissed you right now?"

I didn't wait for him to make his move. I did the moving for him, pulling his neck down and pressing my lips hard against his. He tasted of hops from his beer, and too many other masculine flavors to identify, *need* the most prominent.

I parted my lips, my tongue trying to send a message as it brushed against his mouth. *I want more.* With his hands braced against my waist, his tongue responded, swirling around mine. Together we created a vortex of yearning. I'd never savored anything more satisfying in my life. His chest, firm and robust, remained close, revealing his heartbeat. He was strong in every way, yet his lips remained soft and tender.

I wrapped my arms around his sturdy neck and held on as our mouths remained locked in a dance of passion and newness.

When he trailed his lips down my neck, I thought I was going to climax. My breathing became labored, and my lower half tried to regain some sense of control. He disengaged and examined me, his eyes trying to decide what was going on with this horny woman in front of him.

"I'm sorry." I bit my lower lip, embarrassed. "It's been a while." I half chuckled, hoping he saw the humor. "A *long* while."

Aaron's brow rose briefly. "But didn't you say that you and the other dude just broke up?"

I was happy to set *this* record straight. "Yeah, but things never got that far. Like I said, we hadn't been seeing each other for long." The one thing I *could* thank Justin for was motivating me to get on the pill, anticipating our relationship would eventually head in that direction. "It's been a long time since a man has really *touched* me."

I recalled how Aaron had said that no one had gone into his bedroom when I was asking about cleaning it. At the time, I thought it was a bad sign. Not anymore. I didn't want any other women in his room, except for me.

Aaron seemed to size me up. "So, I take it the men in your world are . . . idiots?" His smile was charming and sweet.

I stared at the floor. "Yeah, I guess." Were they idiots, or was I losing my edge? I often wondered.

Using his thumb and forefinger, he lifted my chin to face him. "Trust me, they *are* idiots. And don't feel bad, it's been a while since a woman has touched me as well. Probably a lot longer than it's been for you." A veil of sadness flitted across his face. "Not that I didn't deserve it."

I waited for his gaze to return to mine, hoping to ease his pain. "So, I take it the women in *your* world are idiots?"

His smile returned, the one I'd fight tooth and nail for.

"Do you want me to touch you now, Aaron?" It was presumptuous of me to ask, but something otherworldly was speaking for me now. What was happening between us wasn't worth fighting anymore. This was real. I knew this as well as I knew the sun would come up tomorrow morning. And having lived the number of years I had, I also understood it was rare.

"I would like that."

I caressed the side of his face and then down his neck. "Do you want me to touch you here?" I tapped his collarbone before placing a tender kiss there.

He closed his eyes. "Mm-hmm."

My hands slid down his chest, his pecs like rocks under my palms. When I touched his left side, his flinch sent up a warning flag. What scars were hiding underneath his T-shirt? What painful memories haunted him? I wanted to erase them all. But this was not the time, so I didn't linger.

I let my hand slide down his stomach, landing on the crotch of his jeans. "Do you want me to touch you here?" The instant bulge answered my question without the need for words.

He exhaled a heavy breath, his pupils dilated. "Let me ask *you* something. Do *you* want me to touch you?"

I nodded. "Yes, I do."

He cupped my breast, nearly turning my insides into molten lava. "How about here?"

I shook my head. "No."

His brow wrinkled. Aaron leaned away from me. "Too much?"

I took his hand and brought it underneath my top and my bra, finding nipples already hard and anxious. "I want you to touch me *here*."

His thumb caressed my nipple back and forth, sending my sexual thirst into a frenzy. He removed his hand, unfastened the waist of my jeans, and inched his touch lower, where a sauna awaited. "How about here?" His fingers stroked my lubricated folds, growing wetter by the second. "Oh, yes, I can feel how much you want me to touch you here."

Cool shivers shot through me so intense I had to grab

hold of his broad shoulders to brace myself. That tingling sensation I had almost forgotten existed had seized control of me now. The only thing I could focus on was feeling more of it. My heart hammered, my lungs gasping for air. I lost all sense of who I was. I wanted to plant his face between my legs and let him lick me to ecstasy. At the same time, I wanted his erection that was bumping against my hip, inside me, stroking my erogenous zone, and driving me wild. I wanted all of it at once. But this orgasm wasn't willing to wait.

Aaron used his free hand to secure me in place as I groaned and hyperventilated right in front of him, his fingers doing all sorts of wonderful things to my body.

An orgasm crashed into me, rendering me as powerless as a rock against a powerful wave. I cried out, "Oh, my god." My entire body went limp, aftershocks still coursing through my lower half.

The hands of a man who saved lives and carried victims to safety, had the ability to send *me* into another realm of existence, a place of pure joy. Once my wits returned, I shied away, realizing how much I had let myself go. What the hell was the matter with me? Had I just made a complete fool of myself? "I'm so sorry. I didn't mean to—"

"Don't talk." Aaron took me into his arms as though my weight were a feather and carried me like a prince would to the one bedroom in the back, a patchwork quilt covering the queen-sized bed. He gripped the bottom of his gray long-sleeved T-shirt as though ready to pull it over his head, but then stopped, undoing the fly on his jeans instead, which he stepped out of, his boxer briefs doing a feeble job of obscuring his massive erection.

Okay, so maybe I wasn't as foolish as I thought.

With his help, my pants came off, my bra unhooked, and

my shirt tossed to the side with them. Aaron spread my legs apart and then looked down at me. "Are you sure about this?"

The eyes of a lion took me in, his breath coming in pants. And yet, he asked me anyway.

"I'm sure."

He hovered over me, his lips suckling my nipples, his hands everywhere. When he entered me, I gasped, feeling the size of him, my moist center ready to see what he had in store. His hips moved slowly at first until we fell into a rhythm, both of us lost in the sensations of the other. His cheeks grew ruddy, his eyes glazed over and unfocused. He held me tight as his hips moved with just the right amount of precision and force.

"Oh, god, don't stop." I could feel that same tingling sensation rising.

Breathless, he said, "Don't worry. I couldn't stop if I wanted to. You feel so fucking good." His lips returned to my neck, then my face. Aaron was a big man, yet he never allowed his weight to dominate me. He hovered, the muscles in his arms flexing their strength.

I got the sense that Aaron needed this release as much as I did, which came a moment later.

"Son of a bitch!" he cried out, no longer able to hold himself back. I wanted that from him, the off-balance Aaron, caught up in passion and nothing else.

I came a moment later, my body still reeling from the last orgasm.

He lowered himself onto me for a brief pause before rolling over onto his side to catch his breath. "That was . . . amazing. Thank you for that."

I smirked. "Thank you back."

It had been over a year for me since I'd been intimate with a man, not a track record I was proud of. Not that I slept around. What was happening here was beyond anything I could explain or understand. The last man I had sex with, Samuel, barely got me off, and it wasn't from lack of trying. Some nights I had faked it to end the misery. I had thought I was losing my sexual drive.

Turned out I had plenty of drive. What I lacked was the *right* man, and by right, a mysterious, gorgeous hunk whose amber eyes made my knees go weak every time he looked at me. A man who made me dinner and snack platters to tide me over. A man who spent an entire week setting up a beautiful campsite to honor my childhood memory. The fact that he was a hero was icing on that hunky cake. Even his pain drew me in. I wanted to know him on every level, to make all his sadness go away.

But did he feel the same way about me? I wasn't sure.

All I knew was that regardless of what happened after today, I was seizing *this* moment. Even if I never saw Aaron again, my time with him would be something I would cherish forever.

Chapter 16

Natalie

We had dinner at the picnic table, neither of us speaking. Aaron would take a slow and methodical bite of his steak or his potato and chew it, watching me. When he popped a piece of buttered bread into his mouth and licked his fingers, his eyes suggested he preferred to lick me instead. I'd never had a man view me that way. I mean, I'd been with my share of horny men, but this was different. If Aaron's gaze was sending a clear message, it was, I want *all* of you. It was both intimidating and captivating, and I couldn't look away.

"How is your meat?" he asked, his voice filled with flirtation. "Did I cook it to your liking?" The words were normal enough; his tone was anything but.

"It's excellent. Just to my liking."

"It's not too tough? I made sure to give you a tender cut." Using his fork, he tucked a piece of filet into his mouth and chewed, his smile both beautiful and open. "Nobody likes a rough piece of meat."

Are we talking about food right now?

"It's just right." I took a bite of potato, licking a drizzle of butter from the corner of my mouth.

Aaron's gaze locked on my efforts like a missile on its target. "You start doing things like that, and I won't be held accountable for what comes next."

"Oh, really?" I stood and leaned over the picnic table, nearly knocking over the lantern. I kissed his spicy lips, savoring the taste of him to the point of pure bliss. "I'll have to remember that."

I lowered myself toward my seat when he held my chin in place with his thumb and forefinger. "You have the most interesting eyes I have ever seen." He stared intently. "Blue with a ring of gold. It's like looking into the universe."

I touched his furry cheek. "I could say the same about yours."

He kissed me. "Nah, you've got mine beat." His gaze traveled my entire face. "You are so beautiful, Natalie." A chuckle escaped his lips. "You and your outfits with doggy prints." His eyes shone with humor.

"Now I know you're pulling my leg. I saw the way you looked at my outfit that first time I came to clean your house." I shot him a look of skepticism.

"Natalie, you could have come here in a grain sack, and I'd have thought you were gorgeous."

Aw. My heart melted. How Aaron made me feel like the most attractive woman on the planet was beside me. Another new experience.

Something dark registered in his eyes. "It had been a while since I'd met anyone new. And I guess I had gotten rusty at it." He pursed his lips. "Sorry if I was rude."

I returned to my seat and took his hand from across the table. "You weren't rude. You were just . . . quiet."

He made a face. "*Pfft.* Yeah, quiet. You're just being polite."

My sympathetic heart embraced his. "No, it wasn't that big of a deal, really." I contemplated my next question carefully. "Can I ask you something?" I raised a palm. "You don't have to answer if you don't want to."

His chin lowered, his eyes staring up at me from under his brow. "What is it?"

"Is the reason you didn't take your shirt off earlier because you were hiding something?" I stroked the back of his hand with my thumb. "Like some scarring? Were you burned in a fire?"

Had I gone too far? Was he going to retreat into himself and ask me to leave? I waited with bated breath.

He pulled his hand away, my fears escalating. "It's getting late." He rose from the table and lifted his legs over the bench before gathering up our plates and utensils.

Should I apologize? I wasn't sure. Instead, I helped him clean. We picked up the mess and brought it all into the kitchen. I stored the leftover steak in a glass storage container I found in one of his cupboards and the potatoes in a small glass bowl, placing both in the fridge to save for another day. While I bebopped around the kitchen, I noticed a small stack of chocolate bars, a bag of marshmallows, and some graham crackers near the fridge.

"Were you planning on making s'mores later?" I asked.

With a new topic on the table, Aaron seemed to snap out of his somber mood. "Oh, yeah, I forgot about those." His gaze stretched across the kitchen to where I stood. "It's probably too late for that, right?"

The clock on his microwave registered nine-thirty-three. Not late, unless he *wanted* it to be. I'd already checked in with Mom, and she and Daisy were doing just fine. I realized that if we had a chance at something special between us, some of his walls *had* to come down. Otherwise, there was no point to any of this, other than some rather great sex. My mother had come to the same conclusion with Harry, minus the sex, although I had no idea about that one.

I crossed the room. "Look, I didn't mean to pry, Aaron, about your body earlier." Sliding my hands around his waist, I clasped them behind his back. "I like you. I know you are a private person. I can respect that. But we don't really know each other, do we?"

Having tossed his hand towel away when I approached, he gazed down at me, his arms lacing around my upper back.

A good sign.

"We know a little about each other." His body swayed in a comforting rhythm. "After all, that's what tonight was all about, right?" He gazed out the kitchen window at the embers of his campfire, still glowing, but losing strength. "If you'd like some s'mores, I can make that happen." He stroked my hair, his fingers brushing along the nape of my neck.

"I'd love that." I nudged him with my arms for emphasis. "But do *you* want that, Aaron?"

He exhaled, fluffing the hair on top of my head. "Natalie, you have no idea how much I want that." This big, brawny man detached himself from me. He rubbed the edge of his jaw along the short beard that grew thick with shades of auburn. "I'm just not." He scratched at his temple with his forefinger.

"You're just not, what? Ready for this?"

He nodded so subtly that I almost wasn't sure of it.

"Does this have anything to do with my question earlier?"

He remained speechless, his eyes downcast.

I had to process what was happening. I could leave and offer him some time to gather himself and maybe decide if he wanted a woman in his life. Or I could press on.

"I don't care if you were burned. You were a firefighter. You were a hero."

He grimaced, his eyes closing tight against my words.

"Aaron, look at me." I stood before him, unwilling to budge. "Bad things happen to everyone, but you were a fireman. Of course, that would raise the risk of danger." I tugged on his sleeve. "Please look at me."

Finally, he opened his eyes. "Two people died on my watch, Natalie. An elderly married couple. Did you know that?"

I knew that, but I wasn't sure I should admit to it. What would he think about me knowing so much about him? It had happened five years ago. Would he believe I had been snooping into his past for a good reason? Would that feel like an invasion of his privacy? I thought about Harry and his reaction the other night. Clearly, Harry felt I was prying, and he didn't like it much. I chose to tread lightly. "No, I didn't know. But I'm sure you did everything in your power to save them."

"How do you know that?" His brow dropped, a storm brewing in his eyes. "You don't know me!" The edge in his voice did its best to push me away. I was touching on something profound and raw.

I gave myself a moment to reply *and* for his shoulders to ease, which they did. This topic was too important to screw up. "I know that because I also know you are a kind man." I fanned one hand toward the back of the house. "You are the type of man who would do something as extravagant as you did tonight for someone you barely know. Just because you were touched by her childhood story." I moved closer. "And I *was* touched. I can't tell you how much. You have to understand: no one has ever done anything like that for me. *Ever!*" I pulled with gentle force on the waist of his T-shirt. "If you bear scars from saving lives, I want you to know, I will only find that more attractive about you. I couldn't care less what the scars look like. You are a beautiful man, Aaron Marino, inside and out."

His arms encircled my waist, and we stood that way for several seconds.

"So, s'mores?"

"Do *you* want s'mores, Aaron?" I gazed up at him with unrelenting resolve.

"I've never wanted anything more."

And so, it was s'mores. We gathered the ingredients and returned to the campground, otherwise known as Aaron's backyard.

If I thought eating steak was erotic, s'mores opened a whole new set of possibilities.

"You've got chocolate on the corner of your mouth."

My tongue responded to mop it up.

"No, wait. I'll clean that up for you." Already perched in the Adirondack chair beside me, Aaron leaned over and licked the sweet goodness from my mouth. His breath smelled and tasted of chocolate and marshmallow, a hint of sugar from the crackers.

"No fair." I feigned disappointment. "I was saving that for later."

The corners of his lips curled upward. "You were, were you? Hmm. Well, there's more chocolate for you to drip all over yourself if you want." He wiggled his eyebrows.

The insides of my thighs shivered with anticipation.

Two finished s'mores sat on a small table on the other side of me. I took one, opened the graham cracker portion, and used my finger to swipe a fair amount of melted chocolate away. Using that same finger, I drew a line down my cheek and onto my neck. "You mean like this?"

Aaron squinted over at me, the fire's glow waving across his cheeks. "I can't see anything."

I made a face. "What do you mean, you can't see anything? You just saw my mouth a moment ago." I pointed at the soiled cheek that I imagined resembled war paint. "It's right here." I knew he was playing, so I performed my part well.

"I'm sorry. I just can't see it. Must be the glare from the fire." A smirk stretched his lips wider. "Why don't you come over here?" He patted his lap. "So I can get a better look."

The benefit of Adirondack chairs was the width, which allowed me to straddle Aaron without much trouble, the heat from the fire coursing across my back with its soothing fingers. "Can you see it now?"

He licked the chocolate stripe away. "Oh, yeah, I can see it now. And it tastes great." His eyes smoldered with new ideas. "Are you cold?" He rubbed my upper arms.

"Not really. The fire is heating me up."

Using delicate fingers, Aaron lifted my shirt off my body, exposing my lace bra, right along with my cleavage. "How about now? I can get you a blanket if you'd like." He used the shirt to drape around my waist.

I shook my head. "I'm good. Not cold at all." In fact, the inferno of adrenaline pumping inside my body was posing as a mini volcano.

He unclasped my bra, gently pulling it off my shoulders and placing it in the vacant seat next to us. His gaze zeroed in on my nipples. "I disagree. I think you *are* cold." He massaged my hardened nipples, firing up my lower half and making me care less about the temperature. His lips surrounded one nipple, his fingers working on the other.

I let my head drop back and moaned. "That feels so good."

Between my legs, Aaron's erection pushed upward. "I agree. I love touching your sexy body."

Ready to take this party to the next level, I rose, pulled down my jeans, and stepped out of them, my panties that matched my bra vacating my body a moment later. I kept my no-show socks on, though—it wasn't quite summer yet—with my shoes nearby.

When I returned to Aaron's chair, he'd removed his pants, his erection hard and eager for attention. For a moment, I contemplated going down on him. The thought of his impressive size in my mouth turned me on, but the crushed stone underneath us warned it wasn't a good idea. I didn't need scraped-up knees.

Instead, I straddled him, letting the potency of his strength pulsate inside me. We'd made love in the camper, but this new position granted me a new perspective and a chance at a much more powerful orgasm. When Aaron continued to stroke my nipples, it became a certainty. Up and down, I moved, Aaron's eyes rolling back in his head. The fire crackled, the scent of chocolate nearby, as we groaned and let nature do its thing. As I had expected, a quiet orgasm amplified until I lost all sense of reality, an orchestra of sensations hitting me all at once. And judging by Aaron's flushed cheeks and crazed eyes, the feeling was mutual. Our bodies exploded with intense pleasure. I fell over him, both of us breathing as though we had just run two miles.

"Wow." I pulled my head away from his chest. "That was . . ." There were no words. The connection I felt with Aaron was indescribable. *For me.* I had to remind myself of that fact. There was no sense in deluding. I was too old for that type of misguided thinking.

"Well said. That *was.*"

I pushed myself up off him and grabbed my clothes, holding them in a bunch over my chest. "Do you mind if I take another shower?" When we had finished making love in the camper, I had taken a brief shower to wash my body, leaving my hair somewhat dry. After this escapade, I decided I needed to clean up properly. I grabbed my shoes nearby and slid my socked feet into them.

Looking like he'd just gone through a psychedelic trip, Aaron exhaled. "No, not at all. Want some company?" The words escaped his lips unbidden, the surprise in his eyes confirming my suspicions.

I had started to walk away, my body shivering from the chill. "Yeah, sure. If you're up for that." I waited for him to recover and change his mind, making one more excuse why that couldn't happen. And it was fine. I understood his misgivings weren't about me.

My handsome companion snapped out of his stupor. He stood and stepped into his jeans, pulling them up around his waist, but leaving the fly open. (He'd ditched the boxers after our first round.) It was sexy as hell. "Let me put this fire out, and I'll meet you inside."

I took my last shower in the upstairs guest bathroom. I sensed Aaron wasn't quite comfortable with me in *his* part of the house. This time, he led me to a rather clean and organized owner's suite. Things were changing between us already.

Just like the rest of the house, the eggshell walls remained bare, a few shoes in one corner, an article of clothing draped over an easy chair. He hadn't made his king-sized bed, but he'd pulled the tan comforter up over the pillows, showing effort. It smelled like Aaron's cologne, or maybe it was his body wash, musky and clean. A large brown area rug offered cushioning from the same hardwood floors that spanned the rest of the house.

Aaron's bathroom was huge: a tiled floor in swirls of white and tan, a double sink vanity with creamy beige granite countertops and black cabinetry. A mirror hung over each sink, where my reflection made me gasp.

"What's wrong?"

I turned to Aaron. "What do you mean, what's wrong? Look at my hair!" It wasn't just disheveled. I was rivaling an Einstein lookalike. My barrette was hanging on for dear life down the side of my face. I thought I'd felt something there. I unclasped it and placed it on the side of the sink.

"Sorry, the hair is my fault. It's soft, by the way. Easy on the fingers."

Had I missed the fact that Aaron was stroking my hair? Given the intense moments between us, it was easy to do.

Aaron opened the enclosed glass shower and turned the nozzle to hot. "My friend's wife left her shampoo and conditioner. You must've seen it in the upstairs bathroom?"

I had to admit, I hadn't noticed. When I was up there, I'd used the body wash and that was it. "I didn't see any shampoo. Are you sure?"

"I'll check. There may be some in the cabinet. I'll get the body wash you used as well."

"Thanks. And towels?"

Aaron approached and kissed me, his tongue gliding along my lower lip. "I'll grab you a couple. Be right back, beautiful."

I practically shivered at the compliment. It was nice to know he still saw me that way after everything we'd done together. A girl never knew how men perceived such things. I had one guy date me for several weeks until we made love, and then I never heard from him again. That was a sucker punch to my confidence as a lover.

I stepped into the shower and adjusted the nozzle to warm, allowing the water to cascade over my chilled body, steam rising around me. A chill had set into my bones, and the warmth was as welcoming as an electric blanket in January.

A couple of minutes passed when I realized someone was watching me. I startled. "Oh, I didn't see you there." I opened the heavy glass door and took the soap and hair products from Aaron's hands, a hint of mango indicating the scent.

"Thanks." I pulled the door closed and lathered up.

What did Aaron do? He stood there watching me again.

I opened the door once more and wiped the water from my face as it drizzled down my nose and mouth. "Is something wrong?"

He hesitated as though unsure of himself. "Nothing wrong. I just thought maybe . . ." He rubbed a hand across the back of his neck. "I thought maybe I'd join you." Trepidation formed a crease across his forehead. His eyes filled with doubt. "If that's okay, I mean."

I tried not to smile or make a big deal of this. "Sure. Come on in." I swiped more water from my nose and mouth and stepped away to allow him inside.

His pants came off first, and I tried with everything in me to avoid gawking at him when he removed his T-shirt next. He entered the shower, his robust body governing the generous area. "Can I wash you?"

"Yes." I handed him the body wash, which he squirted into the palm of his hand before lathering me up, and I mean, everywhere. After being felt up (or down in my case) and making love twice over the past several hours—climaxing three times—my sexual drive wasn't quite as strong as it was, but it hadn't exactly left the building, either. I could appreciate his tender hands that caressed and massaged my body with gentle care. It was sensual on a whole new level. Next came my hair, which he washed with the same devotion. His fingers massaged my scalp so well that it made me yawn several times. I tried not to look at him out of respect, but I knew that couldn't last long. And it shouldn't. He was revealing something to me, and he deserved my utmost respect.

I offered a challenge. "Can I wash you now?"

He paused before he handed me the body wash, his left side turned away from my curious eyes. "If you think you can stomach it, go for it." His expression told me he wasn't sure *he* could.

I set the mango body wash on the tiled bench and grabbed his brand, infused with cedarwood and red sage, flipping open the lid. I started with less incriminating areas of his body, enjoying the feel of his butt and muscular legs. The right side of his chest was perfectly normal—if normal meant stacked with hard muscle and a ripple of washboard abs, his arms sculpted with the same brawn.

Aaron had to work out *a lot* to maintain a body such as this one. And since I hadn't seen any exercise equipment throughout the house, he either went to a gym, which I doubted knowing his reclusive nature, or he had something stored in the basement, the one floor of the house I hadn't ventured into . His current remodel.

"You okay? Can I wash the rest now?"

No words escaped his lips, only a solitary nod, which I knew was difficult for him to achieve.

I held his left hand and kissed it, placing it over my heart for a brief moment. "Don't worry, I'll be gentle."

He tried to smile, not quite reaching his goal.

On his left wrist, a series of flame tattoos started small but grew in size as they crawled up his sinewy arm and across the pectoral region of his upper chest. The tattoo pattern continued its ascent over his broad shoulder, before the artwork crested and fell over the shoulder blade onto his back. Within each frame of imagery, scars peered out, reciting a sad story from his past, the skin a different texture. I made sure I was careful as I washed, kissed, and pampered him , certain he was holding his breath the entire time.

Afterward, I set the body wash on the same bench I had retrieved it from. "I was right."

He tilted his head, his eyes narrowing. "About?"

"You *are* beautiful. Every inch of you."

Tears glimmered in his eyes, which he immediately wiped away with wet hands.

I clutched his arm. "I mean it. You *are* beautiful." I kissed his upper chest where the scars sat more pronounced.

More tears fell from his troubled eyes. "You don't need to say that to be nice." The quiver in his voice caused my heart to pinch with sorrow.

I understood what it was like to put yourself down. After my parents' divorce, I had spent years doing the same, blaming myself for my father's disappointment. When a relationship didn't work out, or a guy had ghosted me, those same feelings of inadequacy returned. I put too much stock in what people thought of me. Or what I *perceived* they thought.

In Aaron's case, it was his honor that had hurt him. For me, it only made him more attractive. How could he not see that?

"You need to stop thinking this way. Aaron Marino, you are *hands down* the most gorgeous man I have ever laid eyes on. You have a body that most men would kill for. You can barely see the scars, but even without the tattoos, you are a work of art." Tears stung my eyes. "I can't stand the thought of you thinking you are anything other than magnificent." I wept. "You have no idea what you have done for me. I never imagined I would ever be with a man like you." I had opened myself completely, my heart exposed and vulnerable. For me, it was worth the risk.

Aaron took me in his arms and held me close, the water providing a soft cloud of white noise around us, steam embracing our dampened skin. "I'm sorry I upset you. I didn't mean to—"

"No, it's okay." I disengaged from his loving embrace and wiped the sorrow from my cheeks. "Just start believing in yourself again. You are too wonderful to waste away inside a world of self-pity."

He clasped my wet head and kissed it. "I'll try. I guess I've gotten pretty good at shitting all over myself. When Paula left with our dog, CB, I was relieved. She tried so hard to reach me, but I was unreachable. And when she got married two years ago, I was happy for her. Even though I spent the better part of that week drunk." He lowered his head to catch my gaze. "And for the record, I never imagined I'd ever be with a woman like you, either." He turned the shower off, the room going quiet. "I'll do my best not to let you down."

We stepped out of his steamy shower, neither of us speaking. He needed a minute, and I was more than happy to give him one, since I needed one myself. Today was surreal. How could someone make me feel this complete? I'd found my own nirvana, and I never wanted to leave it.

Once we dried ourselves off and dressed, I gathered my things for the ride home. This had been an incredible day. Beyond anything I would have expected or even wished for. No one had made me feel as special or as honored as Aaron had. My heart contemplated love. Was it possible to love someone so soon? I wasn't sure. I just knew that Aaron had transformed me in some way. Not only had he showed me in his actions how much he cared about my life and my struggles, he'd opened a locked door to his own war chest, inviting me inside.

When it was time to leave, I grew tearful about it. "Thank you for today." I kissed his cheek, his furry beard tickling my lips. "I will never forget it."

I fished my keys from my purse when a text arrived from Mom.

Daisy is doing just fine. If you get a chance, ask Aaron about Harry. I have to know more about what happened.

Are you sure, Ma? You may find out things you don't want to know.

This isn't for Harry. It's for me. I have to know what happened from someone else's perspective. I need to know what James Logan did to him. I have no one else to ask. If Aaron doesn't want to talk about it, I will understand.

I shook my head and hissed a little. My mother, the pseudo-investigative reporter. Since Harry had shut her out, I couldn't blame her.

"Everything okay?"

I made a face. "Yeah, it's just my mother, trying to dig up dirt on James Logan. She wanted me to ask you about him."

The mood in the room shifted immediately as though someone had sucked all the oxygen away, leaving tension in its wake.

Aaron's entire face transformed, his eyes going dark. His shoulders rose like two mountains. "Why would your mother want to dig up dirt on James Logan, and why would she want you to ask *me* about him?" Two thunderbolts replaced Aaron's eyebrows.

I gulped. Why had I just said that? I'd gotten too comfortable. How could I have been so careless?

And so, I rambled. I told Aaron about Harry and what he'd told us about the fire in Mr. Logan's garage. "Harry's reputation was destroyed. He retired early as a result. He never fought it . . . partly because, according to him, you were the only person who could corroborate his story . . . but you had just been injured in that fire that killed two people." The rotten cherry on top of my rant only worsened the situation. "My mom and I think the fires in the area, the ones authorities suspect are caused by arson, could be set by the same person who may have it in for—"

"Don't you dare say his name again in my presence!" Rage turned his cheeks crimson, his jaw so tight he could bite through steel.

Oh, shit!

Aaron stood back as though I had physically shoved him. He rattled his head. "You know Harry Anderson? And you've known about me all this time? Is that why you and your mother were here last week?" He rubbed his jaw, his feet pacing a small circle in front of me. "You said you didn't know about the fire. So, you lied? *Again?*"

I released a pent-up breath. "I know. I didn't want to upset you—"

"You thought lying to me was the answer?" Hands braced on his hips, he faced me. "What is going on here? Are you another one of those sleazy reporters trying to dig up a story on me? You people will stop at nothing!" He shook his head, his cheeks flaming. "I have to say, this was a new one. I never thought *anyone* would sink this low."

Huh? "What are you talking about? Why would I—"

"You're not the first. A woman came up to me at the local farmer's market. A teacher. She had heard I was a firefighter, she'd said. Wanted me to speak to her class. I told her I wasn't interested. She went on to explain that one of her students had been traumatized by a fire. Lost his dog in the process. She really poured on the guilt. What she did was get me talking. We went to lunch, and she excused herself to go to the ladies' room. Her phone buzzed on the table. It was a text from her editor. He was asking how the story was coming together about the broken fireman. That was four years ago. I thought you parasites had given up."

Parasites?

"Bridgette pretended she was a schoolteacher." He huffed. "If her name was even Bridgette." His angry hand waved in the air. "Is that what you are? Someone who pretends to clean houses so you can get a story?" He shook his head, his eyes engulfed with hatred. He wagged a finger. "You're good. You even went so far as fucking me for information." All at once, his voice changed. "I don't care who you are. I'm not telling you a goddamn thing!"

"I'm not a reporter, Aaron. I knew about the fire, but only because my mother is dating Harry. And I just found out not too long ago. When I first met you, I didn't know anything about it."

"Get out!" Aaron stormed over to the front door and thrust it open. His nostrils flared.

Didn't he hear my explanation? I wasn't sure who I was talking to anymore. Had I fallen for another abuser? What the hell was the matter with me?

I crossed my arms, indignant. "I am *not* a reporter. I do own a cleaning business. Yes, I did know about the fire, but only recently. I didn't want you to think that was why I was here. Just to help Harry. I don't care about any of that. I was being honest with you about everything else."

His face went slack. "Except for dating someone else, right?"

Shit. What sort of hole had I dug myself into? Again? I had never been one to stretch the truth, mostly because my father was so good at it. Was I following in his footsteps?

"That was . . ." There was nothing I could say. I had no explanation. If I had just come clean in the first place, none of this would be happening right now. There was a possibility that

Aaron would never have given me a second glance, had he known the truth, but would that have been worse . . . than this? I wasn't sure anything could feel worse right now.

My shoulders caved. It was as if my heart had stopped beating. My body vibrated with anxiety and dread. All I wanted to do was run out of there and hide in the darkness.

"I said, I want you to leave." He didn't yell those words, but he said them with conviction.

It was definitely time for me to go. I approached his front door. "I'm sorry, Aaron. Today was one of the best days I have ever had. And I ruined it by not being honest with you. But I want you to know that my feelings for you are genuine. I wasn't lying about any of that." I stepped over the threshold and turned back.

The door slammed in my face as Aaron disappeared into his own private hell. He had finally let someone in. Now, he believed I had betrayed him. It wasn't true. But that was how he saw things.

In my car, tears drenched my cheeks. My heart had celebrated the best day of my life and then suffered the worst. The pain was unbearable. Mucus ran down my mouth and chin. I started the minivan and drove out of his driveway, my chest hollow, my stomach tight and acidic. I wasn't sure I had ever felt this horrible. For me, it was as if the world were ending. *My* world.

I drove about a thousand feet down the road when my foot pressed the brake pedal, my hands shifting the van into park. For several minutes I sat there, the engine running idle. My conflicted mind fought over several options. I couldn't leave things this way. If I did, I suspected I would never see or hear from Aaron again. Two weeks ago, I would have been fine with that outcome. Today had changed everything. Aaron had awoken my sleeping heart. He showed me a life that I craved with every fiber of my being. I was falling in love with him. I knew this because in my thirty-six years of dating assholes I had never experienced happiness on this level.

But was I wrong about him? He was so angry.

My tires crept back toward the foot of his driveway, where I cut the engine.

As I traveled up his driveway on foot, my mind worked on the speech that could well be one of the most important of my life. I decided that whatever happened, Aaron was worth the gamble. He'd been hurt. That was obvious. He'd lost his fiancée, the situation with his parents unclear. On top of that, someone had betrayed him. A reporter? How awful. I would never do such a thing to him. And this was my way of proving it.

When I reached his house, a bright light spilled out from the back, tendrils of dark smoke billowing into the night sky. *Oh, no.* Had the campfire spread? Was his beautiful camper now engulfed in flames? When we left things to take our showers, the fire was mostly out. And I swore Aaron had thrown water onto the embers and stirred them, making sure they were out. We were in a euphoric daze, though, so maybe he didn't quite finish the job? I didn't need an additional reason for him to hate me.

My feet picked up the pace as I rushed around the side of his house, coming to an abrupt stop. What I witnessed next defied logic.

Aaron stood at the edge of the fire, lighter fluid in his hands. The flames rose before him. The fire roared as he threw more fluid onto white planks of wood at the center of the flames.

Our Adirondack chair?

The legs of the same chair we had just made love in stuck up like a wounded animal. His back faced me, wide and rigid, and I was grateful for that. I didn't need to see his crazed expression, which I imagined was even more horrifying.

Wood splintering filled the air as Aaron stomped more wooden planks. He flung them into the fire, dousing the chair's remains with more accelerant, inspiring the flames to reach higher. The pieces melted and crackled like a creature being brought down. Its bones crushed by the fury of Aaron's anger. I felt sick; my hand pressed to my mouth to stop my stomach from lurching into my throat. My knees weakened. My head swam. Aaron was upset. I understood that. But this? I didn't know he was capable of such violence.

So much for my no-more-toxic-people-in-my-life mission statement. The wolves were getting harder to spot.

I turned and tiptoed away. The last thing I wanted to do right now was face him. And as I drove home, I wrestled with what I'd witnessed. He'd accused me of such horrible things—all for even worse reasons. He believed me to be a liar. But after what I had seen tonight, I had to wonder, who had betrayed whom?

And if a misunderstanding could set off Aaron's aggressive behavior, what might he do to someone he obviously hated? Someone like James Logan?

Chapter 17

Natalie

When I arrived home, Daisy and Mom sprang from the couch to greet me. Daisy's kisses and leaps of excitement offered my tattered heart a moment of reprieve. My mom's endless questions (*How was the date, Do you think he's the one, and Were you able to ask him about Harry*) did nothing but annoy my tired mind.

"I'm exhausted, Ma. Can we catch up in the morning?" I brought Daisy out for one last potty break and headed to bed, not that I slept any.

Scenes from the day and night played out in my thoughts. The good, the bad, and the, oh so ugly.

Images of Aaron, a dark shadow against the flames, haunted me. Mostly, I tried to sort through how it all came about. Even though I was the one who had lied, I felt betrayed by Aaron. If that was how he had treated Paula and possibly his family, it was no wonder he was alone. All those kind acts and tender words, obliterated in an instant. Decimated, really. Just like our chair. If he were so fragile, why had he allowed me in at all? He was the one who had invited me. His demeanor changed as though someone had flipped a switch in his personality. There was no doubt in my mind that Aaron Marino never wanted to see me again. And while I accepted that reality, my injured heart would take some time to recover, if ever at all. Cruel. What he had done was nothing short. The anger he harbored. Was I even right to trust him?

On Saturday, I had some errands to run, plus a trip to the storage unit to inventory our cleaning supplies. I went before breakfast, knowing a storm was imminent, according to my weather app. I also wanted to touch base with Yaz. Since she'd been sick, we really hadn't caught up with each other work-wise. More importantly, I wanted to be away from customers, and this weekend would grant me that wish.

When I returned home to make breakfast, my mother kept her questions to a minimum. Besides her inquisitive mind, she also had a sixth sense about people (so did Yaz's mom), and something told me she knew things hadn't quite gone as she *or I* had hoped.

She met me at the coffeepot, her hand reaching out to touch my arm. "You okay, dear?"

Not willing to spill more lies, I said, "Not really."

Her face drooped. "Do you want to talk about it?"

The small TV on the other side of the kitchen interrupted our conversation with a breaking news story about another fire in the area. This one occurred at a residential home off Greenwich Drive. The fire had severely burned the man who owned the home, and the authorities suspected arson. As if that weren't bad enough, James Logan had died the night before, *succumbing to his injuries* as they had put it.

My heart dropped like a lead ball into my stomach. And then, the rain came, accompanied by a cold front, bringing with it intense lightning and high winds. The roads weren't exactly safe, so I hunkered down with my mother and my pup for the storm, rain pelting the side of the house. Daisy barked several times, convinced someone was at the door.

After breakfast, I changed into comfy clothes, then made a quick call to Yaz. There was too much to cover over the phone. In all honestly, I wanted to hear her voice.

"Hey, Nat, how's it going?"

"Um, fine."

"You don't sound fine. What's up?"

"Nothing I can get into right now." It was too difficult to open that box. I didn't have the strength. "Things with Aaron didn't work out. That's all." I was starting to think that finding that special someone, my soulmate, wasn't worth the trouble.

"That sucks. I'm sorry. Want me to come over?"

"Nah, the weather is getting bad already. I'll catch up with you later. I just wanted to hear your voice."

Yaz exhaled. "But—"

"Look, I'll tell you later. I promise." I paused and bit my lower lip. "Thanks for always being there for me, Yaz. You have no idea how much I appreciate it." Melancholy was taking over my wounded heart.

"Aw. I feel the same way. Hey, before you go, I need to talk to you about something as well."

Last night was the closest I had ever come to feeling something life-altering. I couldn't fathom why it had happened at all. I cringed inwardly at the sight of him burning that chair, *our* chair. Was he so repulsed by me he wanted to turn what we had done into ash? Only a violent man would do such a thing.

"Are you listening to me?"

"Oh, no. Sorry, Yaz. What did you say?"

"It's okay. Sounds like you have a lot on your mind. I was just saying that I need to talk to you about something else when you have time. I was thinking we could go to dinner next week?"

"Did Ross propose?"

"No, it's nothing like that."

"Are you pregnant?"

"God, no! We can talk next week. In the meantime, I'll be here if you want to share a glass or a bottle of wine over the phone during this storm. And I can come over if you want me to. Ross is gone all weekend, *again.* A couple hired him to photograph their wedding in West Virginia. He was so excited. Kind of makes up for the accident he had at work."

My throat thickened. "What accident? Is he okay?"

"Yeah, that guy, Vic, screwed up again. The jerk was smoking a cigarette near a highly combustible area. Ross ran to tell him to put it out, and he slipped, hitting his head on a pipe. He was so mad that he fired Vic, who wasn't too pleased about it."

"What an asshole. How bad was the injury? Did Ross go to the hospital?" Poor Ross. The man worked so hard to keep everything moving forward.

"He's fine. He got a small cut over his eye." Yaz's tone lightened. "And then he got this wedding photographer job. He told me he's going to quit at the plant soon. He's saved a ton of money, and he's sick of being there."

"Yay. I'm so glad he's leaving."

"Me too. I can't tell you how much." Yaz took a breath. "Anyway, you're gonna be okay, girlfriend. I know it's hard now, but be thankful you just met the guy, and things hadn't gone any further."

Further than what? Falling in love?

* * *

By midafternoon, I was sick of running numbers at my bedroom desk, the same small desk where I used to do homework back in the day, and met Mom and Daisy in the living room for a movie. The wind howled outside our house, cold rain continuing to batter the windows, a stark reminder of how cozy we were indoors. We decided on something funny. Not romantic. And nothing involving fire. Our choice: *The Naked Gun* with Liam Neeson.

Mom sat on one end of her recliner sofa, while I claimed the other. Daisy took the middle seat, cuddled into a little ball, her black-and-white fur resembling a miniature panda bear this time. She was so cute, I couldn't stop stroking her fur and kissing her little head.

"Before we start the movie, how about I get us some ice cream?" Using her feet, Mom kicked the footrest closed and glanced over at me.

Before the divorce, whenever I was upset about losing a game in field hockey or a boy blowing me off, my mother always offered ice cream as a temporary fix. *Ice cream won't solve your problems, but it sure does taste good, doesn't it?* she'd say. *Maybe it can make you forget your woes for just a little while.*

If only that remedy had worked during her divorce, when she could have used a break from her own problems. My mother was a caretaker at heart, but she wasn't one to allow doting on herself. You know the saying that doctors make the worst patients? That applied to moms too. *Don't try to take my job away from me,* she'd proclaim in her defense. *It's all I have.* And it *was* all she had at the time, but not anymore. Her health was improving. She was working, and she even had a boyfriend. Maybe not the third part.

I hoped I hadn't blown things for my mother. At the same time, I worried that Harry had an angrier side to him that he hadn't revealed yet. I had suspected the same thing of Justin, and I was correct. Even Aaron had shown me his inner monster. Could Harry have caused the fire at James Logan's house? I doubted it, but one never ever knew the darkness that lingered within us all when pushed to our limits. James had humiliated Harry (same as Justin), costing him his business and his reputation. Not an easy thing to recover from. But how had James hurt Aaron?

Aaron hated James. *Don't ever say his name again in my presence!* Why? Had James done something to ruin Aaron's reputation as well? Could it have anything to do with the fire in the garage that James had tried to pin on Harry?

I saw the outer scars on Aaron's beautiful body, but I had no idea what remained inside his smoldered heart. Burning the chair we had made love in seemed beyond extreme. The way his body stood before those flames. Could Aaron be the arsonist?

I had to clear my head. This line of reasoning was driving *me* batshit now.

"Ice cream sounds great, Ma." I rose, causing Daisy to do the same. One thing I learned about pups was that they never liked to be alone. *Ever*. She'd follow me into the bathroom if I let her.

A bowl of vanilla ice cream turned into sundaes, with chocolate syrup, chopped pecans, slices of banana, and sprinkles to top it off. We sat on the same couch and consumed our desserts, the ones that came before dinner tonight.

Daisy chewed on her doggy bone.

Opening credits scrolled across the screen.

"Do you want to talk about what happened last night with Aaron?" My mother savored another bite of yumminess as she awaited my answer. The movie on the TV provided a place for our gazes to land.

"I guess. At first, it was a wonderful night. The best. Do you remember when Dad took us camping that year? . . . " When I was finished with my story, my mother had consumed her treat and was sitting sideways on the couch, offering me her full attention, the movie far from our thoughts. I omitted the sex or the burning chair. In her version, Aaron and I had embraced and spent quality time together before I had spilled the beans about Harry, and he had kicked me out.

"That was my fault. I'm so sorry, Natalie. I shouldn't have asked you to do that. It doesn't sound all that bad. Maybe give him a couple of days to process." She stroked Daisy's fur, who remained curled up between us. "What is it about that man?" A hardened expression tightened her face.

"What man? Aaron?"

"No, James Logan." Disgust had her shaking her head. "He sure did have a lot of enemies. It's no wonder someone was out to get him. It's just that . . ." She tilted her head, her mind working on something else.

"What, Ma?"

"Well, as you know, James passed away. But then, another house was burned. And the authorities suspect arson on that one as well." She readjusted herself on the couch, pulling the waist of her sweatshirt down from riding up. "We figured out that James owned the warehouse and the rental property that had burned. And we also know that Bea and Nigel are his parents, so that explains why they were targeted. But another home was burned yesterday, and I can't make the connection."

I couldn't help but smirk. "Ma, you should have been a detective, you know that?"

She waved me off. "Oh, please. I'm just curious, is all. And I know Bea and Nigel, so of course, I pay attention to the reports."

Having already finished my sundae and placed the bowl on a side table, I sat forward on the couch and lightly slapped my lap. I grabbed the remote and turned the TV off. "Well, now is as good a time as any. I'll get my laptop. And let's see what we can figure out." I had to admit; I was curious about this as well. The fact that this story swirled around several people I knew added another level of intrigue, over half of them suspects in my mind. Was I acting like an amateur sleuth wannabe? If anyone saw my Netflix account, they'd think so.

* * *

We spent the next hour doing as much research as we could. Feeling like a real detective, my mother even brought a framed corkboard up from the basement that she had used to keep our schedules straight back in middle and high school. I contributed a stack of index cards, a black marker, and some thumbtacks that we could use to create our makeshift suspect/evidence board. I removed a large piece of artwork from the wall, providing us with a place to hang it nearby.

I sat at the kitchen table with my trusty marker in hand. "Okay, who has a grudge against James Logan?" I made a face. "That we know of."

My mother walked back and forth in front of me, her hands moving this way and that. "Well, Justin has a bad temper, and he's surely got a grudge. And you mentioned the other day that his hand was injured. Do you think it's possible he could have done this?"

I wrote Justin's name on the index card. "I couldn't find much about him online. He doesn't keep up with his social media either. But he's definitely violent. And he hated James for stiffing him on pay and backing out of that contract." I tapped the end of the marker against my chin, the pungent odor making my eyes water, and pulled the marker away from my face. "The only thing that makes me doubt it could be him is all the fires that started weeks ago, before James fired Justin. Or the one at Greenwich Drive, which I suspect is also connected to Logan, somehow." Something occurred to me. "But he's never had a very good opinion of him. He said he was always making him do mundane jobs that Justin thought were beneath him." I stood and grabbed a tack from a cluster already stuck to the board, posting Justin's name there. "Let's keep him up there for now." I returned to my seat. "Who else?"

More pacing from my mother. "Well, according to what you said, Aaron wouldn't even let you speak James's name. Whatever happened between them, it was big."

"I did a deep dive into that fire that burned Aaron. The man and woman who perished were Jennifer and Stephen Anders." No relation to Aaron, not that I had thought they were. I was checking everything. I didn't know anyone named Anders. Could they be Paula's parents or family members? I didn't know Paula's last name.

My mother's hand flew to her mouth. "You don't think . . ."

"No. Aaron's last name is Marino. But he said his uncle and father were both firefighters. I'm pretty sure they still live in Florida, which is where Aaron is originally from. He didn't talk much about his parents, so I don't know anything about them. According to my research, the apartment building had failed several inspections, and some of the tenants had complained about the wiring and the plumbing. In fact, the basement had flooded more than once." I wrote Aaron's name on the card. "Someone dropped the ball there." I gazed up at my mother, who had resumed her back-and-forth stroll. "You should have seen his scars, Ma. They covered his entire right arm, chest, and even portions of his back. He has a bunch of flame tattoos to cover them up." Even with all of that, the man was absolutely gorgeous. His struggles only added to his appeal for me. *Then.* Now, I wasn't so sure. When you witnessed someone doing something you never expected, it altered your perception.

My mother stopped short and faced me. "Wait. How do you know what his chest looks like?"

The jig was up.

"Well . . ."

She quirked a brow. "I see. So, things went a little further than you had told me. No wonder you were upset. And he still behaved that way? Even after . . ." She made a you-know-what-I-mean motion with her hands.

"Yeah, even after." My stomach knotted at the way Aaron looked at me before I had left, hurt and betrayal burning in his amber eyes. The memory of him in front of the campfire burning our chair shoved my sympathies aside.

"Are you okay, hon?"

Hurt, anger, and disappointment rose up my throat and lodged into an uncomfortable ball. "I will be, Ma. Spending time with him was amazing. And all that stuff he did for me." I pursed my lips, my heart grappling with my circumstances. I sighed and shook my head. "I don't know." I rose and pinned Aaron's name to the suspect board, returning to my seat a moment later. "Okay, who else do we have?"

When my mother didn't answer me, I gazed up to see her crestfallen expression. We exchanged a dreadful look.

"Harry." We said his name in unison.

I attempted to assuage her fears. "We don't need to put his name up there, Ma. I'm sure he's innocent."

She paused, rubbing her hand across her forehead as though trying to work this out. "No, put him up there. James destroyed Harry's career. And you saw how upset he was the other night. I haven't heard from him since. I am assuming it's over between us." She lowered her head, her neck appearing to shrink. "I've never met his family." Her lower lip trembled. "He's never asked me to his home. I don't even know where he lives." A frantic ripple dominated her voice.

For a moment, I hated Harry. How could he do this to her? It was hard enough to put oneself out there, but after what my mother had endured, it was nearly impossible. Yet, she had done it.

It was eerily strange how similar our circumstances had become.

"He's such a nice man. I could talk to him about anything. He's supportive of my illness. He used to show me articles all the time about things I could do to feel better. And even though I haven't been to his house, he's made me dinner in *this* house multiple times." A tear ran down her cheek, which she quickly swiped away with her shaky hand.

I rose and went to her, wrapping my arms around her slumped shoulders and pulling her close for a bear hug. "We can put his name up there, but I'm sure it's not Harry. The person causing those fires is now a murderer. Harry would never hurt a flea." I pulled back and braced her shoulders so she could see the resolve in my eyes. "I'm sure it's not him, Ma." I thought of something to get her mind working on something else. "What about our creepy neighbor, Alan?" Our heads turned toward the direction of his house. I made the card and put it up.

Before we called it quits for the evening, I had pinned the names of four suspects on the corkboard, all of them lined up under James Logan's name, which I'd also tacked to the top of the list. Next to each name, I added a new index card with a few notes regarding motive. Alan had a fixation with fire and had exhibited odd behavior *and* lived in Bea's old house. Harry had a dark past that involved James, one that had ended his career prematurely. Justin had some recent altercations with James and could potentially be violent. Aaron. I sighed as I wrote. He must have had some sort of dark past involving James Logan. He'd shown hatred for the man, and had exhibited questionable behavior. I abhorred writing those things, but they were true. As a precaution, I removed the suspect board from the wall and placed it in my bedroom closet for safekeeping. We didn't need Harry showing up unannounced to realize he was a suspect in our amateur sleuthing.

That night, I tossed and turned, unable to relax my mind. The rain had stopped, but clouds stuffed the night sky, the moon unable to shine above. I went to the bathroom, drank a cup of water, and even tried reading. Nothing worked as I lay in bed, staring at the ceiling.

Tap. Tap. Tap. It was so faint, Daisy hadn't even heard. *Just your imagination.*

I checked the digital clock on my nightstand. 3:30 a.m.

Tap, tap, tap reached my ears again. Almost imperceptible.

Maybe it's a branch.

Fingers dragged down glass, the eerie squeak unmistakable. I flipped over, staring out my bedroom window.

A large, hooded figure loomed, framed by darkness. I jerked up in bed and tried to focus my eyes.

The flick of a lighter illuminated a sinister grin.

My toes curled. A scream tore through my throat, startling Daisy, who jumped up and began barking. At what, she had no idea.

Footfalls ran down the hallway, my mother bursting into my room. "What's wrong?" Her hair disheveled, robe half on.

My heart pumped so rapidly that I could barely breathe. "S-someone." I pointed with a trembling finger at the window.

"What?" My mother dashed over to the window. "What did you see?"

I tried to swallow through a constricted throat, my chest sweating profusely. Finally, I coughed the words out. "Someone was standing there! I saw him. He was looking right at me through the window!"

My mother's gaze shot from the window to me and then back again. She bent over and squinted into the shadow of night. "I don't see anyone. It's pitch dark out there. Are you sure it wasn't an animal or a shadow?"

I calmed my breathing. "I'm sure! Animals and shadows don't carry lighters."

Chapter 18

Natalie

At breakfast the next morning, I looked *and* felt like a zombie, a perfect costume for Halloween six months from now. Not only did I stay up the rest of the night, but anxiety had my heart palpitating. I could rationalize the dark figure. As my mother had pointed out, it could have been a tree or a shadow. But the lighter. There was no mistaking *that*. The person at the window, whom I was certain was a man, *wanted* me to see him.

Tap, tap, tap. The sound reverberated throughout my nervous system.

I had added a nightlight to my room to avoid stubbing my toe or running into furniture during the night when Daisy needed to go out. It wasn't bright, but it provided definition, enough that someone could see my bed and that I was lying in it.

How long had he been there?

Tap, tap, tap. What a haunting sound.

The oatmeal Mom made me for breakfast looked more like

paste, my stomach turning at the sight of it. The coffee in my hand, however, became my best friend.

"Have you called the police yet?"

"Not yet, but I plan to."

Perched next to me on her stool at the breakfast bar, my mother didn't look much better than I did. Not only had I stayed up, but so had she, mulling over what had happened. When the sun edged over the horizon, we ventured outside and investigated. Daisy was eager to empty her tiny bladder.

There wasn't much to see. With the rain stopped, the ground was spongy and matted. Footprints were impossible to make out. Given the fact that my bedroom window faced creepy Alan's house, our gazes turned in his direction. His lights were off, no activity to speak of so early in the morning.

Now, we contemplated some more.

"Do you think it's Alan?"

I wasn't sure. "The sad, or maybe the scary, part here, Ma, is that it could have been Alan or Justin, or even Aaron, for all I know. Justin had told me things weren't over between us. And he strikes me as the kind of person who holds grudges. Aaron could be a psychopath, and Alan is just creepy as hell."

With no answers in sight, we could agree on one thing: We'd keep the house locked up like Fort Knox, not that we ever left a door unlocked beforehand. As an added precaution, we ordered additional locks for the windows. I also planned to do some research on creepy Alan and see what I could dig up. But all that *after* I called the police and filed a report.

* * *

It was much harder to find out anything about Alan than I had thought, including his last name. The neighborhood directory was long overdue for an update, missing the names of a few new homeowners from the previous year. I checked various real estate sites, but they only told me how much the house had sold for and when. We tried the HOA, but the board was often neglectful when it came to responses.

We called Bea as a last resort. The poor woman had lost her son and was reeling from the fact that someone had most likely murdered him, with her own gift shop falling prey to the same lunatic. Mom had been in touch with Bea many times to check on her. We also planned to attend the funeral the following weekend. My mom's excuse for calling this time was to ask if there was anything—food or arrangements—that she could help Bea with. Once that conversation had concluded, my mother started her inquiry.

"Hey, Bea, by chance do you happen to remember the name of the man who purchased your house last year?" Mom kept her cell on speakerphone so I could eavesdrop from the kitchen counter, where we both stood.

"Oh, dear. I'm not sure. I'd have to check the purchase contract. Why? Is he not picking up his yard again?"

"Yeah, something like that." My mother shot me a look that implied, *No need to alarm the poor woman*, which I agreed with.

"I'll check and get back to you." Bea's voice was weak and tinny, like a woman who was low on sleep and overloaded with emotion. "I just can't believe he's gone."

My mother took a seat at the breakfast nook table and sighed. "I know, Bea. I'm so sorry."

* * *

I had three cleaning jobs the next day, which was fine, except that I struggled to keep my head on straight. I understood why Aaron was upset about me lying to him. That made sense. But to go to the effort to burn the chair we had been intimate in felt not only wrong but unbalanced.

Was I sure it was the same chair? It was dark, and I was only there for an instant. I didn't know for sure. But why burn any chair? Did he torch the comforter in the camper we had done it on as well? It was such an extreme thing to do. I didn't even know he was capable of such things. And now that I did, it changed how I felt about him. This same argument had replayed so many times already; the subject had gone stale.

"Are you sure you want to use that on the windows?" Hillary Webster asked me, distracting me from my thoughts. She was the owner of the house that I was cleaning. It was a perfectly legitimate question considering I was cleaning her windows with liquid bleach, leaving streaks all over the place.

"Oh, sorry. I didn't get much sleep last night."

The second house was far more stressful. The Robinsons also employed Justin for their landscaping, and it was where I first met him. I had planned to inform Mrs. Robinson that I wouldn't be able to clean for her much longer, even though she had paid on time and kept a fairly clean home, making my job easier. The problem was I couldn't come up with a legitimate excuse. Instead, I rescheduled her usual cleaning job to today, when Justin didn't work, hoping to avoid him.

Though Justin wasn't there when I arrived, he came up the driveway as I was loading up my van.

He spoke in a low voice. "Hey, Cupcake." He'd parked his black truck and attached landscaping trailer next to the curb. "I wanted to apologize for the other night. I had way too much to drink, and I realize I was acting like a douche."

No argument there. Without responding, I returned to the house to collect my vacuum. Unfortunately, he followed me.

"Well, hello, Justin. I didn't expect to see *you* today." Wearing a light-pink tracksuit, Mrs. Robinson sat on a small bench near the entrance, lacing up her sneakers. The forty-something blond ran several miles a day to keep fit, which showed in her thin waist and lean legs. "I was just going out for a run." She stood, her hazel eyes registering confusion. "Did Corey forget to pay you or something?"

"No, ma'am. I was just stopping by to say hi to Natalie."

"Oh." She smiled as though that was sweet and not creepy.

"Take care, Judy. I'll see you in a couple of weeks. Say hi to Corey and the kids for me." I grabbed my vacuum, despite Justin's attempts to carry it for me. "I've got it." I threw a few eye-daggers his way, hoping Judy hadn't noticed.

"Will do. Have a nice week, Natalie. Good to see you, Justin." She closed the door as I traipsed toward my van, Justin right on my heels.

"Can we talk for a second?"

I opened the hatch and thrust my vacuum inside, pushing the button to close it again. "I don't have time to talk right now, Justin. I have another job scheduled right after this one. How did you even know I was here? This isn't the normal day you work here." I approached the driver's side door when he grabbed my wrist.

"I happened to be driving by and saw your van."

Bullshit. Something told me he was driving by a lot. *Stalker* came to mind. I pulled at my wrist to free myself. "Let go of me!"

He removed his hand. "Wait just a goddamn second, will ya?" I could feel his aggravation, even though he tried his best to mask it.

I huffed, growing tired of these confrontations in my life. "What do you want, Justin?" I flattened my lips, my jaw clenching.

He stood back. "I told you. I just wanted to apologize, okay?" He didn't say *sheesh*, but I could tell he was ready to.

"Apology accepted. Now I need to get back to work." I snatched my keys out of my jacket pocket.

He raised a palm. "Just give me one more minute. *Please*?"

I waited with my arms crossed over my chest and refrained from tapping my foot.

"The reason I got so upset before was that I've had a few women cheat on me." He kicked at some stones on the driveway with his work boot. "I've been burned. And I guess I've gotten gun-shy with chicks." His gaze lifted to meet mine. "I was really falling for you, Cupcake. Can't we put this behind us and start over?"

I grabbed the door handle of my van. I knew I needed to be crystal clear about my intentions. "No, I'm sorry, but we can't. I appreciate the apology, Justin, and I'm sorry to hear you've been cheated on." I opened the door, ready to climb in. "As far as you and I are concerned, we are so over!"

He pushed his hand against the door and huffed. "Why? Does it have anything to do with *Hot Aaron*?" Sarcasm intact, the Justin from the other night had returned, only this time, he was sober.

"No, it's not because of Aaron. I am *not* seeing Aaron or anyone else. Not that it's any of *your* business." My anger rose with the force of a geyser in my chest. *These men*. Who the hell did they think they were? People had accused me of being a liar and a cheater—I'd had psychos peering through my window at night—plus, burned chairs, and I was goddamn sick of it. I faced him, causing Justin to back away a step.

"Listen, asshole!"—I poked at his chest for emphasis—"I am *not* interested in you. And if you approach me again, I will file a restraining order against you. I'm not playing around. Take your threats and your stupid nicknames and stay the hell away from me!"

Judy stood at the living room window of her house,

watching us. Maybe that was a good thing. If I needed to cancel my services, after all, she'd know why.

"And if you want to keep this job with the Robinsons, I suggest you back off, because Judy's watching you right now!" I jumped into the driver's seat, fired up the engine, and drove off, Justin standing there with his mouth hanging open.

Good. If Justin was in fact the dark figure lurking outside my window, maybe this would put a stop to that too.

Natalie Dugan was tired of being pushed around!

* * *

When I arrived home after work, feeling wrung out and somber, Mom was making chicken soup for dinner. Rosemary, thyme, and garlic infused the air—staples for her chicken stock—giving the house an inviting ambiance. Comfort food had a way of doing that.

"Smells good in here." I bent down to greet a hyper Daisy who always behaved as though we'd been apart for months, not hours, every time I walked through the door. "Hey, baby girl. . . . Yes, I missed you too." I picked her up, causing her to lick my face as though I'd covered myself with peanut butter, which she loved. "How was your day, Ma?" I put Daisy down. She ran around my legs, her front paws ready to jump up at any moment against my knees.

Stirring the large pot on the stove, Mom tapped her oversized spoon on the rim and covered her soup, placing the spoon to rest on a paper towel nearby to soak up the drippings. "My day was fine. I finished up at two and thought chicken soup would be perfect to comfort my poor daughter."

I took my coat off and hung it in the nearby closet and returned, playing with Daisy some more. "That sounds perfect, actually."

"Bea called about ten minutes ago."

I carried my purse to the breakfast bar, placing it over the back of a bar stool. "Oh? What did she say?"

"She said that Alan's last name is Booker. I figured you'd want to know, so you could look him up."

"So, not the son of Stephen and Jenny Anders, the couple who perished in the fire. I figured as much. I'll grab my laptop and see what I can find out while you cook." I paused. "Unless you need some help?"

She waved me off. "Nope. I've got it covered."

"By the way, Justin showed up at my second-to-last job today."

My mother was approaching the fridge when she stopped dead in her tracks. "What? Did he make a scene? . . . Did he get violent? . . . Should we call the police?"

I patted the air to imply all was well. "Don't worry. I set him straight. He apologized, and I told him to never approach me again."

A strong nod from my mother indicated my response had pleased her. "That's my girl."

"I'll be right back. Grabbing my laptop."

As she finished cooking dinner, I searched online for our neighbor.

I didn't find anything notable about Alan Booker. I checked social media, then Google. While I was at it, I searched for any obituaries for Aaron's parents. I don't know why since he hadn't said they were deceased. The way his face fell at the mere mention of family gave me pause. Could they have had a falling out? If Aaron was so willing to burn furniture for no good reason, what else had he done? He was engaged once until he *fucked it up*. I could see that as well. When Aaron wanted to push you away, he knew just how to do it. The muscles in the back of my neck tensed just thinking about it. I slapped my laptop closed.

I set the table in our small dining room. A meal of this caliber and effort (soup with homemade broth took hours to make, along with fresh salad and steamed spinach) deserved an appropriate presentation. I worked on the silverware and napkins for our place settings, then added the blue floral china, a gift from my parents' wedding. When I finished, I helped my mother carry in the food.

"Have you heard back from the police yet?" Mom placed the white porcelain soup tureen in the center of the table, a hotplate elevating its height.

"No, and I've called them several times. The woman I spoke with initially asked if I had any evidence or proof." I ladled soup into her bowl. "I don't have any evidence that anyone was out here. There was no damage done to the house. I didn't see any signs that anyone was trying to break in, either, did you?" I handed her the bowl. "Be careful, it's hot."

She accepted the bowl with careful hands, then placed the paper napkin I had folded for her in her lap. "No, I didn't. I'm going to notify the HOA so they know *something* happened. It wouldn't hurt to get a few of our nosy neighbors to keep a lookout."

I filled my bowl next, as my mother tonged salad onto her plate. "That's probably a good idea. Good thinking, Ma."

My mind wandered. In the past month, I had dated, if you wanted to call it that, two rather disturbing men. As I'd already contemplated many times, perhaps I should go it alone for a while. The breakup with Justin wasn't anything I would ever regret. He wasn't for me. End of story. The situation with Aaron was borderline traumatic. I really liked him. I opened myself up to him in a way I had never done before. And I allowed myself to believe something profound was happening between us. Life altering. Rising to soulmate status.

All I felt now was empty and shameful that I had ever let it happen. I *needed* to see him for who he was, not who I wanted him to be. Knowing this didn't make the pain any easier.

* * *

I stopped at Coffee Berry in town the next day between jobs, hoping to give my tired brain a boost.

"Well, look who it is? How ya been, Natalie?" Decked out in his dark-navy uniform, holster on his hip and shoulder mic intact, Luis approached from his police cruiser parked across the lot. He opened the door for me, bringing my focus to his left hand, more specifically the wedding band surrounding his finger.

"Thank you."

We walked in together, the smell of roasted coffee beans as inviting as Mom's chicken soup the night before. Customers young and old meandered about, fixing their coffee or sitting at tables chatting. A few students took the window bar where they typed away on their laptops, enjoying a sip of their coffee every now and then or a bite of their pastry. Several young girls performed a continuous loop of selfies at a table in the center of the room.

Most everyone took notice of Luis in his uniform, as most people did when a cop appeared. The crackling of his mic, the gun in his holster, ready to nab a bad guy at a moment's notice. There was always something intimidating about it all. If I hadn't dated the man and slept with him, I would have felt the same.

Instead, I offered Luis a proper hug. "It's so good to see you.

And what is that I see on your finger?" I quirked a brow. "When did you get married? Congratulations, by the way."

Luis lifted his left hand and let it drop. "Oh, yeah. Been three years. Got a two-year-old, and another one on the way. Both boys. Bought a house over in Shady Hills Estates."

We joined the back of the line, where Luis gave my arm a light tap. "How about you? Walked down the aisle yet?" His gaze fell to my ringless hand.

If there was ever a time when a lie would have been the preferable option, this was it. Maybe I *was* becoming my father. "No, not yet."

A guy who looked about college age, donning a full afro, said from behind the counter, "Next." In the same area, employees wore tan aprons over white polos and khakis, working on this drink or that, steam rising, beans grinding in the distance, a constant flurry of activity.

Every so often a barista yelled out a person's name to collect their order, faint music emanating from hidden speakers. Out front, a tall glass cabinet displayed various sweets, all decorated to perfection.

We stepped forward, the strong aroma of various coffees tantalizing my nostrils. "Are you still working downtown at that accounting firm?" The speaker on Luis's radio crackled a few times, but he ignored it.

The guy rocking the afro, again yelled, "Next," forcing the line forward.

"No, I started my own cleaning business. We do offices, stores, churches, and homes. It's really taking off."

His brown eyes smiled as he nodded away. "That's great, Natalie."

"Did you say you have a place in Shady Hills?"

"Sure do. Four bedrooms."

"Wow, that's a fancy neighborhood." Shady Hills was one

of those places where the lawns remained perfectly manicured and the houses were a vision of something out of *Better Homes and Gardens*. I used to drive through that area when I wanted to imagine a posh life for myself. Luis was a cop, and from dating him, I knew he didn't make much money. Not as much as he should have, putting his life on the line and all.

"Yeah, I've picked up a few odd jobs to help make ends meet. Mostly off-duty security."

It would have to be high-paying jobs to afford that area. "Good for you." I smiled my support, wondering how hard this guy had to work to make ends meet. Maybe his wife had money as well?

I just hoped it was legitimate work. Last year, the news reported a scandal that had rocked the Charlottesville police force, with a few officers accepting bribes.

"Next." This time, it was our turn.

Once we had our coffees, we headed for the door. I waited until we were outside to seize an opportunity. "Hey, Luis, do you know much about the recent fires in the area? One of them burned down James Logan's estate. I've been following the stories, and I read the authorities suspect arson."

We had reached Luis's black-and-white cruiser, the word *Police* screaming in large letters across the side, a strip of powerful lights fastened to the roof, unlit and ready to shine brighter than a strobe when the situation required.

"Couldn't happen to a nicer asshole, if you ask me." He leaned back against his vehicle and took a sip of his coffee.

Wow, even the cops hated Logan.

"It's been a hot topic at the station. I haven't been assigned to the case or anything, though. We've got some detectives working on it. Why do you ask?" He lifted his to-go cup to his lips once again.

I swallowed a sip of my coffee, too. The maple spice latte

flooded my taste buds with pure joy. "Our old neighbor was James's mother. Her name is Bea, and her gift shop was also burned. I was just curious about the case. Do they have any leads?"

Luis shot me a look. "They are following up on *hundreds* of leads, to be honest. Most of them bogus."

I hugged my paper cup, the heat warming my palms on this tepid spring day. Since the rain had departed, the weather had decided on sunny, warm, and windy. Dead leaves from last fall tumbled around like confetti across the blacktop. "Do they have any suspects?"

Luis pressed his lips into a thin line. "You know I can't tell you that." He said those words with a slight smile, but I knew he was serious. "It's an ongoing investigation." Low voices emitted from his radio, but he didn't acknowledge them this time either. I figured they must've been addressing someone else.

"Sorry, I guess my mom and I got curious about the case." I made a noncommittal gesture with my hand. "You know, because we know Bea. She said that James had been estranged from her and her husband, Nigel, for a while now, and she's all broken up over what happened. I hope they find the person and put an end to all these fires." I shivered, but didn't mean to. The subject was unsettling.

"Well, if they don't figure out who's doing it soon, they may be shit out of luck." He drank more of his coffee as two cars pulled into the parking lot. A small group of kids—or maybe they were college students—hustled inside the door, all of them offering Luis a backward glance. I wondered how many of them had weed on them.

"Shit out of luck? Why?"

Luis turned as though he was going to get into his cruiser.

"I shouldn't have said that. Listen, Natalie, it was great to see you. I need to get back—"

"Wait!" I reached out a hand to stop him from leaving so soon. "Please, Luis, I promise I won't tell anyone. This case hits close to home. What did you mean?"

He thought for a moment, his eyes working on something.

One thing I knew about Luis was his need to be the smartest man in the room. Not only that, he wanted everyone to know he was the smartest man in the room. I hoped he still harbored those same attributes.

He leaned closer. "Listen." His voice dipped low. "You didn't hear this from me, but the person responsible for all the fires left a calling card." His mouth was so close to mine, I could smell the coffee on his breath. Somehow, that brought back memories of our time together. Luis was attractive, but like Justin—although for a different reason—not for me.

Focus.

"What type of calling card?" I couldn't help but ask. We'd gone this far, and I had to know. Plus, I knew my window was closing.

"They spray-painted a large number in red at the first site. A six. And with every fire since, the numbers have decreased. When they burned Logan's estate, they spray-painted the number one but crossed it out and painted a three next to it. For some reason, they decided to move him up on the list. If the numbers are any indication, we believe there is one more target left. I'm sure you've read that another house burned on Greenwich Drive, right?"

"Yes, I did. They're all linked to Logan, aren't they?"

Luis nodded. "Listen." He pointed. "You didn't hear any of this from me. Let's hope they find the asshole before he does any more damage . . . or kills anyone else." He opened the driver's side door of his car. "Take care of yourself, Natalie. It was good to see you."

And off he went, leaving the facts stumbling around in my mind.

Chapter 19

One More Axe to Grind

Aside from a few unforeseen distractions, everything was going according to plan. The cops and the press still had no idea who was behind the fires. One more job, and it would be over. I would be gone, away from this cesspool of a town.

One more axe to grind.

I watched the news last night. More bullshit. Rich people stealing from the poor. It never ceased. But in my case, and in this little corner of the world, one less douchebag breathed oxygen.

Some may see me as a Dr. Jekyll and Mr. Hyde. Not true. I'd read the book *The Merry Adventures of Robin Hood* when I was a kid. I pored over that story, admiring Robin and his need to help the poor. *That* was me. It was what drove me to be the person I became. Helping others seemed like the right path.

Until I realized five years ago that I was helping people in the wrong way. Cutting off the head of the snake was the only way to truly stop the monsters from hurting others. And yes, I'd hurt a few along the way, but no one who didn't deserve it. *No one.*

The property on Richardson Road belonged to Logan, but that wasn't all. The pedo who lived there didn't deserve a roof over his head. I'd done my homework on the scumbag. He'd served his time, but everyone knew the truth: once a pedo, always a pedo.

Kids lived on that street.

The gift shop I torched belonged to the two people who had created Logan. I didn't know them, but I knew they *had* to be bad. How else could they have raised such a selfish prick?

The warehouse belonged to Logan too. Money lost was my goal. Did he feel me closing in on him? Did I keep him up at night? The stranger who pursued him relentlessly?

And then there was the building manager. The fat fuck who was all too happy to do Logan's bidding, refusing to address the building's issues. There were many. He didn't care about the people who lived there any more than he cared about a bug stuck to the bottom of his shoe.

Once I took care of the so-called building manager, I almost ended my reign of terror. The snake was dead, the scumbags surrounding him marred. But there was still one person out there who deserved my wrath. And I had my plan in place. Soon it would all be over. I could put the ugliness of this time behind me, knowing that I had done my part. Robin Hood. That was me.

Steal from the rich and give to the poor.

Kill the rich to stop *him* from hurting more.

Chapter 20

Natalie

"You're kidding? He's actually spray-painted numbers at every place he's burned as his way of counting down?"

"Yup, that's what Luis told me. But you can't tell anyone, not even Bea or Harry." I wanted to say especially Harry, but didn't want to rub salt in the wound of their relationship. I knew she still hadn't heard from him by the way she kept checking her phone. Not only that, but the shadows under her eyes. The slumped shoulders. It was agony to watch it happen all over again.

It hadn't been that long since Harry had stormed off, so I held out hope for a reconciliation. Part of me felt responsible, but another part—a strong part—felt the jury was still out on Harry. I didn't want my mother involved with someone who had shut her out as he had done. My dad had left scars behind, and she didn't need someone adding to her suffering.

I grabbed the board of suspects from my room, returning to the kitchen, where I hung it up on the wall. "Okay, we know of five places that were burned, right? The rental property on

Richardson Road, the gift shop, the warehouse, Logan's estate, and the property on Greenwich Drive." I bent over the kitchen table and made cards for each structure, pinning them up in a circle, James Logan's name at the center. The suspects remained on the left side of the board.

Standing nearby, my mother watched me work.

"Luis confirmed that all the locations are linked to Logan. We know *the who*. What we don't know is *the why*. Or where his next target will be." I stood back and surveyed the board.

Crunch, crunch, crunch. Daisy remained off in the corner, munching on her kibble.

"I did some checking on the warehouse, but I didn't find out anything notable or sinister, other than the fire had destroyed half of the structure."

"Bea and Nigel's gift shop certainly had nothing sinister about it." My mom kept rubbing her chin as she spoke, her mind trying to process.

"True. I couldn't find out who lived in the Richardson Road house, only that Logan owned the property." I wagged a finger in the air. "But the man who lived in the Greenwich Drive house was the owner, not Logan. His name is Charles Oliver, and he has a strong connection to Logan. That's not all. Charles had a list of complaints filed against his property management company, claiming bad management practices. I found several reports about faulty wiring and power outages. Apparently, the apartment building, he managed—Shetland Apartments—had suffered flood damage years prior that was never fixed properly. Mold and electrical issues were also listed. Residents said they'd lose power for no apparent reason. And from what I read, Charles kept putting a Band-Aid on the problem, never really fixing anything. One newspaper quoted him as saying that 'His hands were tied. He could only authorize what the owner of the building would allow.'" I turned to face my mother. "And guess who the owner was?"

"James Logan?"

"You got it. Not only that, guess the name of that same apartment that burned down five years ago, killing two people and injuring Aaron?"

"You're kidding me." My mother's mouth dropped open.

"Yup. Shetland Apartments." Something else came to mind. "What if the rental houses and the gift shop were warmups for this guy, the warehouse, meant to raise the stakes? Luis had said that at Logan's estate, the arsonist had written a number one and then crossed it out, writing a three next to it. This happened before Greenwich Drive burned. From what he implied, they suspected that the arsonist may have planned to burn Logan's estate last but chose to do it sooner for some reason. Something must've happened that had angered him."

"Are we even sure it's a man?"

"Well, Ma, considering up to 90 percent of arsonists turn out to be male. I checked. Let's just assume for the time being it's a man or a group of men." An uneasy feeling festered in my gut. "Justin was so angry with Logan for canceling his contract and stiffing him on pay. But when I saw him days later—after the fire at James's estate—he claimed it was all taken care of. Could Justin have burned his place to get even? When he lost his temper at Yaz's place, he was like a stranger, Ma. It was terrifying." My mind continued to process the facts. "But Justin doesn't have any connection, that I'm aware of, with any of the other properties."

My mother approached, placing her hand on my shoulder. She softened her tone. "It's all very confusing, isn't it?"

I dropped my head in my hands. "Very."

"When you told me about what happened with Justin, I

was horrified. I'm so glad you aren't seeing him anymore. We need to vet your prospects better."

I lifted my head. It was nice of her to say "we" when it was really *my* responsibility to date normal, sane men, not hers.

"It can't be Justin. He wasn't angry at Logan when the arsonist burned the rental house and the gift shop, or the warehouse, for that matter." I thought about that. "Actually, he *was* annoyed with him. Remember how he had said Logan kept giving him mundane jobs to do, like hanging Christmas lights and picking up dog poop?"

"Uh-huh. But would he kill someone over that? Especially someone who was paying his salary? It sounded like he needed that contract."

"Good point, Ma. And I agree."

"What about the most recent fire on Greenwich Drive? How would Justin be connected to that one?"

I let my mother's question linger for a moment. I needed time to concentrate. "I don't know. He was angry, but how would Justin know anything about all those other people and places? Whoever did this had done their homework. Plus, the timing doesn't sync with Justin signing that contract." I rose from my chair and moved Justin's name to the bottom of the board. "For the time being, I think we need to pass on Justin. He seems unlikely."

My mother sat at the table, facing the board. "What about Harry? What James Logan did to Harry happened years ago. And clearly, Harry isn't over it." She stared down at her hands, clasped on the surface of the table. "Maybe that's why Harry hasn't let me meet his family or invited me over to his place. Maybe he was never planning to see me for long enough, knowing this was going on." Her expression turned grim, her eyes gathering darkness. "For all we know, Harry could also have a connection to the Anders."

I stood next to her, my hand resting on *her* shoulder this time. "Anything's possible. We don't really know enough. Don't forget our creepy neighbor." My mind continued to chew on the problem as though it were a stick of gum. "I'm thinking of contacting Luis and asking him if he can run a background check on Alan. I looked Alan Booker up on the Virginia Police website, but I didn't find anything, like a criminal history. But he may not be from here. I'll do a wider search when I get a chance."

My mom gazed up at me, her eyes filled with sorrow. "You think Luis would help?"

I released an uncertain breath. "I don't know, but something isn't right about Alan, and why was he loading several empty cans of gasoline into his car? I mean, who breathes firebombs in their backyard? I suspect he did that to scare me. And he could be the man who was outside my window the other night. Using the lighter only makes me think he's really into fire-type shit." My mind spun with possibilities. "And then, there's Aaron, who we now *also* know has a grudge against James Logan. And why. He was burned severely from that apartment fire, where two people died. Under his watch." I doubted they were his family, but they could have been people he knew. Or was I trying to make connections that weren't there? "Aaron is a loner. But he didn't strike me as someone who would murder someone." *But you didn't expect his violent behavior either.* I shook my head and flung my hands up. "But who the hell am I to make any sort of judgment about him or anyone? My guy-dar is way off when it comes to men."

My mother stood and smirked at me. "Guy-dar?" She approached the sink to get herself a glass of water, Daisy jogging behind.

I wished I were joking about that, but I wasn't. What bothered me most was how hard I had fallen for Aaron. Whether or not he was a psychopath—and all things considered, he was—I would never forget our evening together. I experienced a consciousness with Aaron that I never knew existed. The man rocked my world. How would I ever accept average again? I wasn't sure I wanted to. In fact, I wasn't sure I wanted to date anymore. The moment it all turned to dust still made my heart ache every time I thought about it, which was pretty much all the time. It would take me a long while to recover—*if* I could recover.

"*Tis better to have loved and lost than never to have loved at all.*" I wasn't so sure, Alfred Lord Tennyson had that quite right.

From the table, my cell phone rang. I grabbed it as an image of Yaz's beautiful face filled the small screen. "Oh, hey, Yaz. How's it going?"

"Good. Hey, could I come over for a little bit? I have something I want to talk to you about."

"Sure. Is everything okay?"

"Everything is fine. I'm already on my way. See you in a few." She ended the call.

"Yaz is on her way over." I pulled the corkboard from the wall. "I better put this away. I don't want her thinking we've lost our minds."

"Good idea. I'll make us some coffee."

Yaz arrived twenty minutes later with Sadie in tow. Daisy went ballistic, chasing Sadie around the house before the two of them entangled themselves in several wrestling matches. Honestly, I still wasn't sure how they didn't hurt each other. But they were sisters, so who was I to try and understand their connection? Who was I to understand much of anything?

"Ma, do you mind keeping an eye on the pups while I talk to Yaz?" My BFF had been trying to tell me something for days.

I'd been so consumed with Aaron and this case that it had slipped my mind.

"Sure, I'll take them into the backyard." My mom walked through the living room to the back door. "Come on, girls, let's go outside." She patted her thighs repeatedly, getting their attention. Both dogs ran to her. In a flash, the room fell silent.

"What's up? Do you want a glass of wine or a cup of coffee? Ma just made a pot." The clock on the microwave told me it was six-thirty already. What I loved about this time of year was the fact that it was still light out. I'd take anything positive at this point.

My stomach rumbled, steering my feet toward the fridge. "Are you hungry? I haven't had dinner yet." I opened the fridge to survey my choices, my nose picking up the garlicky scent of the chicken soup Mom had made. Decision easy.

"Ross asked me to marry him."

I slammed the fridge door shut, my mouth gaping, and diverted my focus toward my BFF. Yaz sat at the breakfast bar watching me, her hand outstretched so I could see her ring.

"What? I asked you that, and you said no."

"I know. I know." She sank into her barstool, looking away. "I wanted to tell you in person."

My hand flew to my open mouth. "Congratulations! I'm so happy for you. Ross is a great guy." I rushed over to her as she slid off the barstool.

We hugged, and then I examined the rock on her finger some more. "Your ring is beautiful. Holy shit. I've been so caught up with my own crap. I had no idea. It's nice to hear good news for a change." I reset myself and motioned for her to return to her seat, which she did. I took the seat next to her. "Okay, I want to hear all the details. How did he ask? *When* did he ask? Have you set a date yet?"

Yaz slapped her hands against her thighs. "Slow down.

You're worse than your mother." She took a stabilizing breath. "Okay, let's see. He took me out to dinner at Mona's, which he knows is my favorite Italian place, followed by a walk in Maybrook Park, where he proposed in the gazebo that overlooks the small lake. You know which one I mean, right?"

"I know exactly where you mean. Didn't we have our prom pictures taken there junior year?"

"Yes!" She flung her hands up and let them fall to her lap. "Well, that's about it." Her cheeks brightened right along with her eyes.

"What did he say when he proposed?" I figured I might never know what this feels like for myself. "Tell me everything!"

She chewed her lower lip, her eyes bashful. "He said that since he'd moved here, away from his family, he'd felt so alone until he met me. He said he loves me more than anyone he's ever known, and that he can't wait to spend the rest of our lives together."

"Wow, Yaz. You found a good one. That is *not* easy." My emphasis on the word *not* was probably a bit too much, but my friend was so happy that she didn't seem to notice.

She continued to giggle like a little girl. "I know. I'm so lucky. He also said he's been working so much so he could save enough for our wedding and to put a deposit on a new home when we are ready."

One chamber of my heart burst with joy, the other chamber wilted, realizing I might never know true love. I didn't mean to be selfish, and I would never admit to those inner demons, but Yaz had found what we both had dreamed about for years. Ross was a good man and devoted to her and their new life together.

"You, okay?" The beaming smile on Yaz's lips faded. "I didn't mean to upset you. I know you've been through a lot lately with Justin and Aaron." She reached out and took my hand.

I squeezed her hand before pulling away and giving her shoulder a slight jab. "Don't be silly. I'm so happy for you. Believe me, I needed good news! Let me see that rock again."

The oval-cut, one-carat diamond shimmered from a band with small diamonds embedded in the shank. Like the proposal, it wasn't anything overly grand, but it was nice, just what Yaz deserved. Just like we *both* deserved.

"It's beautiful," I said, while holding her hand in mine. "Have you set a date?"

That was when Yaz's smile melted away again. She lowered her lashes. "We did. And don't freak out, but it's next month."

As my mouth fell open, a series of questions tumbled through my brain.

She lifted her palm. "We both agreed we didn't want a fancy wedding. Just a few friends at the gazebo that Ross is already working on reserving. We'll have a nice dinner in town, and that is all. My mother has already grilled me about *why the rush*." Yaz's entire face tightened like a balloon filled with air. "My mother is upset that we want a small wedding. No extra relatives. She's worried about offending her family." She firmed her jaw. "But I told her it was *my* wedding. When Naomi got married, she did the big wedding. Ross and I don't want that. And we shouldn't have to pay for one."

Naomi, who was ten years older than Yaz, lived in Thailand, where the rest of the relatives remained. I remembered when Yaz had flown out there for her sister's wedding. From what she had told me, it was extravagant, exhausting, and expensive. Her husband worked in IT for a major corporation there. Naomi was ten years older than Yaz. In the many years I'd known the family, I had only met Naomi a handful of times.

Yaz spoke as if to herself. "Small wedding, no fuss. That's what we want."

For an instant, I wasn't sure who she was trying to convince. But Ross had been good to her, so who was I to judge? Especially with *my* track record. I smiled at my friend. "Then that's what we'll have. I'll be there to support you every step of the way." I gave her my version of the stink eye. "I *am* invited, aren't I?"

She waved me off with a *tsk*. "Of course, you're invited. You're my maid of honor. If you're free, I'd like to shop for our dresses this Saturday or Sunday, or maybe both? Does that work for you?"

I nudged her again. "Yup. Can't wait."

We found Yaz a wedding dress on Saturday, Yaz's mother fussing at her the entire time. "Why the rush? . . . Your sister may not be able to make it. . . . I'm gonna have a talk with Ross about all this. . . . This isn't how you conduct a proper wedding. . . . Will the dress even be ready in time?" (The bridal consultant assured us it would.)

Other than a few minor adjustments, the off-the-rack dress was perfect for my friend and her petite frame, including the V-neck bodice with detailed lace that wrapped over her delicate shoulders and the full satin skirt that cascaded from her tiny waist all the way to the floor. She looked stunning, so much so that her mother stopped complaining for five minutes and gasped, her eyes shining with tears. "You look beautiful, *Chao Fah*."

Yaz mouthed, *Princess*. With a long blink, she shook her head at me.

A luminous metallic satin dress with a halter bodice and an overlapping neckline fit my slim body perfectly. At least something was working in my favor.

Dinner afterward came with more fireworks. Especially

when Yaz mentioned Ross might want to move back to Texas, where he was from. That even shocked me. It surprised me that Yaz hadn't told me about it. I had to remind myself that with her being sick, and my crazy love life, we hadn't had a lot of time to chat. But what could I do? She'd met the love of her life. Things were moving forward. That was how things went, even if it still made me sad.

"It's not definite" was what she kept saying. "He just asked me about it. His father has been ill. He doesn't know how much longer he has."

"Then, go for a long visit. There's no need to uproot your life when you're happy here."

Yaz nodded. "Yes, Máe."

My mother just sat there listening the entire time. She was quiet throughout the fitting and dinner. I knew where her mind was and couldn't blame her.

I drove Mrs. Mounivong and my mother home before I dropped Yaz off, hoping we could have some girl time.

"Can you come in for a glass of wine, Nat?"

"Sure." I was hoping she'd ask. We had a lot to cover.

We polished off a bottle of wine by the time I had finished telling her my story. I also included the makeshift investigation that my mother and I had been conducting, making sure to include that we were total amateurs and getting nowhere with it.

"Jesus Christ, Nat, I don't see you for a few weeks and your whole world blows up. I can't believe that happened with Aaron. And that creep at your window gives me the willies." She outwardly shivered. "Did you call the cops? I would have. By the way, it doesn't surprise me that you and your mom were playing detective." The edges of her mouth tugged upward. "I remember how your mother used to grill you when we were younger. You think I'd be good at interior decorating? Well, you and your mom should start your own PI agency." She smirked.

"Funny." She was probably right. "Okay, let's not get off track here."

Yaz sat on one end of her comfy sofa, and I took the other end, our legs outstretched and intermixed among the cushions. "And yes, I called the cops, but they weren't much help. Probably because we couldn't find any evidence that someone was out there, much less who it was. I do plan to call a friend on the force about Alan. See if he can do a background check or something."

Yaz took a sip of her wine and placed the glass on her side table. "A friend?" Her brow lowered until, all at once, her eyes grew wide. "Oh, you mean Luis? Do you still keep in touch with him?" Her matchmaking eyes shone with new possibilities.

"He's married, Yaz." My tone was deadpan.

She frowned in an obvious way. "Too bad."

"And no, we haven't kept in touch. I ran into him the other day at Coffee Berry." I told her about my latest conversation with him.

"They painted numbers on the crime scenes?" Yaz's eyes bulged. She slapped the cushion of her sofa. "What the hell is going on in this town? I can't believe this is happening. I thought what happened with Justin was bad. But now there's Aaron and this crazy person out there somewhere burning everything to the ground. You've got strangers peering in your window at night. Jesus, Nat, you're gonna have to keep your eyes wide open from now on." She tilted her head slightly. "You know, I remember you being worried about Aaron before your first job with him. How did you go from *that* to sleeping with him?" Her tight cheeks relaxed for a moment as she wiggled her eyebrows at me. "How was he, by the way?"

Sex talk was also our thing. It always had been. For my first time, I was more excited to tell Yaz about it than the actual act. Not that the actual act with Bradley Barns was anything noteworthy. But talking about it sure was. We peed our pants laughing.

I made a face. "Funny you should ask. It was probably . . . no, it *was*, the best sex I've ever had." When I analyzed what we had done physically, it wasn't all that unusual. But the attachment I felt, the way his amber eyes *saw* me, his strong heart so gentle and open, it had reframed my life. I thought of him in the shower, how vulnerable he must've felt, showing me those scars, both inside and out. *I'll try not to let you down.* Not thirty minutes had passed before he had completely changed his tune, right in front of my face.

"Yeah, too bad he's nuts, huh?" My friend's gaze found my sorrowful eyes. At least my eyes *felt* sorrowful. "Sorry, Nat. I didn't mean to be so insensitive. You're obviously going through a lot of shit right now." She scooted across the couch and hugged me. "I'm sorry this is going on. What can I do?" She pulled away but kept her hand rubbing my back. "Do you want to stay here for a few days?"

"Nah, but thanks. I've got Daisy and Ma. And I keep my curtains closed all the time now to ward off the perverts. You are right, though, there is a lot of shit going down lately."

"What about Justin? Have you heard from him?"

I nodded. "Yup, he showed up at the Robinsons' when I was cleaning there. He tried to apologize, but I set him straight. Hopefully, he won't be bothering me anymore. Unless he's a serial arsonist, and he tries to burn my mother's house down."

Yaz grimaced. "Don't even joke." She hugged my head. "I'm proud of you, Nat. If he bothers you again, I'll have Ross pay him a visit." She half smiled.

Ross was a nice guy who never showed any evidence of a

temper. The man had the patience of a saint. If he got cut off on the road, he'd slow down. One time a bee stung him, and he simply said, "Ouch." That was it. Even Yaz's mother never seemed to rile him. *She's your mother, and she loves you.* I'd heard him say those words more than once, during a mother-daughter spat. I had a hard time believing he could pull off being a bodyguard. But I appreciated her offer.

"Too bad Aaron is nuts. It sounds like he'd be a great bodyguard."

My thoughts exactly.

Yaz had a way of reading my mind, and sometimes I felt I could do the same with her. Or maybe we'd spent so much time together over the years, we learned those subtle nuances that told us what the other was thinking.

"Are you sure Aaron was burning the chair you two did it in? That's really messed up." Yaz returned to her side of the couch.

I took a breath, giving her question the proper attention. "I have to be honest, a few times I've doubted myself. But why would he be burning anything right then? I had just left." I grabbed my glass of wine and took a final swig.

She gave me a look, and I knew why. Mind reading at its best.

"Yes, Yaz, I have considered that Aaron could have been the one outside my window and the person causing all these fires. Whoever it is, they have one more target left." I just hoped it wasn't me.

Someone cleared their throat, causing me to startle and Yaz to spin her head around toward the bedroom. "Oh, hi, babe. I hope we didn't wake you." Yaz hopped up from the couch and met Ross as he came sauntering into the room, a small scab over his right eye. "Poor, baby. You are working so hard."

Dark rings underscored Ross's brown eyes, giving them a

sunken appearance. Even his face was pasty, his hair matted on one side, imitating a rooster on the other. For Ross, this was as bad as I had ever seen him. I thought of the ring and the upcoming wedding. Were they planning a honeymoon? I hadn't thought to ask. Was Ross busting his ass to pay for all of that? I knew he'd do anything for Yaz. I also hoped he would leave that dangerous job soon. That Vic guy Yaz had told me about worried me. Could Vic be the arsonist? He had a record. I shook the thought out of my head. Pretty soon, I'd start accusing bystanders if I wasn't careful.

Ross wrapped his tired arms around his fiancée and hugged her, his gaze finding me on the couch. "Hey, Natalie, how's it going? I hope I didn't interrupt anything."

"Not at all. Yaz, I gotta get back. You take care of that fiancé of yours."

Both Ross and Yaz said, "I will."

Sunday morning, I attempted to contact Luis. It took three hours, but he finally called me back. I was grateful he had the same cell phone number I had stored in my phone from years past.

When I asked him to do a background check on Alan Booker, he huffed, and I thought he was going to hang up on me. "I already told you too much the other day. I could get into a lot of trouble for leaking information on an ongoing investigation, you know."

"Oh, come on, Luis." Another fact I knew about my ex was that he had no trouble bending the rules. He'd even taken weed from the evidence locker once to smoke. That was many years ago, and I had to assume he'd matured. He was a husband and a father now.

"I'm sorry, but someone was peering in my window the other night, and it freaked me out."

"What? You never mentioned that. When did this happen?"

I relayed the story. "And I have his license plate number. There is something not right about him, Luis. I mean, who blows fireballs from his mouth? In his backyard, no less. For no apparent reason. And why did he have so many gas cans that time? For all we know, he could be your arsonist. And if he is, you'd be the person who found him." Yes, I was dangling a carrot, but I sensed I needed to. "*Please*, Luis? If you don't find anything on him, no one will know."

I could hear him exhale. "Fine, give me his license plate number."

Monday came, and so did lots of houses that needed cleaning. It was okay. I had some nice clients that I enjoyed seeing, including Mrs. Armstrong, who let me bring Daisy with me. We talked about the warmer weather while I worked.

"My son brought me some doggy treats for Daisy. Mind if I give her one?"

"You are so sweet, Mrs. Armstrong. Do you mind if I take a look at the bag?" When it came to Daisy's health, I checked everything. "They look good, Mrs. Armstrong. Thank you. I'm sure she'll love them."

Perched in her rising recliner, my sweet client bent down to give Daisy her morsel, who gobbled it right up. "How's your mom, by the way? Still seeing Harry?"

"You know, she hasn't seen him much lately." *Why did you say that? This isn't your business.* "But I think they're fine. You know how it is; people get busy."

By the time I had finished cleaning Mrs. Armstrong's house, my stomach was begging for dinner. It didn't help matters that I had brought along a container of chicken soup from my mother's batch, which I had warmed up for Mrs. Armstrong, infusing the air with everything my stomach wanted to devour.

"Stay for dinner?"

"Oh, no. I appreciate that, but I've gotta get back." I wanted Mrs. Armstrong to have enough soup for a few nights, and my staying would dwindle her stock. I also knew her son would be by. He lived close and checked on her often.

Happy that this was my last job of the day, I loaded my cleaning equipment into my van while Mrs. Armstrong kept Daisy happy, not that the pup was ever really happy once I had left her. She wanted to be with me or my mother always. Unless Sadie was around, in which case she forgot anyone else existed.

I took Daisy from her lap. "Okay, Mrs. Armstrong. See you in a couple of weeks. And thank you for giving Daisy a treat."

"You take care now, dear."

I plunked myself and my pup into the driver's seat when I noticed a piece of paper tucked under the windshield wiper. It was so far down that I barely saw it. I placed Daisy in the doggy bed, taking up the passenger seat, and slipped out to grab it. Maybe it was another job? I'd had potential customers leave notes before, but only after I had put the Dust Bunnies decal on the side of the van. "We take the worry out of cleaning" was my idea for our slogan.

Only this wasn't a potential client; it was a handwritten note.

> We need to talk.
>
> A

Aaron?

Chapter 21

Natalie

We need to talk?

About what? That question gnawed at my thoughts the entire drive home. And why leave me a note? Why not text? *Texts can be tracked.* How did he find me? Was he stalking me? Sweet Jesus, was *this* man after me now?

Get in line.

My mother and I pored over the note.

"What does it mean? . . . Why did he leave you a note? . . . How did he know where you'd be?"

"I don't know, Ma!" I barked, hissing under my breath. "I'm sorry. I've thought those same things. None of this makes sense to me either. Should I try to call him?"

My mother returned to the counter to finish chopping garlic and ginger for her broccoli stir fry. The pungent odor offered notes of sweet citrus, the garlic a savory chaser.

Honestly, if it weren't for my mother's cooking skills, I'd be eating takeout on a regular basis. Cleaning houses wasn't the only reason my waistline had diminished.

Her knife chopped away while her mind worked on my latest problem. "I think you should call the police." *Chop, chop, chop.*

I waved the handwritten note in the air. "And say what? This isn't exactly a threat." A thudding boom reached my ears from somewhere outside, and the house seemed to vibrate. "Do you hear that? Do you *feel* that?"

My mother halted her chopping. "Yes, where is it coming from?" She wiped her hands clean with a wet rag and followed me to the front door. Daisy was already barking and rushing around our legs.

"Can you keep Daisy inside?" I rushed out the door, where the volume rose exponentially. If my ears weren't deceiving me, it was some sort of heavy metal music. I couldn't identify the band, and I knew my share of hard rock bands. My head turned toward Alan's house, the source of the noise. Bass pounded against the walls of his house at an alarming decibel. Unlucky for us, we were the only house next to him. On the other side of Alan, a street and a cluster of pines separated his lawn from the other houses in the neighborhood. Behind us, a conservation area restricted building. When my parents bought this place, they loved the privacy. It was a major selling point.

I crouched down and rushed over to a large oak tree taking root in our front yard, hoping it would hide me.

Christ, the bass alone was making his windows shake. My ribs rattled. What the hell was Alan doing? There was a noise ordinance in this area, but I was pretty sure it didn't kick in until late at night. His old maroon sedan remained sad and alone in his driveway, the windows fogged by grime. The man never had people over, which fit right into the psychotic profile I had constructed for him.

Alan was trying to get either my attention or my mother's. I suspected the former, considering the dark figure standing at my window not too long ago, and the fireball he performed in his backyard.

The music stopped, leaving dead silence in its wake. A rush of leaves floated down the neighborhood road, carried by a spring breeze. The sun had started its descent, but not enough to provide me cover. My back matted against the trunk of our tree, bark scratching into my skin. I tried to decide what to do.

A deep laugh crept across the gap between our house and his. Dread filled my chest. *Is he laughing at me?* Had I won some lottery ticket that attracted crazy people? A door opened and closed. Was he outside now? Or was he outside before and was now inside? My mind reeled. I waited and listened for the crack of a branch or a footfall of some sort, my heart hammering against my ribcage.

Mom opened the front door, holding Daisy in her arms. With frantic hands, I waved at her to close it. I didn't want her out here where it was unsafe. She abided; her eyes filled with worry.

I mustered the nerve to peek out from around the trunk of the tree. Nothing appeared to be out of the ordinary. Nothing new, anyway.

Was he done? He wanted to get my attention, and that was it? The sun was dropping lower, shades of deep blue and plum lending an almost bruised appearance.

A light flicked on in his kitchen. I peered over again. He was standing at the window, looking out. Why? *He knows I'm here.*

Alan waved, his large frame silhouetted against the light shining behind him. I couldn't see his face. Somehow, I knew he was smiling. Was he toying with me now? Trying to terrorize me?

Anger bubbled up in my chest at all these recent events with men. Justin felt he had the right to possess me. *This isn't over*. Aaron played with my emotions and cast me out of his life *and* his house, branding me a liar and a con woman. And this psycho was trying to scare and intimidate me. I'd had enough. I came around the side of the tree and faced him. I stuck my middle finger in the air and thrust it in his direction. *Fuck you, asshole!*

Alan's shoulders vibrated. *Go ahead and laugh, weirdo.*

And then I saw.

I rushed into the house, slamming the door shut, and pressed my back against it. I took deep breaths and tried to shake the image of what I'd seen out of my head.

"What happened?" With an excited Daisy in her arms, my mother stood at the window.

"He . . . I . . ." It took me a moment. "He was jerking off at the window, Ma. He . . . he wanted me to see him. He was looking right at me!" My blood turned cold from the sight of it. *Pervert. Sicko.*

While she ranted her outrage, I grabbed my cell phone off the counter and dialed Luis's number. I knew I was pushing it with my ex, but something had to be done about this guy. There had to be a law against exposing oneself, right?

"Officer Lopez speaking."

"Luis, this is Natalie again. Were you able to do a background check on Alan Booker?"

"Natalie, if you don't stop calling me, I'm gonna have to block your number."

"There's something wrong with him, Luis. He was just blaring his music so loud I thought it was gonna shatter his windows. I went outside, and he was watching me from his kitchen window. The man pulled his pants down and started jerking off, for Christ's sake."

Luis exhaled loudly. I imagined him rubbing his eyes with his thumb and forefinger, the way people do when annoyed. "If he keeps his music loud after eleven, you can call in a noise complaint. And what the man does inside his house is none of your business. If you don't like it, don't stand there watching him. You accuse him of being dangerous, but you're the one exhibiting erratic behavior. Don't call me on this number again, Natalie, or we're gonna have a problem." *Click.* The call ended.

"Argh. We're not getting any help from Luis." I tossed my cell onto the kitchen table with a *clank.* I hadn't even mentioned the letter from Aaron. If it *was* from Aaron. *Who else would it be?* They'd signed it, A. *But wait.* Alan also began with an A. Jesus, who the hell left me that note?

"I can't believe this is happening." My mother flitted around the kitchen, carrying Daisy in her arms, who also seemed agitated. I suspected the pup sensed our discomfort. She put Daisy down and cried. "I can't believe my daughter is having to deal with such abusive men. Maybe we should move. We could start your business in another state." Tears pooled in her blue-and-gold eyes.

"It's okay, Ma. We'll figure it out." I kept my voice calm, hoping to ease her worries. "No one has done anything to abuse me. Alan has serious issues, for sure. And I'm not entirely certain how we are gonna deal with him, but we've got this!" I wrapped one arm over her shoulders and jostled her a bit. "Right? We've got this. Just like everything else we've been through, this, too, shall pass." I craned my neck to get her to look at me, which she did. "Right?"

She nodded, wiping a few tears away.

Knock, knock, knock.

We both just about jumped out of our skins, poor Daisy going berserk.

"Jesus, Mary, and Joseph." My mother's hand went to her heart. "If that's Alan, I'm calling the cops. The real ones." She rushed her angry legs to the door while I grabbed Daisy, who was barking so loud it was giving me a headache. I also grabbed my cell from the kitchen table, ready to dial 911.

With her hands curled into fists, my mother looked through the peephole and unclenched her hands, her jaw still tight. She opened the door to reveal Harry standing there, his eyes pouty and his chin lowered. "Good evening, Rose. Is this a bad time?" He stuttered a bit, his hands restless at his sides.

My mother crossed her arms over her chest. "Is this a bad time for what, exactly?" The irritability in her voice did its best to mask the hurt feelings that I knew she harbored.

"To talk? I know I owe you an explanation. And if you allow me, I'll do my best to help you understand my . . . situation." Harry's brown eyes reached out for forgiveness. Or at least, a chance.

My mother uncrossed her arms and held the door handle in her grasp as though ready to close it at any moment. "You stormed out of here weeks ago, and I haven't heard from you since!" She flailed one hand in my direction. "And that is *after* you yelled at my daughter, who is going through some rather troubling times right now. I understand what happened to you was awful, Harry, but you are *not* the only one going through stuff! You shut me out. I spent most of my life with a man who did that to me. I thought you were different."

My mother's words crushed Harry's spirit, his shoulders practically buckling under her ire.

His voice was weak, but carried a strong message. "I'm not perfect, Rose Dugan, and I don't profess to be, but I can assure you, I *am* different."

She huffed. "From my standpoint, I don't believe it." Her head shook with fervor. And then her lower lip quivered.

That was when Harry breached the threshold. "I'm awful sorry, Rose. I know I have acted like an ass. You have tried to be there for me, and I haven't been a good partner to you. I'm sorry

I haven't been there for you and for Natalie." His sorrowful brown eyes shifted his gaze in my direction. "I'm sorry, Natalie. I had no right to speak to you that way."

After what I'd been dealing with, it was refreshing to hear *someone* take responsibility for his actions. "It's okay, Harry."

Once she had realized it was a friend and not a foe at the door, Daisy had stopped barking.

"Can you close the door so I can put Daisy down?"

"Of course." Harry complied, allowing me to free my excited pup from my arms, who ran over to Harry, lifting her front paws against his knees, which she often did when seeing someone she knew. Harry rewarded her efforts with sweet talk and pampering. "How's our little Daisy doing? . . . Yes, I'm glad to see you, too. . . . Aren't you a sweet girl?. . . What a good girl you are."

I went over and grabbed her up again. "I'll bring her into my room. I need to take a shower anyway." I suspected these two needed some privacy.

* * *

After my shower, I sat on my bed and stared at my phone. Soft voices drifted down the hallway from the living room. No yelling or angry footfalls told me Mom and Harry must've made up. I was happy for them. I liked Harry. And having a man around right now—a sane one—wasn't exactly a bad idea. It felt as if the walls were closing in.

While Daisy enjoyed a nap, I sat at my small desk and opened my laptop. My first search brought up a list of security cameras, which I compared and ordered. We needed to be able to see the front and backyards, especially when I was up every night with Daisy. Luckily, she only needed to go out once before dawn, but still. And we had a fenced-in yard. Another advantage.

I was pretty sure the man at my window was Alan. He was a pervert who liked to shock people. But Justin was still a possibility.

I stared at my phone some more. I decided that whatever was going on with Aaron, I needed to face it. It had been a week since I had left his house with no contact from him.

I wrote four text drafts before I came up with something that I was comfortable with.

> Why did you leave a note on my car? How did you know where I was? And what do you want to talk about?

I waited for those three dots to tell me he was typing his response. Only none appeared.

Maybe it *was* Alan. I doubted it. Alan lived right next door. Why would he follow me around town? *We need to talk* also didn't fit. The note came from Aaron.

The sound of knuckles tapping on my bedroom door lifted Daisy's head. My mother cracked the door open and spoke in a low voice. "I just wanted to tell you that dinner is ready. Harry is going to join us. I hope that's okay." Her red eyes shone with tears, her face revealing a few emotional blotches.

"Everything okay between you two?"

She shuffled her slippered feet into my room and closed the door with a gentle *click*. "I think so. We have a lot more to discuss, but we're on the right track. Harry divorced his wife seven years ago, and from what he told me, it was bitter. His only son was grown by then, but apparently Lisa worked hard at making him look bad in front of Bryton. When Logan caused all that trouble, Lisa sided with Logan. It was one of the reasons Harry chose to let things go."

Harry hadn't felt supported back then, even by his family. I could understand his apprehension about opening that can of worms. "Poor Harry. How are things now? I mean, with Bryton?"

"Better. But he doesn't want to do anything to hurt the progress he's made with him."

"Makes sense. I'm glad things are better." I blinked, my heart drawing sympathy for my mother's man. "His ex sounds like a real bitch."

"I agree." A slow smile stretched her lips wide. "He's invited me over for dinner next weekend. If it's okay with you, he may stay over here tonight." The blotches flourished, creating a full-on blush. "He asked me to stay over at his place." Her voice lifted with those words. "I told him I don't feel comfortable leaving you here alone. But I could do dinner."

As much as it shamed me to admit, I didn't feel comfortable being alone either.

Standing next to me, she brushed one palm over my hair in a soothing way.

"That's great, Ma. I like Harry. And at least one of us has found someone nice." I didn't mean my words to sound as pathetic as they spilled out.

"Oh, Natalie. You'll meet the right person, I'm sure of it. You're just dealing with some unsavory characters right now. I can't make sense of it." She inhaled and released a calming breath. "As you said, 'We've got this.' We'll figure it out. Together." I loved hearing her optimism. I needed that from her. When I was younger, she wasn't capable. I never blamed her for her shortcomings, but that didn't reduce the need for a mom's supportive shoulder.

I pushed my chair back and rose. "I ordered surveillance cameras for the front and the back of the house and paid for rush delivery. If that isn't enough, I may even get us a security system."

"That's great, honey. I bet Harry can install them."

* * *

Even with Harry in the house, the promise of security cameras on their way, and my curtains closed, I tossed and turned. At midnight, my phone vibrated on my nightstand.

It was a text from Aaron.

> I wasn't stalking you. I happened to be driving by and saw your van. I wanted to apologize for my behavior the other day. Figured it best to do something like that in person.

More dots flashed on the screen.

> Would you be up for a visit this Saturday night? The camper is still out there. We could pick up where we left off?

Huh? The man had kicked me out of his house. And after accusing me of being a liar and a schemer. There would be no *picking up where we left off*. How odd that he would suggest such a thing. It seemed out of character for him. Just like with Justin, I was getting whiplash from his mood swings.

No dots responded from my end. I was glad it was late, so he wouldn't know whether or not I had seen his confusing text. His message was not only insensitive but also arrogant, something I had never sensed from him. This only proved that I didn't know the man at all. I'd opened myself up to a complete stranger. And I'd suffered the consequences as a result.

Big mistake.

It was noon the next day when I finally replied.

I appreciate the apology, but I have plans this weekend. Thanks, anyway.

But we shared something special, Natalie. Let's not let my attitude come between us. I am sorry about my behavior. I really am. And I didn't mean what I said. Not one word. Except for the good stuff.

I stared at my phone in disbelief. "What?" This didn't sound at all like the recluse who struggled to trust people. Aaron was really putting himself out there. *Maybe he feels he has to.* It was flattering but made me a little weary. What if I went all the way out there to find Mr. Hyde had returned? On the other side of that coin was the hope that he meant what he said. Or texted, in this case. *I'll try not to let you down.* That was also Aaron, and I had heard him say those words with my own ears.

I thought long and hard about his offer. That took me several days. Flowers arrived on Friday.

Please forgive me. A.

I finally settled on a reply.

Thanks for the flowers. But I think it's best if we don't see each other right now.

It was difficult to text, but if anything had taught me about men lately, it was to tread lightly.

A week passed, and a letter arrived in the mail.

Dear Natalie,
I know I screwed things up with you. And I don't

blame you for not wanting to see me anymore. I've been alone for so long, I've forgotten how to treat people. I know that's no excuse. You think that because I was a fireman, I am brave. I'm not. I'm a coward, which is why I'm writing you this letter and not calling you. The truth is, I've never been brave. I've only done what everyone else has expected of me. And I failed. I didn't deserve the badge I wore. But none of that was your fault. All you did was make me happy.

I drove by a campsite the other day, and it reminded me of us and our night together. That was the night I fell for you. I hope someday you will forgive me. I am a selfish man, Natalie. Help me change that.

Until then, my heart belongs to you.

A

I scrutinized that letter, so much so, I caused the paper to thin. Aaron was everything I wanted in a partner. He messed up. Was it worth my helping him try to fix it? I knew what my heart wanted to do.

I texted him.

I forgive you. Aaron. It's okay. I'm fine.

Please come see me Saturday night. Let me show you how much I care.

My fingers answered before my brain could stop them.

I'll think about it. I can't do this Saturday, though. I have plans with my best friend. But maybe Sunday I could stop by.

It was kind of a strange lie, but I didn't want to be so available. I also preferred daytime to night.

I could have asked him to come to my house, but I wasn't sure I wanted to expose my home or my mother to so many unknowns.

See you then. Can't wait.

I called Yaz immediately. "Got any plans Saturday night?"

"I don't think so. I'll check with Ross, but I think he's working on Saturday photographing a wedding. I think it starts at four. His last job recommended him. I'm hoping this will allow him to leave that job at the plant even sooner. Sorry, I didn't mean to rant. Why do you ask? What do you have in mind?"

"I don't know. Dinner out, maybe hang at your place afterward. Aaron contacted me."

"And you waited till now to spill those beans. You should have started with that. What did he say?"

* * *

Friday arrived, my stomach already tight and uncomfortable about my trip to Aaron's house on Sunday. Yaz wasn't feeling well again. This time her stomach was acting up.

"I hope we can still get together," she'd said over the phone.

"Well, let's see how you're feeling tomorrow. We can always reschedule."

"But wasn't I your alibi for Aaron?"

"Meh, he won't know whether or not we got together. At the time that I told him that, I was just trying to be . . . not so available. You know what I mean?"

"Oh, yeah. I totally get it."

"Do you think you have a stomach bug?"

"Not sure. I'm just really nauseous, especially around Ross's aftershave."

"Yaz, maybe you're pregnant."

"No, I don't think so." The waver in her voice hinted uncertainty.

"Maybe you should get a test and find out. And no wine in the meantime," I said with mock annoyance.

"Yes, *Mom*."

I spent my Friday night at home with Mom and Harry. The three of us sat around the dining room table, sipping a bottle of cabernet—compliments of Harry—savoring roasted cauliflower, pulled pork sandwiches, potato salad, and coleslaw for dinner, also brought by my mother's main squeeze. He even came with a rack of ribs. I licked my fingers with every bite. When the conversation steered toward James Logan, we had progressed to our second bottle of wine.

"That man is . . . *was* not someone you ever wanted to cross. He was one of the most evil men I had ever met. He cheated everyone he knew. Your mom told me about the research you've both been doing and the places that burned. And the suspects you came up with." After Harry pushed his plate back, he rested his elbows on the table, clasping his hands in front of him. "I can't say I blame either of you for including *my* name on that list."

I shot my mother a you-told-him? look. I couldn't believe she had done that.

She just shrugged.

Harry seemed to notice. "It's okay, Natalie. I gave you plenty of reasons to doubt me. So, let me set the record straight. As I assured your mother, I have never been a violent man, and I'm too old to start now." His smile spread wide before the humor left his voice. "No, Mr. Logan has his own crosses to bear, wherever he is now. I don't think you have to worry about Aaron either. He's a good man."

"Even good men can be pushed over the edge, Harry. Aaron has a deep-seated hatred for Logan. Or did have."

Unclasping his hands, Harry stared down at his now empty plate. "You can't go from being someone who would risk their life to save others, only to turn into a murderer. I've met Aaron more than once. He was severely injured in that apartment building blaze, but that wasn't all. From what his friends at the firehouse had told me, he struggled more with losing two people on his watch. Your mom said the building wasn't being managed well. Just another Logan trait. Have you considered that whoever is behind the fires is related to the couple who died? Or knew them?"

I had just taken one last bite of my ribs and had placed the remnants on my plate, the tangy barbecue sauce coating my tongue with a smoky tang. I swallowed quickly. "Yes, many times. The couple's names were Stephen and Jenny Anders. I've cross-referenced their names with creepy Alan next door and even Justin and Aaron, but I came up short." I wiped my mouth with a wet nap before I worked on my fingers. My fingernails looked like I'd been digging in the dirt, so I worked on them as well. "I agree with you that the fires could be related to their deaths. Given the condition of the building from the complaints I read, the fire was 100 percent preventable. So, if someone related to Stephen and Jenny is holding a grudge, I wouldn't be surprised."

"Did the couple have any kids? Seems like that would be a good place to start."

* * *

Harry's observations reignited my inquisitive mind. The fires had to be related to what happened at Shetland Apartments, which burned on March 17th, five years ago. The recent fires began on the same date. It was too close to be a coincidence.

Yaz still wasn't feeling well the next day and canceled our plans via text.

Did you get a pregnancy test yet?

I checked the calendar, and I should be starting my cycle any day now, so I wanted to wait a day or two first. We've been careful, so I don't think so. And I hope not. My mother would kill me! 😳

She was right about that. Her mother had certain standards when it came to her children's relationships. Ross stayed over with Yaz all the time, but her mother was never the wiser. Plus, the whole rushed-wedding thing. I was sure it wouldn't take much to send Mrs. Mounivong into a frenzy. It was silly, really. Yaz was a grown woman in her mid-thirties.

You cleaned for the Fletchers this past week, didn't you? Didn't they have a stomach bug not too long ago? 🤮

I did clean for them! And yes, they were sick, but that was weeks ago. Like in March, right? 😨

Hard to believe it occurred a month ago, the middle of April sailing by.

If it's a stomach bug, it's a mild one. I haven't thrown up, but I've come close. Ross had to put away his aftershave.

I was pretty sure that becoming sensitive to smells was a

symptom of pregnancy, but I figured she didn't need my two cents on the matter. We'd find out soon enough. I offered one thought that would hopefully ease her worries.

If it turns out that you are pregnant, you're getting married in like three weeks, Yaz, and you can always fudge the timeline. You lived with Marty back in your twenties, and your mother never knew. Don't worry about it. 😬

Thanks, Nat. 🩶 🩶

Want me to bring over some chicken soup? We have plenty.

How about tomorrow? I'm too tired for company tonight. 😵‍💫

I wasn't an expert on pregnancy, but being overly tired seemed like another possible symptom. And since I considered Yaz my sister in all ways but one, I was excited about the idea of becoming an auntie. She loved Ross. They had a future together. This wasn't awful news. And we weren't getting any younger. The thought of her moving away was another story. My gut wrenched every time I thought of it.

Okay, I'm supposed to go see Aaron tomorrow, but I'll check-in with you before I go.

Are you sure that's a good idea? I still don't think you should go out there alone, Nat. ☠️

See, you're already acting like a doting mom. 😇

I'm serious! 😠

She did her best to appear mad, but I knew she wasn't, not really. Just worried. I was too.

I know. I spoke to Harry about Aaron, and he thinks Aaron is a good person. And he wants to apologize. You know his location, and so do Mom and Harry. I'm good. We can even do our protocol if you want.

Talk tomorrow, Nat. Love you. 

Love you too. Feel better. 

I was about to search for Stephen and Jenny's obituaries when my phone chimed with a text from my bedroom desk.

It was Aaron again.

Tonight is supposed to be a beautiful night. If your plans change, I bet we could spot some Or even afterward. I really miss you, Natalie. Let me show you how much.

That one made my insides go slightly weightless, like something you'd experience on a roller coaster.

Aaron was trying really hard to convince me he was sorry. I appreciated his efforts, knowing it couldn't have been easy for a man who had been alone for so many years. It also helped to ease my trepidation about seeing him again.

I'll check with my friend. Maybe I can switch things around.

Yes, I was lying to him again, but he deserved this one.

Great! Let me know. I'll keep the stoked.

Aaron was putting himself out there. Big time. Then again,

texting had a way of allowing a person to communicate without having to speak or stumble over one's words. I'd used texting in the past to deliver a message that I might not have been able to speak as clearly, once breaking up with a man who would have cut me off every third word. Maybe Aaron was doing the same, only in this case he was trying to fix things, not end them.

I went back to work on my pseudo-investigation. What I discovered was that Stephen and Jenny had one son named Kevin. The information was in their obituaries. Interestingly enough, Kevin was about my age. He was a high school science teacher at the time of their death. *Science, huh?* It made me think of the show *Breaking Bad*, where a science teacher turned meth dealer. Could Kevin have gone to the dark side? *Could Alan be Kevin?* He was also about my age.

Flashing blue lights permeated my drapes. I peered out just as several police cars skidded into Alan's driveway.

Chapter 22

Natalie

I threw on a sweatshirt and a pair of sneakers, my leggings already offering cover, and rushed through the house toward the kitchen door. My mother and Harry were watching *Jeopardy* from the couch, Daisy on the floor asleep.

"What's going on?" My mother's back stiffened, curiosity widening her eyes.

I felt bad about alarming her once again. "I don't know. A bunch of police cars are over at Alan's house. I'm gonna go see what's what."

Mom and Harry flew off the couch, Daisy at their heels. "We're going with you," my mother said as she tried to calm Daisy, who was frantic.

I was out the door in an instant.

Wearing standard police garb with a name tag that read *Officer Helen Jones*, a young policewoman with high cheekbones, dark skin, and short black hair—covered mostly by her department-issued baseball cap—stepped forward and raised her palm. "Miss, you need to stay back."

"Why? What's going on? Has Alan done something? Is he the arsonist?" I craned my neck to see inside his house. The lights were on and shadows moved about.

With her hand raised like a Stop sign, Officer Jones kept her tone firm. "I cannot answer that at this time. For your own protection, miss, please keep your distance. Do you know Alan?"

Daisy's barks emanated from the house. Poor thing, I should have carried her out. She was probably scared, wondering what was happening.

"Sort of. I know he's strange. I actually called—" I stopped speaking.

Alan burst out of his door outfitted in his typical sweatpants and a not-so-white T-shirt. A policeman held one arm; a policewoman held the other, Alan's hands cuffed behind his back. Together, they ushered him over to one of the cruisers and folded him inside, making sure his head didn't hit anything solid. A familiar face came hurrying over to me. Luis looked at Officer Jones holding guard.

"I've got this, Helen. I know her. I'll take care of this."

"Copy that." She pointed as she stepped away. "Hey, nice work on this one, Lopez." Officer Jones then spoke into her shoulder mic as she walked away.

Luis placed one hand on his hip, the one sporting his holstered gun.

Luis widened his stance. "I finally did a background check on your neighbor. And you were right; this guy is bad news. His last name isn't Booker. It's Baker. He's wanted in three states for sexual assault and battery. He also robbed two convenience stores. Apparently, he skipped bail and has been on the run since, using a stolen identity." His eyes grew sheepish as he rubbed his jaw. "You had said he blew fire in his backyard, which reminded me of a story I had heard about a year-and-a-half ago."

You could have told me that sooner, Luis. I tried to hide my annoyance. Mainly because I wanted to hear more.

"Apparently, Alan has done the fire-breathing exercise in front of several women as a scare tactic. It had become his calling card, only he never stayed in one place long enough for us to apprehend him. He paid cash for that house. Not sure where he got the money, but we intend to find out." He met my gaze. "Anyway, I know I was rude to you the other day, and I felt bad about it, so I checked into him."

I tightened my jaw. "Why didn't you call me?" *Calm down, he's telling you now.* In all the battles I'd waged as of late, I didn't feel up to another. "I *knew* something wasn't right about him. What about the fires? Is he connected to them?" Shoving my annoyance toward Luis aside, having Alan gone amazed and relieved me.

Luis shook his head. "We don't believe so. Those cans you saw contained lamp oil for fire breathing, but it can be used in arson. We will be conducting an extensive interrogation. For now, it appears he's not involved. That's not his typical MO, but we will look into *everything,* including searching his house."

The arsonist was connected to James Logan. That much I knew. Considering Alan was new to the area, I doubted he even knew who James Logan was, even if he'd bought his parents' house. Creepy, yes. But probably not the arsonist they were looking for.

"It must've been him at my window the other day." I shivered outwardly, and not because I was cold. In fact, the mid-April temperatures were holding steady in the low seventies during the day, the low sixties at night.

Behind me, my mother spoke up. "What a pervert. Maybe next time you'll listen to my daughter when she tells you something, *Officer*!" She wagged her finger at Luis. "That man was harassing her."

"Yes, ma'am." Luis looked down and then up at me. "Again, I'm sorry, Natalie. My bad."

"Hmph." My mother, still agitated, shot daggers from her protective eyes, her chin defiantly high.

Daisy continued to fill the void with her distress from the house.

"Come on, love, let's get inside. Before Daisy blows a gasket. Nothing going on out here anymore." Harry wrapped his arm around her shoulders and guided her back into the house as the police cars dispersed.

I loved that she had someone who cared for her on this level. My father never did.

"I will need to get a statement from you and your mother." Luis made a motion with his hand between us. "Are we okay? You made me look good today. I appreciate the assist. And I won't forget it."

Assist? I had handed him the whole enchilada. I shifted from one foot to the other and back again, my legs restless. When it came down to it, what did it matter? They'd solved the case. They'd apprehended Alan. One less name on our murder board. "Yeah, we're fine. When do you need our statements?"

Luis's radio crackled from his shoulder, causing him to turn away and address whomever was contacting him. When finished, he took a few steps away. "Tomorrow is fine. We want to do it soon, though. Witnesses tend to forget the details over time, but we have enough on this guy to put him away for a while. Quite the rap sheet." He raised a hand in a sort of half-wave. "I can even come by here to save you and your mom a trip to the station. I'll call you tomorrow morning and set it up. Anyway, thanks again for the tip. Take care, Natalie."

"Yeah, you're welcome, and you too." I wanted to grill him about the arson case, but chose not to. Instead, I shuffled back into the house, where Daisy greeted me at the door.

With one case solved, I was feeling pretty good about myself. I called Aaron, which would go a long way in easing my apprehension about driving to his place. Mom and Harry resumed their recorded *Jeopardy* episode, while I dialed Aaron's number from the kitchen and waited. No answer. A half hour passed, and I tried again. Same nonresponse. The phone rang through on both calls. It didn't go right to voicemail, indicating his phone was at least on. I didn't leave a message.

Hmm. *So, you won't talk to me, but you'll text?* Or was he away from his phone?

> I tried to call you. I feel we should have a conversation before I drive out there.

Again, no response. Maybe he was asleep? It was eight o'clock. He didn't strike me as someone who would keep his phone close, given he avoided people at all costs.

The next day, I finally received my reply at 9:00 a.m.

> Sorry, Spent most of my ray in the woods yesterday choping woode. And then I cut hnd with Dy axe. Had to drive Charloppville To get stitches. I'm at the hospital nW. I cNt wait to see you.

I had to decipher his text a bit, but considering the condition of his hand, he'd done a better job texting than I would have.

I'm sorry about your hand. How bad is it? Isn't it hard to text? Want me to call?

Nh, I can txt. Not sURe of damge. WRApped in Band-Aids and a cloDth. NT MUch help..

Send me a pic of your hand.

Why did I ask him to do that? My inner voice answered: *You want to make sure he's not lying*. I wasn't sure why I would think such a thing, but I did.

A moment later, a pic came in that was rather gruesome. Layers of white cloth wrapped around his hand, blood seeping through the material. Had he ripped a sheet to make the bandage? The frayed edges indicated as much. There was also a lot of dirt on the cloth. I almost gagged at the sight of it.

Ouch. That looks nasty.

YGH, I neede oto watCh what I'm doing. Ttal bonehd MOove.

What time will you be done? Do you want me to come another day?

No PloeaSE Cm 😍

I had wanted to touch base with him, maybe bridge the gap between what happened when I was there last, but given his injured hand and the fact that he was probably sitting in a waiting room with several other potential patients around him, this didn't feel like the appropriate time.

Text me when you get home. I'll leave soon after that. And I'll pick up pizza with my two good hands. 🩶

YoU gt it. WIShe me 🍀

Good luck! 🍀🍀🍀

Several shipments had arrived from a place I'd found that sold cleaners at wholesale prices. I took Daisy with me to deliver them to the storage unit. By noon, I still hadn't heard from Aaron. I knew visits to the emergency room could take some time from when Jack had broken his leg jumping off our roof during a snowstorm when he was younger, the one Dr. Clark had set. We were there for hours, the snowstorm causing multiple car accidents on the highway that day.

The cleaning supplies weren't the only thing that had shown up on our doorstep. While I waited, I helped Harry install the video cameras for the front and back of the house. They also allowed viewing of both side yards. Mostly. Given that Alan was gone, the need for such security had dwindled. Then again, one never knew what strange event was coming next. I thought of Justin, who had hopefully moved on. Men like Justin and Alan needed to come with warning signs: *This man could be hazardous to your health.*

Being an electrician, Harry was of great service to me and had the equipment installed like a pro. As the hours ticked away, I worried that Aaron's hand was in worse condition than he had surmised, possibly needing surgery if the wound was deep enough.

At two o'clock, my phone chimed from the side table in the living room, where Daisy and I were cuddling on the couch watching a romantic comedy. Mom and Harry had gone out to visit his house for the first time. My mother was so excited to see his place, and I couldn't wait to hear all about it. Harry also told her that he wanted my mom to meet his son, Bryton. Life was moving in the right direction for them. Since the cops had apprehended Alan, she was easing up on her watchful eye over me.

The text from Aaron read.

> I'm on my way home. Why don't you come around five? Much easier to text through dictation. Loving CarPlay.

> How's your hand?

> Hand is sore. Fifteen stitches. I'd call, but I'm about to enter a dead zone. I may lose you.

> No worries, see you at five. Drive safe.

With Mom gone, I called Yaz to see how she was feeling and to ask if she felt well enough to watch Daisy for me, since Mom was occupied.

"Sure, Sadie will love to see her."

I showered and primped before Daisy and I traveled to Yaz's apartment an hour later. I was dying to know how she was feeling. Did she change her mind about purchasing a pregnancy test? I was beside myself with curiosity.

Yaz met me at the door, Sadie trying her best to run outside, despite Yaz's efforts to stop her. I hurried inside to make her job easier. Daisy was moving so erratically, I practically dropped her as I attempted to put her down.

"Okay, okay, chill out, Daisy. Sheesh."

The two pups dashed into the living room to wrestle and reacquaint themselves. "Thank you for watching Daisy. I won't be gone too long." I stood near the door with my shoes on.

"No problem. I took your advice and bought a test. I started thinking that my symptoms were too strange for a bug. Anyway, when you said you were coming over, I took the test. I was going to wait for you, but I had to know." She was pale, her expression hard to read.

"And?"

She exhaled. "I'm pregnant."

I fanned my hands out wide. "What? Congratulations!" I wrapped my arms around her and held her tight. "I'm so happy for you, Yaz. You're getting married in a few weeks and starting a family." I pulled away and held her shoulders firm. "Have you told Ross yet?"

"No, not yet. I'm hoping when he finds out, he'll leave that job for good. I rarely see him these days." Her eyes registered that something else was going on. "He really wants to move to Texas, Nat. His father is ill, and Ross is worried he's running out of time to be with him. I told him to go already, and we can figure out what to do long term when he gets back. He also has aunts and uncles and cousins there. He said he feels the need to be closer to his family." Unlike the pregnancy news and the proposal, Yaz's tone didn't carry that same enthusiasm. "I'm not crazy about moving so far away, but I think I can talk my mother into moving with us. The problem is, I don't want to leave *you*."

I didn't want her to leave me, either. "When does he want to do this? What about our business?"

Her shoulders slumped. "I know, I've tried to explain that to him." Tears glimmered in her eyes, which she quickly wiped away. "I'm such an emotional mess." Her hand covered her mouth as though hoping to block the flood of emotions. "Is that normal for pregnancy?"

I shrugged, unsure. "It's okay, Yaz, if you move, we'll still see each other. You could start your own decorating business. I've always told you how good you'd be at it, and when the baby comes, I'll visit. *A lot.* So, make sure you get a nice big guest room for me." I was masking what I really felt, which was sad, so very sad. I never had a sister, and Jack was thousands of miles away. I shuddered at the thought of what my life would be like without Yaz. It would be one thing if I had a healthy relationship of my own. Heck, even my mother was moving on. And here I was stuck, right where I had been for most of my life. Single and lonely.

"I told Ross I'd think about it. But I couldn't make any moves right away. I still have to hide the fact that I'm pregnant from my mother. You know how our moms are. They seem to know everything."

I shook my head. "You got that right."

"I suspect she'll figure it out. But I'll hide it as best I can until we're married. I have a life here. And I have you. What if I can't make any friends there? What if his family doesn't like me?" More tears spilled, distress shaking her entire body.

I wrapped her in another bear hug. "Look, you have a lot on your plate right now. Take a few days and let this sink in. I can understand Ross wanting to be near his family. He wants to share them with you. And I know he loves you . . . very much." I let go of my friend. "I'll text Aaron that I can come another time. I don't want to leave you like this."

Yaz rolled her shoulders back and shooed me with her hand. "No way. Go. I'll be fine!"

"I can't leave you like this. You're my best friend." If I had my way, I'd never leave her.

Yaz wiped her cheeks dry with her hand, the dogs rushing past her feet to chase each other some more. "If you think this guy is worth it, you need to see this through. I know you, Nat. You don't give your heart to just anyone. If you want, I can follow you with the dogs in my car."

"I appreciate that, but it's not necessary. I've been in touch with him enough that I think it's fine. And Harry vouched for him as well. He's not going to do anything." I placed a hand over my heart. "And I'm not going to do anything either. That's not why I'm going."

Sniffling a few more times, Yaz gave me a once-over. "Your outfit says otherwise." She giggled at me before she chose a more serious tone. "Why are you going, then?"

I took a deep breath. "I don't know exactly. Something meaningful happened between us, Yaz, and I guess I want to see what it was. I have never felt that way with another man. Don't you think it's worth finding out if it was real?"

I watched her face for an answer. She nodded. "I do."

I put my hand on the doorknob.

"Just be careful. I've pinned his location and call if you need anything at all. I can be there in no time."

* * *

After texting Aaron from the pizza place that I was running late, I arrived at his house at twenty minutes past five. Fashionably late. I had to remind myself that Aaron was lucky I came at all. My hands were literally shaking as I checked my reflection in the mirror and straightened a few strands of hair away from my face. I chose a pair of tight capris jeans and a form-fitting light blue top for this occasion. I even wore my high-heeled sandals that laced up my calves. It was the sexiest outfit I owned, something Yaz had taken note of. I figured if this was my last time seeing Aaron that I wanted to make him suffer.

I grabbed the pizza—the scent of fresh tomato sauce and garlic making my stomach growl—and climbed out of my minivan, my feet dragging my nervous heart to his door. When I arrived there, I rang the bell and held my breath.

Through the beveled sidelight, a shadowy figure emerged,

the door opening to reveal Aaron in all his glory before me. And man, did he look good, his white *short-sleeve* T-shirt hugging his chest and arms in all the right ways, his faded jeans sexy as hell. No longer hiding, the flame tattoos riding up his arm bore witness to his suffering. All those feelings I harbored for this man returned in an instant. His amber eyes watched me, his mouth pursed. What was he thinking? Did he still want me here? Riveted in place, I was unable to speak. My heart, however, was beating out of my chest, the magnetic force between us nearly unbearable. I didn't just want Aaron. I ached for him.

He took the pizza from my hands and dropped it on the table in the foyer. He was back in no time, staring me down.

His lips twitched. What would he say to me? *I'm sorry?*

Hunger grew in his expressive eyes before he thrust himself forward, grabbing my face with both hands and planting one of the most passionate kisses I had ever experienced. His need for me overpowered. The strength of his essence against mine rendered me helpless. I opened my mouth and invited his tongue to roam, *my* tongue desperate to connect and rekindle what we had. His robust body moved so close I could feel the torment pumping his heart against my chest. What words couldn't provide, our bodies communicated.

My purse fell to the floor.

After the kiss, he held my forehead firmly against his as though unable to let go.

"I'm sorry." He spoke in a whisper. "I'm glad you're here." He grabbed my waist and lifted me up, my legs wrapping around his body of their own volition. Slamming the door shut, he carried me into the living room, where he kissed my face and neck like a man possessed. His powerful hands rode under my shirt, finding my breasts, where he excited my nipples, hardening against his touch. Before I knew what was happening, my sandals came off along with my capris.

Aaron knelt on the floor, pulling my panties off next, before he took my legs and draped them over his shoulders. Wasting no time, he plunged his face between my legs, his tongue riding up and down my center with the sole intent of driving me wild.

My back arched, my mouth groaning. "Oh, god." I grabbed his head to tether myself before an orgasm seized control. The entire scene took minutes, yet it felt as though I'd been gone for an eternity. The potency of his acts turned my muscles to jelly. It was then that I realized what had happened, common sense returning.

Aaron lifted his head, his eyes glowing with pride. "I should have done that last time you were here. I should have worshiped every inch of you, never letting you go. That was my mistake. And I never should have let you leave the way you did. I hope this begins to make up for my behavior. I told you I'd try not to let you down, and that is exactly what I did."

As I gathered my clothes and redressed, Aaron stood. The bulge in his pants was hard to ignore. It had to be uncomfortable.

When we were in the camper, and he had told me not to speak, his gaze intense, he carried me into the back and made love to me. I sensed the same urgency rippling off him now, yet he didn't make a move.

"Can I do something for *you* now?" I wasn't sure what he wanted. Pleasing him after what he'd just done for me was a no-brainer. Of course, I was all in. The tension between us had dissipated. *For me.* What did he feel?

His demeanor told me he struggled with conflicting ideas as he stood there, hands on his hips, staring at the floor. Finally, he lifted his gaze to meet mine. "You don't owe me anything, Natalie. You've already given me more than I deserve. After the way I behaved, I'm surprised you want anything to do with me anymore. But I want you to know that I didn't mean any of those things I said to you. I've been fucked in the head for years, and I'd gotten pretty goddamn good at keeping people away. Even though you probably didn't realize it, you've challenged me to be different. From the moment I met you, I found myself wanting things again I hadn't wanted in a long time." His eyes glistened with intense feelings that were boiling to the surface right in front of me.

He *was* sorry for his actions. It wasn't a ruse. More importantly, I now knew that what we felt for each other was real. It was as though we were linked by some higher power that had the ability to transform both of us into something better than ourselves when we were together.

It was my turn to come clean. "You know, Aaron, I've had friends over the years and boyfriends who came and went from my life. Aside from Yaz, few people have stuck around long enough to learn much about me, mainly because I kept my private thoughts to myself. Like you, it was easier to keep them away. My feelings about my parents, the divorce, and what it had done to my mother. Even the good memories, such as the summer of camping, I kept them all locked away. No one was interested enough to ask. Yet, with you, I was comfortable opening up about all of it. You made me feel safe and respected. Not only did you listen, giving my life your full attention, you paid homage to those memories, showing me how much you cared. When I said no one had ever done anything like that before, I wasn't kidding. If I've helped you see another path, I'm thrilled. You are too great a man to waste away blaming yourself for things that you couldn't possibly have prevented."

There it was. *My* truth. I laid bare who I was. A private person who wanted so desperately to share my life with him.

He let his head drop. "I don't want to be alone anymore, Natalie." His voice shook, tears falling to his feet like droplets of sad rain.

I went to him, wrapping my arms around his large frame, my hands caressing up and down his back. "You don't need to be alone anymore, Aaron. All you have to do is ask." I rested my head against his powerful chest before I looked up at him.

Wiping his cheeks dry, he gazed down into my eyes, his amber orbs surrounding me with a sense of warmth and adoration.

"I love you, Natalie. I want you with me always."

My soul filled with light. My heart blossomed with the prospect of spending my life with this man. Was it too soon for such thoughts? Not for me, it wasn't. I'd spent thirty-six years without him. "I love you, too, Aaron." As we stared into each other's eyes, the heat between us began to rise. My hand found the crotch of his jeans. "Now, let's take care of this. Shall we?"

His bulge remained ever present.

Filled with newfound energy, I knelt before him, unzipped his fly, and lowered his pants, right along with his boxers, which puddled around his ankles. What he had just done to me, I did for him, licking, suckling, and stroking his impressive erection with everything I had, leaving no area untouched.

"You don't have to—"

"Don't talk." I followed that command with one more. "Sit!"

He did as I instructed. I made myself at home between his knees, going to work on him with the sole intent of rendering him as helpless as he had rendered me.

Aaron rested his head back against the sofa and enjoyed the ride I was more than willing to provide for him, his hands gripping the sofa cushions, moans of ecstasy slipping from his lips. Soon, he was panting, his face tight and his body ready for release. "Holy shit." His mouth gaped open as his lungs gulped a lungful of oxygen.

When he was finished, I left Aaron on the couch with a dazed look in his eyes. I rushed off to his bathroom to finger brush my teeth and to check my makeup and hair. When I returned to the living room, Aaron was gone. The faucet in the kitchen told me his location, where I found him doing the same thing I had just done.

I approached the kitchen sink with one thought in mind. Where would we go from here? We'd professed our feelings. What would come next?

"Thank you for having the courage to invite me here, Aaron. And sending me those beautiful flowers, along with that letter. I'm not sure I would have come otherwise." I smiled with genuine love in my heart. "I couldn't be happier that I did. Are you up for that pizza now? Let's eat and talk some more. Figure this thing out."

Aaron turned and wiped his mouth and face, tossing the kitchen towel he had used onto the counter. His brow tensed. His eyes narrowed. "Um. Yeah, we can talk for sure. But what do you mean? I didn't send you flowers or a letter. And I didn't invite you here, Natalie. I thought you came on your own." He reached out to me. "I wished I had. I've been thinking about you nonstop since—"

"Wait, what?" I rattled my head as a sense of foreboding crawled up my spine like a poisonous spider. *His hand.* How had I not noticed before? I was so wrapped up in the moment; it had slipped my mind that *his* hand wasn't wrapped at all. "What do you mean you didn't invite me here?" My thoughts stumbled. "You sent me a text asking me to come here. Several texts. And how is your hand? Why isn't it bandaged?" My mouth ran dry as confusion drew his brows together.

Aaron stepped forward, spreading his hands out cautiously.

"Natalie, I don't know what you're talking about." Concern clouded his eyes. "Are you saying someone texted you to come here? Someone also sent you a letter that was supposed to be from me? You didn't just stop by on your own?" A tense breath escaped from his lungs. "I don't have my phone. I think I lost it somewhere in the basement. Truth be told, I was too busy feeling sorry for myself to care."

What? The room spun. "Aaron, we have to get out of here."

A throat cleared. "You can't find your phone, asshole, because I have it."

Chapter 23

Natalie

Aaron and I turned our heads toward the back door of the kitchen, where a man stood, a cell phone in one hand, a pistol in the other.

I felt as though lightning had struck me. Blood pumped through my veins at an alarming rate. Was I seeing things?

"Ross? What are you doing here? I just left Yaz. I don't understand what is happening right now."

Face lacking any semblance of kindness, Ross waggled his gun at us. "I figured I'd give you both one last hookup before you meet your maker. Now sit down and shut up!" The man who had never so much as raised his voice in my company, motioned with his gun toward the kitchen table on the other side of the room. "Now!"

I jolted at Ross's voice as Aaron lunged forward, causing Ross to shoot over his shoulder, shattering the glass door of an upper cabinet.

I screamed, my body crouched, my hands holding my head.

"Don't push me, scumbag. The only reason you aren't dead

right now is because I want you to understand *why* you soon will be. I said, sit down, now!"

Aaron took my forearm and guided me over to where we both claimed our seats. "Listen, man, I don't know who you are." He slid his gaze toward me and whispered, "Is this the dude you were dating?"

Horrified, I shook my head no.

Aaron returned his attention to Ross. "Whatever has pissed you off, it has nothing to do with me or Natalie. If this is a robbery, take whatever you want. I gotta warn you, I don't have much."

"Did I tell you to speak? You'd be wise to keep your mouth shut right now." Ross closed in but kept a safe distance. "And that's where you are wrong. It has *everything* to do with you, Aaron Marino."

I saw before my eyes what was happening, yet my brain struggled to comprehend it. This was my best friend's soulmate. How was this possible? A large bandage covered his left hand, revealing a dark truth that sat in my gut like razor blades.

"It was *your* parents? Wasn't it? Who burned in the fire? You told Yaz that they lived in Texas." My voice caught in my throat, my insides twisting into knots. Fear had nearly choked the oxygen from my lungs.

"Whose parents? I don't understand." With sweat beading across his brow and blood rushing to his cheeks, Aaron looked over at me again for an explanation.

"But Stephen and Jenny's last name was Anders. Your last name is Parker. Their son's name was Kevin."

Clarity registered in Aaron's eyes. He knew those names. And I was pretty sure they haunted him. "You're Jenny and Stephen's son?" Aaron's face turned white as his gaze fastened on Ross's.

An eerie glint sparked in Ross's eyes. "That's right, jackass." His shark-eyed gaze slid over to me. "My mother's maiden name is Parker. And my middle name is Ross. Kevin Ross Anders. I left her maiden name and my middle name out of the obituary. That's where you got your information, right?" He smirked, but it lacked any humor. "Nice to meet you, Natalie." He lifted the bandaged hand. "And thanks for forcing me to send you flowers, write you letters, and cut my own hand to get you here."

The cut above his eye. Was that a lie too? "B-but you told Yaz your parents . . ." This had to be a mistake. I'd known Ross for years. Had he hidden this side of himself all this time? "You're marrying my best friend. How can you do this to me?"

"That is unfortunate. Too bad you hooked up with this loser. You would've been better off with that lowlife, Justin. At least you'd get to live."

Aaron flew to his feet, his chair tumbling over backward with a bang that startled the life out of me. His muscled frame leaned into his message as his hands curled into fists. "Look, you may have a problem with me; that's your business. But this has nothing to do with Natalie." He pointed at me. "Let her go, and you can do whatever you want with me."

No, he can't. I'd just found Aaron. I couldn't lose him now. What kind of joke was this? Had the universe forsaken me my whole life?

Cool, collected, and filled with evil, Ross chuckled at Aaron's heroics. "Isn't that sweet? You want to protect your girlfriend." Levity drained from his eyes. "Well, who protected my parents when they needed it? Not you!" His gaze found me again. "Nothing personal, Nat, but Yaz is never going to go away with me while you are still around, anyway. It's better this way. She'll mourn the loss of you. And I'll play the supportive husband. She'll see the benefit of leaving here." He placed Aaron's cell phone on the counter. "You two have a volatile history. Natalie told Yaz all about it. She didn't trust you, *Aaron*." He held the cell phone up in the air. "And now, there are texts between you about this little rendezvous of yours. With a little help, the cops will believe that Aaron lost his temper, which her best friend already knows about, probably her mother, too, and he burned the house down with you both in it. Just like he burned the chair Natalie told Yaz about."

I remembered how Ross had come out of the bedroom that day, all sleepy-eyed. Was he listening the entire time? Did he also hear the stuff about Luis? Was that when he had put this plan together? And there was Justin. Ross had thrown him into the lineup as a suspect. He was looking for people to pin his crimes on.

A wrinkle forged across Aaron's sweaty brow. "What chair?"

Ross ignored him. "It was a crime of passion. Happens all the time." He set the phone down, clearly enjoying himself. "And from what I saw earlier, you two have a lot of passion."

"What chair?" Aaron asked again, his pitch rising.

"The chair you burned the night you told me to leave? I came back to apologize and saw you out back burning the chair. *Our* chair."

Aaron rattled his head. "What? I wasn't burning that chair. I was burning the old, rickety table that you put your wine glass on. And I had planned to burn it all along. It was garbage. I would never burn our chair." He stared at me, his expression crestfallen.

I had assumed the worst, my overactive imagination running on steroids. Of course, Aaron wouldn't burn our chair. I couldn't for the life of me figure out why I would think so. It felt so significant at the time. Now, it seemed futile. I should have spoken to him that night. If I had, I would have known the truth. What a mess. I grabbed my stomach, the acids trying to burn a hole. "How can you do this to us, Ross? You're sick. You aren't the only one who has suffered. Aaron has burns over half of his upper body. He regrets not saving your parents. He stopped being a firefighter because of it. Aaron has remained hidden here for years, torturing himself. He lost his fiancée and his life."

"Natalie, stop." Aaron sounded so defeated. Had he returned to the darkness?

"You're right about it being someone else's fault. James Logan was the one who orchestrated all of this. That was why I burned his properties *and him.* And if I hadn't seen him the other day, you and your boyfriend would already be dead by now, and I'd be torching Logan's house, instead of yours."

Words squeezed past my tightened windpipe. "If you know it was his fault, then why hurt Aaron?"

Ross's shoulders pulled back, his gun aimed directly at Aaron's chest, who stood there like a mountain as though ready to strike at any moment.

That had to be intimidating for Ross. Aaron was twice his size, gun or no gun.

I wanted to stand, too, but I feared I'd topple over if I tried.

"Because *he*"—Ross pointed the gun at Aaron's head, his voice rising with each threatening word—"was in charge of his crew that day. He ordered them to evacuate. Said it was too dangerous. He gave up on my parents. He should have tried harder." Ross kept waving the gun as he spoke, and I feared it was going to fire prematurely.

Aaron shook his head, his chin lowering and then rising to face his assailant. "It *was* too dangerous. There was nothing we could do. I ordered them out, but *I* stayed." He pulled his T-shirt off, some of it tearing, to expose his scars. "I tried my best. I wasn't conscious when they pulled me out of that building. I would have died to save them!"

Tears ran down my cheeks at the sight of him, his chest and arms maimed by his gallant efforts, tattoos of flames engulfing his body as though the injury was still burning him whole. Aaron had suffered so much from that day. What I found when I had met Aaron was a shell of the man he used to be. A broken spirit.

Aaron slapped his chest so hard it made a hollow sound that threatened to upend my stomach. A red welt showed the force of the impact. "Like I said, do what you want with me. I don't care anymore. But let her go. I won't even fight you. Please, she's done nothing to you."

His pleading tone ripped my heart at the seams. This warrior, whom I loved with every ounce of my soul, was so willing to give his life for another, no matter what the stakes. And now, he was staring down the barrel of a gun because another had saved his life, even when Aaron didn't have the strength to do it for himself. As he said, he would have died in that fire. It was *his* truth. There was no denying it.

"How can you be so cold? This wasn't Aaron's fault. You have to know this. What would your parents think of what you are doing? Or Yaz? She's pregnant!"

Ross staggered, unsteady on his feet, eyes vacant. "She's pregnant?" His voice lowered, barely discernible.

Aaron pounced, using the moment to his advantage. "I'm not gonna let you hurt her!"

Bang. That awful sound echoed off the walls of my heart, the smell of gunpowder ripe and unforgiving.

I closed my eyes, terrified of what it meant.

A gasp reached my ears before the sound of a body thumped to the floor.

I pried my eyes open to find Ross standing over Aaron, who lay on his back with blood dripping down the side of his chest. Ross's eyes widened, his mouth gaping open, and the gun still in his hand, but now dangling by a thread.

"What have you done?" I raced over, dropping to my knees and trying to determine if Aaron was still alive. "Aaron?" I touched him, trying to be gentle, but wishing I had the strength to fling his hulky body over my shoulder and carry him to safety, something he would never hesitate to do. I covered the wound with my hand, blood seeping through my fingers. "Aaron, stay with me." I touched his face. I listened to his weakened heart. "We have to get him to a hospital." Tears flooded my eyes.

I gazed up at Ross, who stood over us, watching, his expression blank as though lost in his actions.

"I can't let you go." His voice was no longer firm, but wavering and uncertain. "I-I didn't want it to go this way, Natalie. I didn't even know you were seeing Aaron until you told Yaz the other day when I was there. But you see, you provided me with an out. And I will always be grateful to you for that. I will take good care of Yaz and our baby. I promise you that."

Aaron's eyes fluttered, his head rolling back and forth. I could feel him slipping away, the wound in his upper chest oozing through my fingers and down his ribcage, creating a small puddle on the floor.

I ran to the kitchen sink, grabbing the same dish towel Aaron had used to wipe his mouth and face, and brought it over, pressing it hard against the wound. How close was the bullet to his heart? I shuddered. "He's alive, Ross. You can come back from this. But we have to get him to a hospital. I'm going to call 911." My phone was in the foyer where Aaron had carried me off, but Aaron's sat on the counter right above my head. Inches from me. Following my gaze, Ross grabbed the phone before I could.

"I'm sorry, Nat, but I can't let you do that. It's too late now. Things have gone too far. There's no turning back." He placed the phone in his back pocket.

I knelt down and pleaded with everything in me. I even made praying hands. "It's not too late. He's still alive." Was he? I couldn't tell anymore.

Ross watched me. "You don't understand. I've already killed someone, injured others. I've burned several properties in the area. They won't let me get away with that. And I won't go to jail for avenging my parents' deaths. This is my final score. It all goes away after this. I can return to the man I used to be."

He was right about going to jail. Of course, he was. My mind grappled with his logic as my stomach clenched. Ross had murdered James Logan. It was premeditated. It didn't take a genius to realize that was first-degree. "How can you say that? How can you ever look Yaz in the eye or your child, knowing you have killed innocent people? I didn't know you before, Ross, but I can tell you that you will never be the man you were." I tried to swallow. My parched throat made it difficult to speak. "But if you stop this now, that counts for something. You could make this last act something you can be proud of. And you can leave. Right now. I won't tell a soul."

Ross stuffed the gun in the back waist of his jeans and pulled me off Aaron, his jaw muscles flexing, his eyes feral.

"Stop, Ross. You can't just let him die. You can see his scars. What happened wasn't his fault. He tried to save your parents."

As he dragged me away, kicking and screaming, I thought of a new approach. "You were right about James Logan. He was an evil man. I know a lot of people who suffered because of him. They could testify on your behalf."

A bag sat near the back door that Ross grabbed, one I hadn't noticed before. Using one hand to restrain me, Ross pulled out a rope. Another struggle ensued between us as he dragged me over and tied me to the kitchen chair. Aaron remained unconscious on the floor, the towel on his chest growing redder by the second. He was bleeding out. How long did he have?

The speed at which Ross's hands moved defied logic. He had trained for this. And he was much stronger than I had ever given him credit for. The knots were professional-grade, cutting into my flesh and strangling my circulation.

Returning to the counter, Ross retrieved Aaron's phone from his pocket and texted something. He set the phone down, rushed into the foyer, and returned a moment later with *my* phone. He texted some more. "You came here to break things off with Aaron."

"You just texted Yaz that Aaron was unstable. You were scared. You didn't know what he was capable of. When they find you both, they will see that Aaron had a gun." As Ross spoke, he texted his rant. "Aaron torched this place with both of you inside. He confessed to killing Logan and burning all those other places. He blamed Logan for ruining his life. You fought with him, shooting him without meaning to. This gun is untraceable." He wiped the gun clean, placing it on the counter.

Ross bolted through the back door, leaving me alone. I wiggled my chair back and forth until it tumbled over sideways. My shoulder and face collided with the marble floor; the impact feeling like a baseball bat to the head. Didn't matter. Whatever injuries I suffered would be nothing compared to what was coming.

And what was coming was a large gas can, which Ross used to splash the surrounding area after he burst through the back door. The pungent odor made it difficult to breathe. Nausea swelled in my stomach.

I had burned myself on the stove once. The pain was so intense. I never forgot it. What would this feel like?

I had never been so scared in my life. Facing death wasn't something I had prepared myself for. Everyone died, but not me, and not now. I wept, my entire body quaking to the point of convulsing. Vomit burned my throat. I thought of my mother. How would she handle losing me? Jack would have to be there for her, and so would Harry. Thank god she had them both. What about Daisy? My little pup who hated it when I left her. How long would she wait for me to come walking through the door?

I tried to move toward Aaron, but with the chair as my anchor, I made little progress. I craned my neck to see him.

With the room soiled and wet, Ross stood back, surveying the damage. "I'm sorry, Natalie. I really am, but I have no choice anymore. You know too much." He pulled a long lighter from his bag, the one that contained the rope, and stood before me. "I wish I could shoot you, first, spare you the pain, but that wouldn't support the story I have created." He flicked the lighter.

I held my breath; my eyes slammed shut. In an instant, it would engulf me. *Please, God, let this be quick.*

"Ross, what are you doing?" The voice belonged to the last person I ever expected to hear again. *Ever.*

Time stood still, silence stretching through every crevice of this horror show. I pried my eyes open.

The old Ross's voice answered, the one that showed kindness, not hate. "Yaz, what are you doing here?"

Her footsteps entered the room, but I couldn't see her. I sensed she was nearby, or maybe I wanted to believe she was close. "Your work called and said that they hadn't been able to reach you. I was your secondary contact. They also said you hadn't been to work in two weeks." Alarm spiked Yaz's voice.

"Where have you been? And what is going on here? Why is my best friend tied to a chair on the floor? Is that gasoline?" She took several quick breaths. "I knew something wasn't right."

All Ross could manage was "Why are you here?"

This would change everything for him. There was no pretending anymore. There was no returning to the life he had. The woman he loved now knew the truth.

"I was worried about my friend, so I called my mom to watch the dogs and came to check on her. On my way, I received a text from her saying Aaron had lost control, and she feared for her life. I rushed over." Her sneakers came into view, her hand touching my restrained arm. "Natalie, are you okay?" Her hands worked the rope binding me to the chair.

"I think so." Tears bubbled, as did the hope in my chest. "I sure am glad to see you, Yaz."

"You don't understand, sweetheart. It has to be this way." Uncertainty cracked Ross's voice. "Natalie said you're pregnant. Is that true? Are we going to be a family?"

The knot loosened, freeing my hands, which I used to untie my feet. I wiped my mouth with my shirt, the bitter taste of bile rampant.

"What have you done, Ross? Please explain this to me. What am I seeing here?" Yazmine helped me stand.

"James Logan was the one who owned the building where my parents died. He was the one who cut corners on the living conditions. What happened to my parents was *his* fault. It could have all been prevented."

"You said your parents lived in Texas." Her quick breaths told me how overwhelmed my friend had become.

I stood beside her, my gaze landing on Aaron, who I swore had just moved. Was he still alive, or did I want to believe he was?

"I know, sweetheart, I should have told you the truth. Logan stole everything from me. He deserved what he got."

Yaz fanned a hand out in my direction and Aaron's. "And what about them? What did they do? Ross. She's. My. Best. Friend!"

Ross stepped forward, his free hand—the one not holding the lighter—reaching out to her. "You don't understand, my love. He was the firefighter in charge on that day. He gave up on my parents. He should have saved them."

"And her?" Yaz hooked her arm in mine, pulling me close. "What the hell did my best friend do to deserve to be burned to death? That's what is happening here, isn't it? Who were those texts from?" Her gaze found my phone on the counter near her fiancé. Next to the gun.

If only I could grab it, but I was too far away.

Ross lowered his chin. He exhaled as though not sure what to do or say.

"Yes, I am pregnant." Yazmine unhooked her arm from mine and pulled the engagement ring from her finger. She threw it across the room. "And, no, I will never marry you now. I don't know who you are, Ross Parker. If that's even your name."

He lifted his face to see her. He set the lighter down and retrieved the gun.

My fears escalated. I stepped closer. I'd protect Yaz and her baby if I had to.

"My name *is* Ross. Kevin Ross Anders. My mother's maiden name was Parker. But what difference does it make, Yaz? That's just a name. I love you. I want us to be a family. I had to avenge their deaths. Otherwise, they died for nothing. They didn't deserve it. They were good people. Burned to death. My mother's face melted to the carpet. Did you know that?" His eyes spilled with tears, his nose with mucus, all of it dripping down his deranged face.

My friend practically choked out her next words, her gaze pivoting between Ross and the gun in his hands. "I didn't know that. And that must've been a horrible way to die. But did you just say, 'What difference does it make?' Are you serious? How can you say that? And how can you do to these innocent people what James Logan did to your parents? You hate the man, but you are no different. We will *never* be a family." She placed her hand over her stomach. "And you will never be part of this child's life." A steady stream of tears ran like a waterfall down her cheeks. "How could you, Ross?" I could feel her heart breaking open. This was the man of her dreams. The man who *got her*. The man she had planned to spend the rest of her life with.

"You don't understand. This is all wrong. You weren't supposed to be here." Ross lifted the gun higher, his eyes predatory.

Sweet Jesus, what is he planning to do now? He wouldn't hurt Yaz. Or his unborn child. I had to believe that.

On wobbly feet, he stepped closer, the gun loose in his grip. "It's not too late, Yaz. I will let them go. Just come to Mexico with me."

I had wondered why Texas. Now I knew.

"We have to leave right now. The cops are figuring things out. She's friends with one of them. No one else needs to get hurt. I'm sorry about all of this. We can put it behind us. I can't live without you. I have money saved for this. I will make a good life for us and our baby."

The look she gave him said it all: a stony stare with the absence of any love she had ever felt for the man. Instead of answering, she nudged me. "We need to go."

"We can't leave Aaron!"

Ross reached his hands out, including the one holding the gun, which remained pointed at me this time. "Please, Yazmine. It's me, Ross. I'm still the man you fell in love with. We can make a life together. But we have to leave now. We can live comfortably. I can take care of us." A shadow slid across his face, his jaw muscles flexing. "They will turn me in. I have no choice. We have to leave."

Yaz firmed her own jaw, her hands clenched into fists. "You have always had a choice, Ross. And if *they* don't turn you in, I will! Go ahead, leave. I will never be with you again. You are not the man I thought you were." She spoke through tears, her voice drenched with torment.

Her courage floored me. I was in awe of my friend.

"No, no, no." Ross tapped the gun against the side of his head. "This isn't how I wanted things to go. I can't lose you. I can't lose our baby." He moved closer, causing Yaz and me to back away. "You'll understand once we leave here." He pointed the gun at me again. "I'm sorry to have to do this, but if you won't come willingly, I will have to force you." He chambered a round. "I won't hurt her . . . unless you leave me no other choice."

My eyes surveyed the floor where Aaron's body had fallen. The soiled dish towel had taken his place. Behind Ross, Aaron rose to his full height. He reached around Ross and grabbed the arm holding the gun. Another fight ensued as Yaz and I ran behind the wall that stood between the kitchen and the living room.

"You're not going to hurt anyone, asshole!"

I peered around the corner as Aaron pulled the gun from Ross's grip, slamming his other fist into Ross's jaw. The gun in Aaron's hand came down next, the metal colliding with Ross's skull. A haunting sound. The second blow landed Ross on the floor. Blood trickled down the side of his face.

Yaz stood in place, visibly shaking. "He can't hurt us anymore." She dashed into the kitchen, finding the lighter on the counter and heaving it out of sight.

Aaron slumped over the same counter; blood smeared over his pecs.

I grabbed my phone and dialed 911, explaining the situation as best I could. I took Aaron's shirt from where he had flung it to the floor and used it to apply pressure to the wound. His face turned ashen, his eyes droopy. I helped him with great difficulty over to the couch in the next room to await the ambulance. Aaron never let go of the gun.

He fell back onto the sofa, his lips trying to form a smile. "I'd much rather use this couch for what we did earlier." He chuckled, but the pain he was experiencing forbade it. He cringed instead.

"Don't push yourself right now. The ambulance is on its way. Save your strength."

In the other room, Ross cried. "I'm so sorry. I don't know how I let things get so out of control."

Yaz offered what little comfort she had left, never once promising anything for their future. I knew my brave friend. This was a bridge too far. It wouldn't matter, anyway. What Ross had done would put him behind bars for years to come. I kept my ears perked in case he got violent again. I suspected he wouldn't. The jig was up. No sense in pretending anymore. Ross had lost his battle.

While I listened, I sat close to Aaron, making sure he remained conscious. "Thank you for saving us." I kissed the side of his sweaty forehead.

"I think you've got that wrong, Natalie. It was *you* who saved me. And as much as I hate the guy, Ross did the one thing I didn't have the courage to do: he got you here." He took several measured breaths, his voice fading and his eyes fighting to close. "I love you."

"Don't talk. Save your strength. The ambulance will be here in no time." My gaze shot between the living room window that overlooked his driveway and him. How far was the nearest EMS?

"No, I have to get this out." He inhaled and exhaled while I kept my hand on the wadded-up T-shirt bound to his wound. "After the fire, I felt responsible for Jenny and Stephen's deaths. Ross was right. I *was* in charge that day. We had so many residents to get out, pets included. His parents lived on the top floor. Ross's mother had trouble walking. His father wouldn't leave her. He yelled to us from their window. We brought the bucket up just as an explosion shook the ground. The fire engulfed the upper floors. I tried to get to them."

He closed his eyes as though imagining every moment of the inferno he was describing. "I instructed my crew to get out. The roof wasn't stable. These were family men and women. I refused to tell their families they weren't coming home. I chose to go in one last time. As I reached the stairs on the second level, the roof caved. I felt it hit me, knocking me to the ground. The flames were everywhere. The smoke made it impossible to see. Two of my best, Rodney and Chuck, pulled me out, risking their own lives. They're the same men who came to see me recently and the same men who have come every year since. They refused to give up on me." He blinked back new tears. "I had never lost anyone before. I knew I was burned, but I didn't care. Skin grafts and surgeries meant nothing to me. I should have gotten them out. I couldn't move past it. Being a firefighter herself, Paula tried to reason with me. We had a wedding to plan . . . a family to start. I couldn't do it, not anymore. Finally, she gave up trying. I never blamed her. I made her job as difficult as I could. It was a relief to cut her loose. My father came and tried to reason with me. So, I pushed him away too. I said things to him I can never take back."

I wiped his tears away; my heart wrenched with his struggle.

"After the fire, and then Paula left me, I lost interest in pretty much everything and everyone. I just wanted to be left alone. I haven't spoken to my parents in five years. The only people who still come around are Rodney and Chuck." Aaron tried to smirk. "They are almost as stubborn as I am. On his last visit, Rodney said I looked different. I didn't know what he was talking about." He took a measured breath.

"I bought the house to get away from people. I could focus on fixing it up on my own. That was my plan. I got pretty crafty at being alone." He shifted his gaze to meet mine. "Until you showed up at my door to clean my house in your doggy-print outfit. The minute I saw you, I felt something . . . a spark." He released a tense breath. "I don't know, exactly. And at first, I didn't like what I felt. I figured you'd leave and that would be the end of it. Only I couldn't stop thinking about you."

He shifted his body toward me, a grimace pulling the corners of his mouth downward, his face even paler. "I know it sounds sudden, but what I feel for you, Natalie, has changed my life. And I can't explain to you why. I just know it does. I loved Paula, but it was different with her. We were both firefighters. We knew the risks of the job. She was a tough woman, but fair. And we worked well as partners. There was physical attraction, but it wasn't this, what I feel with you . . ." He pressed his lips into a thin line, words unable to express their true meaning.

I understood exactly what he was struggling to put into words. I had dated many men over the years, but what I felt with Aaron was not of the same caliber.

"Hell, we don't even know each other all that well. I just

know that I want you with me from now on. For as long as I have left on this planet."

His saturated T-shirt refused to collect anything more, and I didn't dare go grab another one. Instead, I pulled my shirt off and used it to staunch the bleeding. "Don't talk anymore, Aaron. The ambulance is on its way." I realized his eyes had closed.

"Aaron? Aaron, stay with me."

His head slumped to the side.

Chapter 24

One Life for Another

"Come on, just one more push. You got this! You're almost there." I held Yaz's hand tight, fearing her forceful grip might just crush the bones of my hand. No parents, siblings, or friends crowded the room. It was just us. My sister and I.

Monitors around us beeped. One doctor and two nurses were ready to deliver her baby boy.

"Okay, Yazmine, you need to push." Doctor Yates sat on a backless stool with wheels, ready for the delivery, her two male nurses there to support her every effort.

Yaz's entire face pinched, her cheeks on fire, and sweat dripping down the sides of her temples. "Ahhhh!" She tightened her grip on my hand. "It hurts!"

I moved my head closer to face her. "Focus on me. You got this. You're almost done. It's almost over. And then, you'll have your beautiful baby boy."

Thirty minutes later, on December twenty-second, Joshua Niran (named after Yaz's father) Mounivong was born at 8 pounds, 3 ounces. Yaz's little bundle of sunshine came into this world donning a full head of black hair, along with Yaz's beautiful dark eyes.

As Yaz's family hurried into the room, I sat on the side of her hospital bed, offering Yaz sips of water and cooing over her adorable baby. The sounds of paging personnel and people shuffling past our hospital room door—a few babies crying in the distance—did little to drown out the oohs and aahs from Joshua's new grandmother and aunt.

"You did good, Mommy." I touched the top of Joshua's head, which was unbelievably soft and spongy. "So did you, Little Joshy." At the advice of her nurse, Yaz had Joshua latched onto her breast for sustenance already, which the poor little guy needed. He could barely keep his eyes open. He'd taken a long journey from his comfortable womb to the real world, which was bright and loud and much colder than his 98.6 cocoon.

Mrs. Mounivong and Naomi, remained bent over Yaz on the other side of the bed. My mother, Harry, and Aaron waited out in the hallway to join us.

"Okay, I owe you a chicken pesto ciabatta from Panera." I stood, ready to get my BFF her favorite takeout, something I had promised her during labor. Given the amount of pain she was in, I would have offered her the moon and the stars.

"And one of those cookies I like." She smiled down at her son. "Mommy needs to keep her strength up."

"You got it. A cookie it is." I slid off her bed and located my coat draped over a lime-green chair in the corner.

Naomi met me halfway across the room. "Let me go. I'll take Mom. She could use a break and some fresh air."

I had just shouldered one arm into my fleece coat. "Are you sure? I don't mind making the trip."

"I don't mind at all. Mother, you up for a trip to Panera?"

* * *

After they left and before I invited my side of the family into the room, I rejoined mother and son, perching myself on the same bedside I had just left.

"How are you feeling about . . . things?" I didn't need to say any more; my psychic sister knew what I meant.

"Well, there's nothing I can do about his father." She played with Joshua's tiny little fingers that looked smaller than a doll's against his mother's, his skin a beautiful shade of olive.

"Will you tell Joshua about Ross?"

"I don't know. Maybe when he's older and can handle hearing about what his father did." She spoke lightly as she gazed down at her newborn as though she were reciting a nursery rhyme.

After a long trial, the judge had sentenced Ross to life in prison for first-degree murder, first-degree arson, aggravated arson, reckless endangerment, and too many other charges to keep track of. Later, the courts stripped him of his parental rights. He'd done a lot of damage in this town, all of it premeditated, which did nothing to help his case. His *extra* jobs as a wedding photographer and an appraiser for the county were also a ruse. (He'd used stock photos of wedding couples to fool Yaz.) The camera he used for his lies provided him a way to survey the area, which he had done for years, planning his nightmare.

Yaz cried for months over it. She mourned the loss of the man she believed Ross to be. But with her tummy growing by the day, she had to put those hurtful feelings aside and take care of herself, the baby her new priority. For the remainder of her pregnancy, that was precisely what she did.

I attended the trial with Yaz and her family. Yaz never spoke to Ross, nor did she visit him in prison. It was difficult for her to tell her mother all that had happened. And on top of that, she was pregnant. Although Mrs. Mounivong was a stickler for all things socially acceptable when it came to her daughters, she rallied behind Yaz when the chips were down, like all good mothers did.

"I had no idea Ross had such a darkness hidden inside of him." That was where mother and daughter could agree. Mrs. Mounivong doted on Yaz during her entire pregnancy. She also attended all the court hearings, never once criticizing Yaz for putting herself in such a dire situation. It wasn't Yaz's fault, and we all acknowledged that. It didn't hurt that Yaz had also saved mine and Aaron's lives. Like Aaron, she was a hero.

I refocused my attention on my friend and the beautiful new boy in her arms. "Well, when the time comes for you to tell him, I will be right there with you." I took her free hand and held it firmly. "We've got this!"

Tears glimmered in Yaz's hormonal eyes. "Good, because I'll be a single parent."

I shook my head. "Nah, if I count both our moms, your sister, and me, not to mention Aaron and Harry, you've got half a dozen parents, all ready to step up when you need us." I smirked. "And when the time is right, I'll help you get back out there. We'll make sure we vet the next guy." I winked, hoping she appreciated the humor.

Her soft smile told me she had. "Thank you, Nat. You always know just what to say. And I'm glad you and Aaron are together. He's good for you. And you're good for him." She smiled at herself, almost laughing.

I let go of her hand. "What?"

"Maybe once I get my figure back, you can have Aaron set me up with one of his single fireman friends."

We both shared a laugh. "Knowing you, you'll have your figure back by next week. And you can count on it. Aaron did mention he has a buddy who divorced two years ago. His name is Connor, and according to Aaron, he's a good man. If he's the person I think he is, he's also pretty darn cute. Tall and built like Aaron, only with black hair and brown eyes."

Even though we joked, I knew her meeting someone new was a ways off. Still, it was fun to dream.

After what happened with Ross, Aaron agreed to seek counseling. And he really needed it. When he was able to stop blaming himself for things that were out of his control, the healing began. Much to the persuasion of his best friends, Rodney and Chuck, the two heroes who had saved Aaron's life, my fiancé returned to the firehouse. And that was only recently. He also resumed CPR classes and his EMT work.

He called his parents two months ago, asking for their forgiveness. They responded by showing up at his door the following week. He also contacted Paula, offering her the same olive branch, which she took without hesitation.

Aaron had always been a good person. He had bad things happen to him, and he blamed himself for those unfortunate events. None of that was unforgivable. In fact, the people who returned to Aaron's life were more than happy to do so with open arms.

As far as Aaron and I were concerned, we'd been busy over the past eight months, trying to get his life in order and mine, not to mention my best friend's budding family. Aaron finished his basement.

I rehung The Fireman's Prayer above his mantel, a reminder of the risks and the sacrifices.

We hadn't had much time to discuss our future, but it didn't matter. We loved each other with everything in us. I knew this because we said so all the time. We did, however, breach the subject of children. I reminded him I wasn't getting any younger, and that was when he proposed.

"I didn't say that to get you to propose, you know." As I typically did, I'd placed my hand on my hip for effect.

Down on one knee, Aaron jumped up from the camper where we had just made love when all of this came about. We chose Sandbridge Beach for our mini vacation, kayaking and collecting shells, and watching incredible sunsets at night. Daisy loved the sand. So much so that she wanted to eat it.

On that fateful night, Aaron had darted out of the camper and into his truck. He returned in a flash with a beautiful diamond ring in his hand. "I've had this thing stored in my dresser for two months now, just waiting for the right moment. I was going to wait until Christmas Day, but that also felt wrong. You shouldn't have to share your proposal with anyone, including Santa Claus." He smirked.

We decided on a September wedding, providing Yaz time to adjust to motherhood and for me time to plan. Our wedding would come a year-and-a-half after I had met Aaron. Hard to believe all that had happened in such a short time.

Back in the moment, I stood from Yaz's bedside. "Are you ready for the other side of your family to join us?"

"Yup. Send in the troops."

Joshua detached from Yaz's nipple and cooed his approval.

My mother entered first, carrying a bouquet of balloons. Harry and Aaron followed behind, rushing in to gush over Yaz and Joshua as I stood back to take it all in. Not all families came in the perfect little package, with the perfect little nuclear organizational chart. In fact, some of the most supportive families were often unconventional. What Yaz had was a circle of people who loved her and Joshua dearly, and who would do anything for them. As I often reminded myself. She was my sister in all ways but one. We were a family. And together, we would make our lives the best they could possibly be.

What could be better than that?

"Would you like to hold him?" Yaz directed her question at Aaron, who nodded hesitantly.

"Uh, sure." With careful hands, he took Joshua into his big, muscular arms. "Aren't you a little cutie?" He'd said the same thing to Daisy when he'd first met her. On instinct, he began to bounce and sway, touching the baby's tiny fingers with his own, which appeared gigantic in contrast. "You know what you need, little man?" Powerful emotions flushed Aaron's cheeks as he gazed over at me and winked from across the room. "You need a playmate. Aunt Natalie and I will get to work on that for you. Would you like that?" Joshua cooed and squeaked his tender voice as though he understood.

"Oh, he needs a playmate, does he?" I beamed back at my fiancé. "Well, you'll get no argument from me." I was excited about the prospect. In fact, I couldn't wait.

Tell me what you think ...

I'd love to know how you felt about this book. And I would be grateful for an honest review on Amazon and Goodreads. A few words are plenty and can make all the difference in how I plan my next novel.

If you don't have time to write a review, a rating will do just fine.

Acknowledgments

I am beyond excited to bring this book to you. Suspense and mystery have always been two of my favorite genres to read. I love not knowing who the villain is as much as I love finding out the truth. Unexpected twists and turns fuel my inquisitive mind. I hope that *Burning Vengeance* did the same for you.

I continue to appreciate and adore Melissa Shelton Harrison, who has become more of a right hand to my work. Melissa understands where I want to take my books and meets me there every time. Her skills as an editor, proofreader, and overall friend are beyond anything I could ever hope for. I am grateful for Melissa every day!

My proofreader Hattie LaRochelle is not only family, but she is gifted at finding blemishes in the work to the nth degree. I look forward to the bottle of celebratory wine and inspirational card from Hattie every launch!

Another growing tradition is sending Laurie Geraci a copy of my book before everyone else. I do this because Laurie is a champion reader and book blogger. She is also a huge supporter of my work. A launch wouldn't be the same without her input and support. As a bonus, she is also a sweetheart of a person.

There are important aspects to publishing that have little to do with editing. Maddee and Riley at Xuni.com for website work as well as Amy and Lauren from Indie Penn PR present my books to the world in a thorough and professional manner.

They make me look good, and I am grateful to them for the many hours involved to make it so.

A big thank you to my wonderful hubby, Bob, who has been there since this idea of publishing spawned. He celebrates the wins and consoles the losses. And I am truly grateful that he is with me on this exciting journey.

And no acknowledgement page would be complete without thanking my readers, subscribers, and friends who have stuck with me. Terry M, Anna P, Cheri G, Dawn M, Robyn X, Mary and Jess T, Marta M, Michael B, and Craig H (Craig writes the best book reviews on the planet), thank you all for being on my team. And to everyone else who I haven't mentioned here, but I keep warm in my heart. You all honor me with your presence in my life.

About the Author

Tricia T. LaRochelle is the award-winning author of the Sara Browne Series, a gripping romantic suspense along with *Sun in My Heart*, *A Collision with Love*, *Let Me Go*, and *Burning Vengeance*, her stand-alone romances with a twist. Gut-wrenching romances with unforeseen plot twists are where she thrives. Her apologies ahead of time for the tears. 😊

Coming from a background and education in Marketing, Tricia has spent the past eleven years pursuing her author endeavors. She now lives in Virginia with her husband and new pup, Daisy, who keeps her on her toes. She enjoys long walks with her hubby, time with her two grown sons and DILs, and board games that bring out the silly.

Subscribe to her newsletter https://www.example.com, where you can receive updates on her work, announcements, and giveaways, or follow her on social media.

Barcode to my website

Also by Tricia T. LaRochelle

Sara Browne Series Romantic Suspense:

Flickering Heart - Book 1 (Available on Audible)

Revive - Book 2 (Available on Audible)

Handfast - Book 3

Bleeding Heart - A Holiday Romance - Book 4

Stand-alone Contemporary Romances:

Sun in My Heart (Available on Audible)

A Collision with Love

Let Me Go

Burning Vengeance

Look for another new stand-alone coming this summer!

www.ingramcontent.com/pod-product-compliance
Lightning Source LLC
LaVergne TN
LVHW100516110826
845146LV00002B/657

* 9 7 9 8 9 9 0 9 1 0 7 7 5 *